D1478303

BREAKING FREE

JULIA TANNENBAUM

Wicked Whale
Publishing

Tannenbaum, Julia

Breaking Free/ by Julia Tannenbaum

Summary: A high school junior fresh out of treatment for an eating disorder must overcome real-life challenges to stay in recovery with the help of her friends and family.

ISBN: 9781732555426

Wicked Whale Publishing
P.O. Box 264
Sagamore Beach, MA 02562-9998

www.WickedWhalePublishing.com

Published in the United States of America

This book is dedicated to Uncle Gary.
Thank you for supporting me through thick and thin.
I love you.

1

I t's snowing again. In the dim light of the lamppost outside my window, I watch as the fluffy flakes descend onto the winding driveway of 16 Woodland Lane. I'm not sure how long it's been snowing for—I stopped keeping track of time after midnight—but judging by the size of the flakes and the speed in which they plummet to the ground, I'm certain that unlike the last snowfall two days ago, this time they will stick.

I feel badly for whomever has to shovel later today.

In the twin bed next to mine, my roommate Liv sleeps soundly beneath her massive lavender comforter. Every so often, her lips part to mumble an incoherent word or two, then settle back into a scowl. Even asleep, she's as sullen as ever.

Liv is the fourth roommate I've had since I was admitted to The Center for Healthy Living, Southview House, six weeks ago. First was Lilly, a quiet, artistic brunette, then eighteen-year-old Dakota, a down-to-earth Bostonian who'd suffered a relapse during her first semester of college.

My third roommate was Gracelyn. Despite having similar names, we were polar opposites. She would keep me up until eleven o'clock—an hour after "lights out"—endlessly chatting about her boring interests, her thriving social life—even her YouTube channel, where she uploaded makeup tutorials and fashion hauls.

"You're a pretty girl," she once told me, "but you need to do something with your hair. Have you thought about cutting it? I bet you'd look ah-mazing with a pixie cut!"

I couldn't tell if I felt more relieved or guilty when her insurance dropped her four weeks later. Either way, at least with Liv, I can have a semi-normal sleeping schedule. She's not too keen on conversation.

Tonight, however, sleep is impossible. No matter how hard I try, I can't quiet my active mind. My thoughts are like a tornado, plowing through my brain at breakneck speed and obliterating any small shred of tranquility in its path.

In a few short hours, I'll discharge from CHL. Although I've sworn to everyone who has asked that I'm excited for this transition, there's no point in lying to myself: I'm scared. I haven't been home in close to two months. What if I'm not ready? What if I relapse, like I did the first time I falsely assumed that I could handle life outside of a treatment facility?

Around three in the morning, Jackie, one of the night staff, quietly ascends the staircase to the third story to check on Liv and me. "Grace?" she whisper-asks. "Are you still awake?"

I squint into the blinding beam of her phone's flashlight and nod. "I can't fall asleep. There's too much on my mind."

"What are you thinking about?"

"Discharging," I admit. "I knew I'd have to leave eventually, but it's all happening so fast."

"You aren't the first person who's felt that way." Jackie sits on the edge of my bed and gently pats my hand, her fingers grazing my green *Strength* wristband. "How long have you been here?"

"Almost six weeks. I came on New Year's Day. I remember because everyone was watching a recording of the Times Square Ball Drop. It was raining a lot there."

Jackie nods. "My mom lives in Manhattan. She said it was even worse than it looked on TV."

"The people seemed happy though," I say. "I wish I could be that happy again."

"And I wish you'd shut up," Liv grouches. She raises her head from her pillow and shoots me a sour look. "Has anyone ever told you that you suck at whispering?"

"I'm sorry," I apologize. "I'll be quieter."

"And I'll go check on the others," Jackie says. "Goodnight, girls."

"'Night," I echo, while Liv continues to grumble under her breath. "I really am sorry. I'm just having a hard time sleeping."

"Pretend you're in school," she says.

"Huh?"

"When I can't sleep, I pretend I'm in class, and my teacher is giving a lecture about something super boring, like politics or cells or whatever."

"I did doze off in bio a couple times," I say.

"You see? That's why it helps."

"Okay, I'll try it. Thanks, Liv."

I wait for her to respond, but after several seconds pass, I realize that she's not going to. So, I turn on my side, close my eyes, and visualize myself in biology last year, nodding off to Mrs. William's monotonous lecture on cellular reproduction.

"There are two different ways that cells reproduce. The first, mitosis, is a process that creates almost an exact copy of the original cell. Now meiosis, however . . ."

I'm asleep in minutes.

Six o'clock arrives much quicker than I'd anticipated. I'm immersed in a dream about returning to school, which, like discharging, has been on my mind a lot lately, when I'm woken by someone shaking my arm. When I open my eyes, another counselor named Bridget is standing over me. Her blonde hair is parted into two uneven braids, and she's wearing a tight grey shirt with *The Future is Female* scrawled across the front.

"Get up," she says. "It's time for your weigh-in."

"You know it's my last day, right?" I mumble into my pillow.

She ignores me. "I've left a gown in the bathroom, so when Liv is done in there, put it on and come downstairs, okay?"

"Whatever."

Bridget walks away, her high heels clickety-clacking against the wooden floor, while I blink into the sunlight seeping through my sheer shades. Several inches of snow coat the ground like a sea of sparkling white. I shiver. Even though it's warm inside, the sight alone makes me cold.

Cold and sad.

I know that any minute now, students across Connecticut

will wake up to the exciting news that school is cancelled. I can see the smile on my brother Jamie's face; hear the joy in his gentle voice as he skips around our house. I wish I could be there with him. I wish I could curl up on the couch with him and play *Ticket to Ride* or *Life* or perhaps *Monopoly* if we had the stamina. I wish, for one day, that I could be a normal kid again.

"Grace! You don't have all day!"

With a sigh, I change into my gown and amble downstairs. I wait behind Julie, a slender blonde who arrived two days after me, outside the second-story bathroom to get weighed. While Liv takes her turn, Julie clamps her hand around her wrist, rechecking for the umpteenth time that her fingers overlap.

"Did you see the snow?" I ask.

Without tearing her gaze away from her wrist, Julie nods. "Uh-huh."

"I just hope the roads are good enough for my mom to drive on," I continue. "She said she'd be here at seven, but I'm worried that she'll get stuck in traffic."

Liv strolls out of the bathroom with her lips pursed in their trademark scowl. "She's ready for you," she tells Julie.

"'Kay. Wish me luck."

"Good luck," I say even though we both know that luck won't influence Julie's number. We're all on Exchange-based meal plans that vary depending on our weight. Lose a pound or two, and your Exchanges increase. Reach your target range, and *voilà*; you're back to eating reasonable portions.

Despite the counselors' efforts to keep our numbers on the down low, I know from this rational that I'm in my range. My Exchanges have been stable since Week Three, fluctuating only a starch or fat when I'm having "poop problems"—as eighth-grader Jack puts it—or consumed too much salt at that week's restaurant outing.

As a result of my consistent Exchanges, I'm able to take walks on pleasant days with Chanelle, a strict counselor who also manages our schoolwork, and anyone else who is weight-restored. It may only be through the neighborhood, but I still enjoy getting exercise after spending most of my time holed up in the house.

Once Julie is finished, I enter the bathroom. As I approach Bridget, who's waiting in the corner behind a digital scale, I glance at the large vanity mirror mounted on the wall. The glass is covered in dozens of colorful Post-it notes, each with a positive message written on them in Sharpie. *Beauty is not a size. Shine like the star you are. You are worth something.* In the top-left corner is mine: *Only you can change your ways.*

Bridget watches as I remove my socks and pull my underwear down to my ankles to confirm that I'm not hiding anything weighted in them. Then I turn around and step backwards on the scale, waiting until I hear a shrill *beep!* to get off.

"Can I go now?" I ask Bridget.

"You may," she responds.

When I return to my room, Liv, her brown hair wet from the shower, is rummaging through her dresser in a white camisole and striped boxer briefs. I watch as she yanks a purple long-sleeved shirt over her head, frowning when her hair dampens the fabric.

"Fucking shower," she gripes. "Did you know it's bad for your hair to wash it every day?"

"It is?"

Liv nods. "My sister said that. She's a hairdresser."

"I didn't know you had a sister."

"How would you? You never asked."

I glance at my nightstand, where a photo of Jamie and me sharing a massive plate of blueberry pancakes at our favorite diner in California is propped up against my retainer. Of all the times I'd talked about him with Liv, had I really never bothered to ask about her family?

Some roommate I am.

As Liv pulls on a pair of black leggings, I fish a grey sweatshirt and jeans out of my cluttered dresser and disappear into the bathroom. The mirror is still foggy from Liv's shower, so I rub my palm against the glass until my face is visible. Besides the bags under my hazel eyes, I look healthy: my skin glows, my dirty-blonde hair is thick and sleek, and my cheeks, once hollow and bony, are full again.

The longer I look, the more confused I feel. I've seen this face for my entire life, yet for some reason, I barely recognize the girl staring back at me. I don't know who she is.

I stay in the shower longer than usual, letting the hot water wash over my body until my pale legs adopt a reddish hue. When I finally reemerge into the chilly bathroom, I realize I forgot to shampoo my hair. I'm eager to tell Liv, but by the time I'm dressed, she has already left our room. So, I stuff my dirty clothing in my duffel bag, lug it down two flights of stairs, and abandon it next to a beige console table in the elegant foyer, my arms aching from the weight of everything Mom has brought me over the last six weeks.

As I'm walking to the kitchen, I pass my therapist Karoline's office, and I'm surprised to hear Mom's voice talking inside. I guess the snowy roads hadn't slowed her down after all. If anything, she's early.

Lowering the volume on a sound machine projecting a soothing ocean atmosphere, I press my ear against the door and curiously listen in on their conversation.

"So, she'll start her Partial Hospital Program on Tuesday?" Mom asks Karoline.

"That's correct."

"Okay." Mom takes a shaky breath. "And, uh, what if this happens again?"

"She'll always have a place here," Karoline responds. "If worst comes to worst, we'll readmit her."

"But she's doing better, right? With her weight and all?"

"She's weight-restored, yes, however that's only part of the process. You should begin looking for an outpatient therapist while she's at her PHP, so she'll have support when she discharges."

"And what about her father?"

"What about him?"

"Well, did you talk to her about what happened?" Mom presses.

"I tried to more than once, but she insisted that she'd moved on."

"So . . . that's it? That's all you got out of her?"

"I can't force her to talk, Kira. Grace clearly stated that she was uncomfortable with the subject, and I had to respect that. Would I have liked her to be more open with me? Of course. But at the end of the day, this isn't my recovery or your recovery. It's hers."

"What'cha doing, Grace?"

Alexa, my closest friend at Southview, touches my shoulder, and I jump. "Nothing!"

"You spying on them?" When I don't respond, she laughs. "It's cool. I'm not judging."

Alexa and I were roommates at Mistlyn, my last psychiatric hospital. When I met her, she was completely different than the kind, quirky fifteen-year-old I've grown to adore: she was sullen and distant and irritable to the point where I genuinely couldn't stand being around her. Now, however, I'm saddened by the thought of leaving her behind.

"So, you must be psyched to get out of here," she says. "How long has it been; seven weeks?"

"Six," I correct, "and yeah, I guess I'm excited."

Alexa raises her eyebrows. "You could have fooled me."

"I mean, it'll be nice to see my friends and family, and obviously I'm looking forward to having more privacy, but I'm also . . ."

"Nervous?"

"Yeah. There's so much uncertainty. I know I have support, but sometimes, I feel like people forget how hard recovery is, and that scares me. I don't want to disappoint them."

"You can't please everyone," Alexa responds simply. "Do your best, and if that's not enough for them, screw 'em."

"Screw 'em, huh?" I laugh. "I'm gonna miss you, Alexa. I'm gonna miss all of you."

Alexa rolls her coffee-colored eyes. "Oh, don't get all sentimental on me."

"I thought I heard voices out here." Karoline emerges from her office with Mom and stands in front of Alexa and me, her hands on her shapely hips. "What are you two doing?"

"We were, um . . ." I glance at Alexa, who shrugs helplessly. "Talking?"

"Outside of my office?" Karoline chuckles. "Shouldn't you girls be making breakfast?"

"Jack is taking forever in the kitchen," Alexa says. "He burnt his bagel, so he had to start over again."

"Why am I not surprised?" Karoline jokes. "Grace, did you have your Goodbye Group yet?"

I nod. "Yesterday. You weren't there."

"I know. If I hadn't had to be at the Northview House, I promise I would have come."

"It was pretty dope," Alexa says. "Grace read a poem she wrote to her ED, and for her Goodbye Song, she chose *Shake It Out*, which everyone was really into."

"The Taylor Swift song?" Mom asks.

"No, that's *Shake It Off*," I correct. "*Shake It Out* is by Florence & the Machine. I'll play it for you in the car. You brought my phone, right?"

"Yes, it's in the console."

"Awesome."

"Well, I'm glad you had a nice farewell," Karoline says, "but you really need to get started on breakfast. You know Chanelle doesn't like waiting."

Rolling her eyes again, Alexa takes off down the hallway. I hurry after her, struggling to keep up with her quick pace. For just shy of five-two, she's surprisingly fast. When we reach the kitchen, Chanelle is standing by the stove with her arms folded across her chest. Her diamond engagement ring sparkles in the dim overhead lighting.

"Where were you two? Everyone is waiting."

"Sorry," I apologize. "I was talking to Karoline. Do you have Cheerios?"

Chanelle nods. "There's a new box in the cereal cabinet. What are you having, Alexa?"

Alexa scans her Exchange Sheet. Since she's on Level Two, she's required to record her snacks and meals the night before, whereas my Level Four privileges allow me to decide in the moment. "Greek yogurt with a quarter-cup of granola and a banana."

Chanelle opens the refrigerator and hands Alexa a tub of yogurt. She watches her measure two-thirds of a cup, while I shake approximately one cup of cereal into a bowl and pour a glass of apple juice.

Once we've prepared our breakfast, we join the others in the dining room. Chanelle sets a timer for thirty minutes and instructs us to begin eating. As I munch on my Cheerios, I look around the table at the five teenagers who, for the last six weeks, have essentially become my second family.

I meant what I said outside of Karoline's office. I'll miss them: Alexa, Nate, Julie, Jack—even grouchy Liv. I'll miss the inside jokes, the competitive card games, and the weekend mornings we spent watching *Friends* on Netflix. I'll even miss the Monday car rides to the phlebotomist, where we'd sing along to catchy pop songs on the radio and play Sweet and Sour at the expense of other drivers.

Above all, I'll miss being around people who genuinely understand me. We may not share the same experiences, but we've all carried the burden of mental illness. We all know the struggle of having to dig ourselves out of a seemingly bottomless pit of numbers and secrets and lies. Here, I could share whatever was on my mind without feeling ashamed; out in the real world, I had to pretend to be someone I wasn't so I wouldn't humiliate myself.

It's not fair, but then again, neither is this world. You don't have to be mentally ill to understand that.

Forty-five minutes later as I follow Mom out the door, I glance behind one last time. Whereas everyone else has disappeared, Julie has remained by the front window and is staring out with a pensive look on her face. But when I raise my hand to wave goodbye, I realize that she isn't looking at me. No, her eyes are trained on a navy Nissan that's just pulled into the driveway. The girl who's going to replace me clutches a pink drawstring bag to her chest while her father, a lanky man with sad eyes, hauls an olive suitcase out of the trunk of the car.

"Are you coming, honey?"

"Yes, Daddy," a familiar voice responds.

"No way," I say under my breath. I steal another glance at the girl, and sure enough, it's her; a thinner, meeker version, but still the same girl I knew a couple months ago.

When she sees me, her chapped lips lift into a small smile. "Hi, Grace."

"Hi, Chloe," I say.

"Here, Chloe." Her dad hands her a beige pompom hat, which she shoves over her pin-straight hair. I recognize the hat as well; she'd often wear it to The Center for Adolescents with Disordered Eating on cold or windy days. "Ready?"

"Ready as I'll ever be," she responds with a sigh. To me, she says, "Maybe I'll see you around."

"See ya," I echo.

As Chloe's father guides her towards the door, I join Mom

in the car. She hands me my phone from the console. "Sorry, it's a bit cold."

I take it from her. "Thanks."

"You're welcome. Who was that girl?"

"Chloe. She was at CADE, remember?"

"I knew she looked familiar." Mom glances behind us at Chloe and her father, who are standing on the porch. Even from a distance, I can easily see the fear on Chloe's gaunt face. "I thought you said she was doing better."

"I thought so too," I respond quietly.

Mom starts the engine and cautiously reverses out of the driveway, her tires skidding against the icy asphalt. Although it's still frigid, the sun has emerged from behind the grey clouds, casting a blinding glare against the metallic hood of the car.

"Do you want to play that song for me?" she asks.

"One moment."

I turn on my phone and, ignoring the dozens of texts and notifications on my lock screen, open my music app. When I glance up, we're approaching the end of Woodland Lane, nearing the small ice-covered pond that we would pass on our weekly walks. Suddenly, I'm overcome with anxiety. I close my eyes and force myself to breathe deeply as I count to ten in my head.

One . . . two . . . three . . . four . . .

"Grace? Are you all right?"

When I look at Mom, her hazel eyes are filled with concern. Nevertheless, I nod. "Yeah, Mom. I'm fine."

2

Emilia has a new couch.

That's my first observation when she invites me into her office for my intake at the Center for Adolescents with Disordered Eating. It's much nicer than her last one; instead of the ugly leopard print, the soft fabric is a pleasant shade of blue that reminds me of the ocean.

"When did you replace your couch?" I ask.

"The end of December. It was a Christmas gift to myself."

"Oh. I like it."

"Thank you," she responds, smiling warmly. "So, how are you? It's been a while since we last spoke."

"Almost two months," I say.

"I imagine they've been an eventful two months, yes?"

"I guess so. Like, getting used to residential was weird at first, but after I'd adjusted to all the rules, it was pretty boring. It was a lot like the hospital, only the place was homier and I had more freedom. I even got to go to the movies once I was on Level Three."

"What did you see?"

"Just some PG action flick. It wasn't my genre, but it was nice to get out of the house. We also went to Panera for lunch that day. I got Creamy Tomato Soup—have you had it?"

"I have. Broccoli Cheddar is my favorite though." When I wrinkle my nose, she says, "What? You don't like it?"

"No, it's too cheesy."

"Ah, well, we'll just have to agree to disagree. And how were the other kids at Southview?"

"They were nice, and they understood what I was going through for the most part, so that was good . . ."

"But?"

"But there were times that they could be super overwhelming," I finish. "That's another reason I like being home. It's a lot easier having one sibling than five."

"How is Jamie?"

"He's good. I missed his thirteenth birthday, so I'm trying to think of something fun to do with him when I have time. Maybe I'll take him to laser tag or an escape room."

"I bet he'll like that."

"I hope so. I wrote him a note, and Mom used my money to buy him an Amazon gift card, but it just wasn't the same. You know, when we were younger, Mom and Dad would hide our presents around the house and give us clues to find them. We'd spend thirty minutes looking under furniture or opening drawers or going through closets. This one time, they hid my gift in our crawlspace. It was a Ballerina Barbie. I was eight."

"That sounds like fun."

"It was. I know it's stupid, but I miss it."

"It's not stupid, Grace. It's not uncommon for people to want to relive fond memories."

"And forget about the not-so-fond ones," I say.

"Exactly."

"But you can't," I continue, "because bad memories don't go away."

"Neither do good ones," she points out.

I chuckle dryly. "I don't know which is worse: remembering something awful, something you never want to relive, or remembering something you do but knowing you'll never be able to again."

Behind her rectangular glasses, Emilia's almond-shaped eyes narrow. "You've changed."

"You can tell?"

"Yes. You seem . . . older."

"My mom said that too. She also said I was more stubborn, which isn't the first time I've heard that from her." I roll my eyes. "And she wonders why I don't like talking to her."

"I take it that things are still difficult between you two?"

"Mom and I are figuring a lot out," I say. "I think it will be a while until everything is back to normal."

"You'll get there," Emilia says. "Take it day by day—isn't that what Lou would tell you?"

"Minute by minute," I correct.

"My mistake."

"It's okay. I'm surprised you even remembered."

"Why is that?"

I shrug. "I guess I'm just used to people forgetting."

Minute by minute, our session crawls by. It's nearly identical to my first intake at CADE mere months ago: Emilia asks about my health, my mood, if I'm actively restricting or having urges to harm myself (I'm not), so on and so forth. Thirty minutes in, Brooklyn, who oversees the program, brings me a grilled cheese sandwich, a bowl of salted popcorn, and an apple, which I nosh on while Emilia promptly picks up where we left off.

Around two o'clock, as I'm starting to grow impatient, she finally runs out of questions. I leave my lunch tray in the kitchen and join five girls in the Art Room for Dialectical Behavioral Therapy. I sit on a plastic folding chair next to Miriam, who's snapping a rubber band against her wrist under the table.

"Hey," she says.

"Hey," I respond. "How was Utah?"

She makes a face. "I don't want to talk about it."

"You were at Southview, right?" a pale girl with long dark hair to Miriam's right asks. In one hand, she clutches Silly Putty, while in the other is a half-drunk vanilla protein shake. Per CADE's rules, if we lose more than half a pound at our weekly weigh-in, we're required to supplement with a shake.

"How did you know?"

"I was at Northview," she explains, referring to the other Center for Healthy Living house. "I remember seeing you on one of the lunch outings. Chipotle, I think."

Now that she mentions it, she does look familiar. "Oh, yeah. I'm Grace."

"Maggie. So, what's your deal?"

"Huh?"

"Are you anorexic? Bulimic? Something else?"

"I, um . . ." I trail off, not sure how to respond.

"Ignore her," a tall girl wearing a preppy plaid outfit says. "She doesn't have a filter. I'm Mia by the way. That's Kimmy," she points at another tall girl in a baggy sweater and bootlegged jeans, "and—"

"Brenda," the final girl—a thin blonde with oversized glasses —whispers.

"Brenda was also at Northview with me," Maggie says, "but she was only there for nine weeks. I was there for twelve."

I glance at Brenda. Behind her glasses, her eyes are averted to her lap.

"You know, when I was admitted, my starch number was twenty-one," Maggie continues. "My therapist said it was the highest she's ever seen."

I can't tell if she's boasting or simply informing, so I merely nod. "Wow."

Teagan, one of the more annoying counselors at CADE, clears her throat. She's sitting at the head of the table, her piercing eyes shifting around the spacious room. "Grace, today we're learning about Interpersonal Effectiveness. Interpersonal Effectiveness is a dialectical behavioral skill that helps us build and maintain healthy relationships. Here you go."

She hands me a worksheet titled *Relationship Effectiveness: GIVE*. Below, a brief explanation of the acronym states:

Gentle

Don't attack, threaten, or express judgment during your interactions.

Interested

Show interest by listening to the other person without inter-rupting.

Validate

Acknowledge the other person's feelings and respect their opinions.

Easy Manner

Try to smile and act lighthearted.

When I'm finished reading, I sigh. After five months of therapy, between the hospitals, CADE, and Southview, I'm so over DBT.

———

"So, how was Program?" Mom asks as she turns onto our exit. A delivery truck swerves into her lane, and she honks. "Sorry."

"Program was boring. Literally nothing happened."

"Nothing?"

"Nothing," I reiterate. "It's such a waste of time."

Mom sighs. "I understand you feel that way, however you're at a point in your recovery where treatment is nonnegotiable. If you can't manage at CADE—"

"I know, I know," I interrupt. "I'll go back to the hospital."

"And that's the last thing anyone wants," she finishes.

I chew on my thumbnail. "Did you go shopping? It smells like tomato soup in here."

Mom sniffs the air. "You don't say. After I dropped you off, I went to Stop&Shop. I got vanilla yogurt, strawberries, burger buns, soup—obviously."

"Cheerios?"

"Ah, damn. I knew I forgot something."

"But I was going to have Cheerios for breakfast," I protest. "What am I supposed to eat now?"

"You'll just have to be flexible," she says. "If I have time tomorrow, I'll pick up another box."

"Tomorrow is Multi-Family."

"Then I'll go on Thursday." Mom is quiet for a minute. Finally, she points out the windshield at an illuminated ranch-style house. "I can't believe people still have their Christmas lights up."

"It's the same every year. Look, that house has an inflatable Santa."

Mom chuckles. "Some people have such a hard time moving on."

"Isaac still hasn't taken down his tree. We're hanging out on Sunday if that's okay with you."

"As long as his mom is home, it's fine. I'm taking Jamie shopping at two, so I'll drop you off on our way. Sound good?"

"Yeah. Thanks, Mom."

"You're welcome."

Half an hour later, Mom pulls into our driveway and parks next to her boyfriend Kevin's silver Kia. We head inside, where he and Jamie are playing Spit at the kitchen table. He places down his cards and greets Mom with a kiss on her cheek.

"How was the drive?"

"Good. Not too much traffic."

"We're in the middle of a game!" Jamie exclaims.

Mom laughs. "My apologies. Grace, are you ready for snack? I bought a pack of Milanos while I was out. I hope you'll have some with me."

I shake my head. "I want Goldfish."

"Didn't you have those last night?"

"So? What's your point?"

When she doesn't respond, I find an unopened bag of Parmesan Goldfish in the snack cabinet and shake some into a bowl. Mom places two Milanos on a plate, and we walk into the living room so we won't disrupt the boys. We make small talk about Oscar nominations and the weather—the forecast predicts another snowstorm on Monday—until I finish my snack. Then I put my bowl in the sink and head upstairs to face an enormous pile of review sheets that will supposedly help me pass my midterms.

After careful consideration, I select a ten-page math packet, because I know if I don't start it now, I likely never will. I'm halfway through the first page when my phone buzzes. My best friend Lou Jackson's name appears on the screen. I briefly consider ignoring the call, but since I haven't spoken to Lou in days, I stifle a yawn and reach for my phone.

"Hey."

"Hey!" she says enthusiastically. "What's up?"

"Nothing much. Just studying for midterms."

"How's that going?"

"Awful. I have no idea what I'm doing." I sigh dramatically. "I'm so screwed."

"You're screwed? You should see my grades! Ma's gonna murder me when she gets my report card."

"It's that bad?"

"One B, three Cs, and a D+ in math. I'm not doing so good in gym either. Last week, we were learning how to square-dance, and I was paired with Tommy Kershaw."

"Gross!"

"I know, right? On the second day, he tried to grab my ass, so I kneed him in the balls. Everyone thought it was a riot—except Coach Berger. He gave me detention and called Ma, who was super pissed. I'm still on house arrest, but at least I have my phone back."

I force myself to laugh. "I wish I was there to see that."

"I wish you were too. So, when do you take your midterms?"

"Next week. My tutor sent my mom the schedule, but I'm pretty sure I'm doing English and math on Tuesday, Euro and Spanish on Wednesday, and chem on Friday. I'll have to get up early, since Mom and I leave for my program at eleven."

"Oh, shit! I totally forgot! Today was your first day, right?"

"Yeah, but it's not a big deal," I say, thinking about my conversation with Mom. "I'm basically picking up where I left off."

"Is it the same group?"

"No. Miriam's back from Utah, but aside from her, I don't know anyone. It's all girls this time, which I thought was a good thing until I realized how cliquey they are."

"What did you expect?" she asks, and I can almost see her rolling her eyes on the other end of the phone. "I gotta say though; I'm surprised you've known so many boys with eating disorders. I thought that was, like, super uncommon."

"Not really. A lot of boys just don't talk about it."

"How come?"

"I think it has to do with stigma. Ryan, my roommate in the hospital, said his dad told him that only girls have eating disorders. The same thing happened to Jacob with his soccer team."

"Man, our society sucks," she grumbles. "Speaking of boys, have you seen Isaac yet?"

"No, but I'm going over to his house tomorrow."

"Sweet. What'cha gonna do?"

"Catch up. We'll probably watch Netflix too."

"Netflix . . . and chill?"

Even though she can't see me, I roll my eyes. "You're sick."

"Grace?" Mom raps on my door. "Are you on your phone?"

"Gotta go," I tell Lou.

"Okay, I'll talk to you late—"

Mom enters my room without invitation. She sees my phone before I can slip it in my pocket, and her eyes narrow. "I told you to leave that thing downstairs. You need to concentrate."

"Oh, give me a break," I snap. "I'm tired and bored, and I haven't spoken to Lou in days. Can't you cut me some slack for once?"

"You don't have to yell at me," she responds. "How about this: study for thirty more minutes, and then we can play Scrabble. Is that fair?"

"Okay, but I can't do anymore math tonight. It's, like, literally killing my brain cells."

"Dramatic much?" She laughs. "Try another subject then. You always have tomorrow."

She kisses my forehead and walks away, closing the door behind her. Ten minutes later, as I'm reviewing my notes on the Scientific Revolution, Jamie comes upstairs. He turns on his music, and *Chandelier* blasts through the entire upper floor.

I pound on the wall. "Headphones, Jamie!" When he doesn't respond, I set down my notes and barge into his room. He's sitting on his bed, painting his nails a vibrant shade of red. "Jamie, what the hell? I'm trying to study."

Jamie lowers the volume on his phone. "Sorry, I didn't realize—"

"It's fine. Just keep it down, okay?"

"Okay," he responds meekly.

"Really, it's fine," I assure him. "I didn't mean to snap at you. I'm just stressed—that's all."

"Because of midterms?"

"Because of a lot of things. You wouldn't understand."

"I might."

"No, you wouldn't," I disagree. "You have it easy."

Jamie finishes painting his pinky and places the polish on his nightstand. "You're not the only one who has struggles, you know. Don't you remember what happened with Zack?" His eyes drift to the clarinet case in the corner of the room. "I can't even play my clarinet without thinking about him smashing it in my face."

"Zack was expelled. You don't have to worry about him anymore."

"Sure. It's not like there are hundreds of more Zacks out there who'd love to pick on someone like me."

"Jamie, I didn't mean . . ." I sigh. "Look, if something is going on, you can tell me. You know I'm here for you, right?"

He stares down at his penguin-patterned socks. "There's nothing to say."

"Okay." After a long beat of silence, I say, "Well, goodnight then."

"'Night," he echoes.

Back in my room, I close my notebook and collapse onto my bed. I insert my earbuds and turn on an alternative playlist to distract myself from overthinking "my struggles." At first, it seems to work, but then *A Long December*—a song I frequently listened to in treatment—comes on, and before I can make sense of what is happening, the daunting memories from my own long December fill my mind. I see myself standing on the Jackson's scale; feel the touch of the razor blade against my wrist; hear the desperation in my mother's voice as she begs me to eat; taste the bitter retaliation on my tongue.

I hate you! You're ruining my life!

I rip my earbuds out and chuck them across the room. Burying my face in my pillow, I scream into the soft fabric until my throat is raw and my mind has stopped racing. Then, I take three deep breaths, fix my disheveled hair in the reflection of my phone's camera, and head downstairs. Mom is lounging in the TV room watching a CNN segment on the latest presidential drama.

"Ready to play?" I ask.

She flips off the television and nods. "Bring it on."

3

"Ms. Nielson is home, right?"

"For the hundredth time, yes. Can I go now?" Mom unlocks the door, and I step out of the car, eager to escape her maternal paranoia. My beige Uggs sink into the mushy snow. "Gross."

"I'll pick you up at five thirty, okay?"

"Okay. Bye, Mom."

"Have a good—" she begins to say, but I close the door without waiting for her to finish.

As she disappears down the street, I cautiously walk up the Nielson's icy driveway. I ring the bell and wait for someone to answer, shivering in the brisk wind. Glancing down at my thin fleece jacket and lycra leggings, I chastise myself for not wearing more layers.

"Hey, Grace," Isaac greets me. "You look cold."

"Yeah, it's freezing out here." The second I step foot in his kitchen, his Golden Retriever Dasha jumps onto my leg. "Hi, girl," I say, bending down to ruffle her silky fur. "You're getting big."

Isaac nods. "I know, right? She's growing like crazy!"

"I thought I heard a familiar voice." Ms. Nielson walks into the kitchen carrying a bag of dog food in her arms. Dasha eagerly claws at her fitted black sweatpants, but she nudges her aside with her foot. "How are you, Grace?"

"I'm okay. How are you?"

"Exhausted. Isaac, take this." She hands him the food and checks her Apple Watch. "I called the plumber. He's coming over shortly to fix the leak in the basement, so I'll be with him if either of you need anything."

"Grace and I are gonna hang out upstairs," Isaac says.

"All right. Just keep your door open, okay?"

Isaac rolls his eyes. "Whatever. C'mon, Grace."

After saying goodbye to Dasha and Ms. Nielson, I follow Isaac up to his room. It's drastically different than the last time I came to his house in early December. Gone are the FIFA posters, the trophies—even his soccer-patterned bedspread has been replaced by mundane grey sheets.

"I see you did some redecorating."

"There's no point in having all that stuff if I'm never playing again," he says. "It's depressing."

"I understand." I lie on his bed and gaze at the blue ceiling, squinting into the blinding overhead light. "I can help you find new posters on Amazon if you want."

"Like what?"

"I dunno. Bands, maybe."

"Cool. I'll ask my mom for some money." He lies beside me and rests his head on my shoulder, his face inches from mine. I feel his warm breath on my cheek as he exhales deeply. "It's good to have you back."

"It's good to be back."

"I bet. That place must have been hell."

"You'd be surprised. Besides having to follow a bunch of stupid rules, it was actually kind of . . . nice."

"Nice?"

"Well, not nice like I had a good time. Nice in the sense that it was an escape. I was with people who understood what I was going through, and the only thing I really had to worry about was food. Of course, I'm happy to be back, but sometimes I miss it. Does that make sense?"

Isaac shakes his head. "No."

"You never felt that way about the hospital?"

"Are you kidding? I couldn't wait to get out of that hellhole."

"Oh. Okay."

"Whatever." Isaac strokes my cheek with his thumb. "I'm just glad you're here now."

"Me too." Suddenly, Dasha leaps onto the bed, and I flinch. "You scared me, girl. I didn't even hear you."

"She does that sometimes." He pats the empty space next to him, and Dasha lies down, resting her head on his lap. "Good girl."

"She makes me miss my dog," I say.

"You had a dog?"

I nod. "Tiana. She was hit by a car when I was six. Since then, all we've had is a goldfish Jamie won at some school fair. But I'll have to wait until Mom ends things with Kevin to ask for another dog. He's allergic."

"Kevin?"

"Her boyfriend. They started dating while I was at Southview."

"What happened to Trevor?"

"Same thing that always happens. They realized how little they had in common, and then they started fighting, and before long, he got fed up and left."

"My mom used to date a lot of guys too," Isaac says, "but a while ago, she just stopped. Now she hasn't been on a date in years."

"I wish my mom would just stop," I respond. "At least she met Kevin at work and not on some dating app. Those guys are always the worst."

"Have you checked out his Facebook yet?"

"Of course. Want to see?"

"You know I do."

I open Facebook on my phone, type *Kevin Osborne* into the search bar, and click on his profile. Beneath a cover photo of the sunset, Isaac and I skim through information about places he's lived, his education, his relationship status—in a relationship, as of January—and other random details including his Episcopalian religious views and his spoken languages: English, Spanish, and . . .

"Norwegian?" Isaac remarks. "Who speaks Norwegian?"

I'm laughing as I move on to his photo collection. Aside from a few unflattering selfies, most of his photos are of vacations or sports games. Isaac studies a picture of Kevin and a tall woman with his same grey eyes and strong jaw posing outside of Fenway Park.

"He kind of looks like my dad," Isaac remarks. "Before my dad put on twenty pounds anyway. Since he got engaged to

Ashley, he's been gaining weight like crazy. Downside of marrying a cake designer, I suppose."

"Do you miss him?" I ask.

"I see him every month, so not really. I miss his cooking though. He was a boss chef."

"My dad was too. My mom tries her best, but it's not the same."

"Do you miss your dad?"

"I don't know," I respond truthfully. "I think I just miss the life I had when he was around. If he hadn't left, none of this would have happened. I'd still live in California, and I wouldn't be in treatment, and everything would be . . . better."

Isaac considers this. "You wouldn't have met me."

"That's true . . ."

"Things happen for a reason," he continues. "It sucks—believe me, I know—but it's not all for nothing. You're a lot stronger because of what you've been through. You're not like most kids our age, who live this fake fairytale life where their biggest issues are acne or getting a bad grade."

"What if I want that life?" I ask. "What if I want to be normal?"

Isaac situates himself so we're facing each other and stares into my eyes. "But you're not, and that's okay. That's why I like you."

"You like me 'cause I'm a weirdo?"

"Well, when you put it that way . . ."

I laugh. "I'm kidding. Thank you."

In response, he gently kisses me. "You're welcome," he says, brushing his nose against mine.

I feel a smile creep onto my face, but when he places his

hands on my hips and tries to pull my body closer to his, I imme-diately recoil. "Your mom is downstairs."

"So what? She's in the basement. She won't hear anything."

"I know. I just . . ." I sigh. "Let's do something else, okay?"

Reluctantly, Isaac retracts his hands. "Like what?"

"Um . . . have you seen any good shows lately?"

"I started *American Vandal* a couple days ago. It's pretty interesting."

"Oh, I've been wanting to watch that for a while." I grab the remote off his nightstand and hold it out to him. "What do you say?"

Although his pout implies that he's still irritated, he takes the remote and flips on the television. A NCAA playoff game between Florida and LSU is in its last minute, the score tied at seventy-six. "Come on, Gators," he says. "Don't let me down."

"I didn't know you liked basketball."

Isaac's eyes remain trained on the television. "I like March Madness. When I lived in Florida, my cousins and I would make brackets, and whoever did the worst had to do some dumb dare like dye their hair or prank call Domino's. Some-times, my dad would get in on it too." A Gator's center swishes a three-pointer, and he fist pumps the air. "Fuck yeah!"

"So . . . are we watching this now?"

"It'll be over soon. Anyway, I'm already a few episodes into *American Vandal*. It makes sense for you to catch up before we start watching together, don't you think?"

I don't, as a matter of fact, but since I'd rather not create more tension between us, I nod. "All right. Basketball it is."

Isaac's charismatic smile returns. He raises the volume so

we can hear the commentators and slings his arm around my shoulders. "I knew you'd understand."

EVERYTHING IS WHITE WHEN I WAKE UP ON MONDAY morning. Raising my head, I peer out the window at the thick layer of snow coating the ground. On my nightstand, a text from Isaac, sent at eleven-o-eight, lights up the lockscreen of my phone.

Isaac: *forgot this at my house. dasha already misses you.*

Below his message is a picture of Dasha lying on my fleece jacket.

Grace: *so cute. ill pick it up later. can u believe this snow!?*

I wait a minute for him to respond, and when he doesn't, I figure that he must be sleeping in. I'm surprised I hadn't slept later considering how tired I've been. *Maybe tomorrow*, I think as I pull my UConn sweatshirt over my pajama shirt. By the looks of it, I doubt I'll be going anywhere for at least another day or two.

When I come downstairs, Mom is sitting at the kitchen table sipping a mug of coffee while she responds to emails on her computer. She glances up when she hears me. "Good morning."

"Did you have breakfast yet?" I ask.

"No, I was waiting for you. What would you like?"

"Cheerios."

"You sure you don't want something different? I could make pancakes or eggs or—"

"I'm good, Mom. Really."

"All right. Let me use the bathroom, and then we'll get started."

While I'm waiting for her, I wander into the TV room and flip on the television. I watch news coverage of the brutal snowstorm, which has even caused power outages in some parts of the state, until she announces that she's ready. She hands me the box of Cheerios and a bowl with strawberry and banana slices at the bottom. Her own cereal—a blend of Special K and Grape Nuts—is already on the table.

"Do you want raspberry or apricot jam?" she asks.

"Raspberry." I add a splash of milk to my cereal, then reach for the jar and pop the lid.

Mom watches as I spread a thin layer onto the crispy surface of my toast. "More, Grace."

"It's just jam, Mom. Chill." I balance the sticky knife on top of the jar and slide it towards her plastic placemat. "Are you gonna sit?"

With a quiet sigh, she sinks into her chair. She looks even more tired than I feel; I can tell by the dark bags under her eyes.

"Are you okay?"

Mom clears her throat. "Your cereal is getting soggy."

"Uh-huh." I stick a small spoonful in my mouth, chew until it's mush, then pause to wash down my morning medications with a sip of my water. Mom is halfway through her cereal by the time I resume eating.

"It looks like the snow is lightening up," she says. "Can you help me shovel after breakfast?"

"Okay."

"Thank you."

"No problem."

She waits until I finish my cereal and toast to carry our dishes to the sink. "The winter clothing is in the hall closet. Dress warmly—it's cold out there!"

I open the creaky closet door, where sure enough, a massive box labeled SNOW CLOTHES is buried under a pile of TJ Maxx returns. I move the latter and bundle up in snow pants, a puffy ski jacket, boots, waterproof gloves, a hat, and a wool scarf. Mom fights back a smile when she sees me. "What's so funny?"

"Nothing," she lies. "The shovels are in the garage. I'll meet you outside in a few."

I feel like I weigh two hundred pounds as I drag myself across the kitchen and thrust open the door. Immediately, I'm greeted by a gust of snow flurries. Blinking furiously, I grab a shovel and begin hefting the heavy snow onto our lawn. My arms are aching when Mom joins me five minutes later. She says something, but the wind is blowing too loudly for me to hear her.

"What?"

"How are you doing?" she yells.

"My arms hurt!" I yell back.

"Bend your knees! It'll make it easier!"

"Okay!"

"What?"

"OKAY!"

We spend the next thirty minutes tirelessly attempting to clear our driveway. By the time we're finished, however, a fresh layer has already begun to coat the frozen asphalt.

"We'll try again later," Mom says. "You can leave the shovel by the door."

I do as she instructs, then follow her inside. We hang our

soaking clothing in the basement and change into warmer outfits—grey sweats for me; a mauve sweater and loose-fitting jeans for her—before we return to the kitchen. While she prepares lemon tea, I unlock my phone and google *how many calories does snow shoveling burn?* The results do not disappoint.

"I made chocolate chip banana bread while you were asleep," she says. "How about you have a slice with me?"

I close the tab and slip my phone in my pocket. "I told you I prefer it without chocolate chips."

"I'm sorry," she responds. "I must have forgotten."

I don't buy that for a second. "If you say so, Mom."

"I'll take that as a yes." She slides the bread off the cooling rack and onto a cutting board. It's flatter than usual with a deep vertical crease running down the middle.

"It didn't rise well," I remark.

"That happens sometimes. Do you want me to cut your slice?"

"No, I can do it." I take the knife from her and line up the sharp edge with the sugary top. My hand trembles as I sink the blade into the dense dough. Realizing that the slice is going to turn out too large, I tilt the knife towards me to shorten the bottom half.

Mom sighs. "Grace, what are you doing?"

I pretend I don't hear her as I place my uneven slice on a plate. "Mmm. Smells great." I try to hand her the knife, but she keeps her arms crossed.

"It's too small. I'll take it, and you can try again."

"It looks fine," I disagree.

"No, it doesn't. You just shoveled for half an hour. You need to replace the calories you burned. If you won't fix the slice, at least add cream cheese."

"I don't want cream cheese." I grab my plate off the counter and retreat to the TV room before she can protest. I flip on the television and scroll past more news coverage, cartoons, and dozens of sports stations, most of which we aren't subscribed to, until I find a *Chopped* rerun.

"Grace—"

I raise the volume so the sound of Vidalia onions sizzling in a frying pan drowns out her grating voice. An overweight man hastily dicing cucumbers nicks his finger. Blood squirts everywhere.

"Yikes," I mumble. I tear off the lower right corner of my bread and take a small bite. Flatness aside, it's not half bad.

Mom sits next to me on the couch. "Who's winning?"

"I'm not sure. It's the entrée round."

"What happened to him?" She points at the overweight man. He's standing off to the side while a medic wraps a Band-Aid around his bloody finger.

"He cut himself."

"Bummer." Mom glances out the window, where snowflakes continue to fall from the sky. "I got a text from Brooklyn that Program is cancelled, so if you need help studying for your midterms, I'd be happy to quiz you before I go to work."

"Maybe. I think I'm in good shape."

"If only I could say the same thing about the roads," she responds. "Driving is going to be hell in these conditions."

"I hate snow," I gripe. "I miss living in California. It was so nice and warm there."

"I know. I miss it too."

"Can we visit sometime? I know it's expensive, but we haven't been back in years, and I think it would be good for all of us."

"We'll see."

"So . . . no?"

"You know I'd like to visit too, but with everything that's happened, I—"

"I get it," I interrupt. "It's fine."

Mom and I fall quiet for a couple minutes; my eyes trained on the television, hers on my barely touched bread. When *Chopped* breaks for a commercial, she grabs the remote from me and mutes the television.

"What's going on?"

"Nothing."

"Then why aren't you eating your bread?"

"I'm taking my time. Do you want me to get a stomach ache?"

"Of course not. I just—"

"Mom, is school cancelled?" Jamie wanders into the TV room wearing red pajama pants and a clashing purple sweater. He settles beside me and rests his head on my shoulder, his overgrown hair reeking of strawberry-scented shampoo.

Mom nods. "Yes."

"Sweet!" Then he notices my bread. "Ooh, can I have some too?"

"It's on the counter," she informs him.

"Dope." Jamie hops off the couch and skips into the kitchen. Three minutes later, he rejoins us with a thick slice lathered in cream cheese.

On *Chopped*, the overweight man has just been eliminated.

He offers a few parting words about how great the experience was and walks away while the two remaining contestants prepare for the dessert round.

"Who are you rooting for?" Mom asks.

I point at the young blonde woman on the right. "Her."

"Me too."

Ted Allen permits the contestants to open their baskets, which contain puff pastry, watermelon, chocolate chips, and sriracha. We watch the final round with bated breath, and when the episode ends—the blonde woman placing second to a man with a thick southern accent—Mom and Jamie disappear into the kitchen to make him hot chocolate, while I head upstairs to take a shower.

After I've gathered clean underwear from my dresser, I close the door to the bathroom, turn on the faucet, and undress. I hold my hand under the running water, and, once it's warm enough, step in. I shampoo and condition my hair and scrub my skin with my coarse loofah until it hurts. I wish I had my razor to shave my hairy legs, but Mom confiscated it after my first hospitalization and has yet to return it to me—even though I'm nearly four months clean.

The mirror isn't as foggy as I'd anticipated when I get out of the shower, so I flip off the light to refrain from staring at my hideous body. I'm seriously regretting agreeing to eat Mom's banana bread. I should have opted for a Clif Bar, like I do every other morning. I should have been safe.

I'm applying lotion to my legs when the door abruptly opens. "Jamie!" I exclaim, fumbling for the towel. "Haven't you heard of knocking?"

"I—I'm sorry," he stutters. "The lights were off. I thought . . . why *were* the lights off anyway?"

"Never mind that," I say. "Do you need something?"

"My moisturizer."

I open the cabinet under the sink and find the silver bottle with a pumpkin-scented air freshener. "Here."

As I hand Jamie the moisturizer, his eyes glimpse at the scars on my wrist. "Did it hurt?"

I pretend I don't hear him. "Jamie, if you don't mind, I'd like to get dressed now."

"Right. Sorry."

I wait until he leaves the bathroom, closing the door behind him, to pull on my underwear and sports bra. I'm blow-drying my hair when my phone dings, so I shift the dryer to my left hand and use my right to open iMessage.

Isaac: insane. mom made me shovel :(

Grace: lol so did mine. my arms ache!

Isaac: same haha. what r u doing now?

Grace: hw.

I place my phone on the counter and pile my hair into a sloppy bun. Isaac still hasn't responded by the time I'm dressed, but I'm too tired to care. I head to my room, tossing my dirty underclothes in the hall hamper on the way, and crawl into my bed. Surrounded by the sounds of Jamie's distant laughter and our next-door neighbor's snowblower rumbling outside, I drift into a restful sleep.

4

G as doesn't have a definite volume because the particles move too fast. That's why it can fill the entire volume of a container.

I place my pencil down and stretch my hands over my head, yawning loudly. My tutor Marilyn, who's sitting across the kitchen table from me, cracks a small smile.

"Finished?"

In response, I close my chemistry test packet and thrust it towards her. "Take it. I never want to see it again."

Her amused smile broadens. "Gladly. How did it go?"

"Better than math—that much I know," I say, as no amount of studying could have prepared me for Mr. Lipschitz's brutal midterm. "So, I'm done, right? There isn't a surprise essay question or anything?"

Marilyn shakes her head. "Nope."

"Thank God. That was exhausting." I yawn again. "Hey, Mom?"

Mom pokes her head into the kitchen. "Yes?"

"Can I skip Program today? You know, as a reward for finishing my midterms?"

"Very funny," she says. "If Marilyn doesn't have any other work for you, you can take a thirty-minute nap. I'd like to leave a little early since the roads are still a mess."

"They're not *that* bad."

"Well, Kevin said it took him nearly half an hour to get to CTC, and Manhattan is much further away."

"Fine," I reluctantly agree. "Marilyn, are we good?"

She nods. "Read up to Chapter 20 for English this weekend and do two chart entries. I'll check them on Monday."

"Coolio."

Marilyn places my midterm in a blue two-pocket folder and stands. Mom comes to her side as she's pulling on her jacket: a puffy silver parka with a magenta interior. Even though the snow has mostly melted, it's still freezing outside—twenty-three degrees, according to the thermometer on the counter.

Mom hands Marilyn a plastic bag with four chocolate chip cookies. "I made them this morning. Think of it as a small thank you for everything you've done for Grace."

Marilyn places the bag in her leopard-patterned purse. "It's my pleasure. These look delicious." To me, she says, "You did well. You should be proud of yourself."

"We'll see about that."

She chuckles. "When are you going to stop doubting yourself? You're way more capable than you give yourself credit."

"Uh-huh. So, I'll see you Monday?"

"Yes. I'll see you then."

Through the kitchen window, I watch Marilyn climb into

her minivan and whip out of our icy driveway. Mom slings her arm around my shoulders. Her oversized burgundy sweater smells like chocolate and molasses.

"She's right, you know; you should be proud. You've worked hard."

"I'm going to take my nap." I shrug off her arm and unplug my phone from its charger. "You don't have to wake me. I'll set an alarm."

"Thirty minutes."

"I know. You already told me."

I toss my crumpled Clif Bar wrapper into the trashcan and leave the kitchen. Upstairs, I crawl under my blankets and close my eyes. I lie on my side, the seconds crawling by, as thoughts about midterms, Program, and food—to name a few—invade my mind.

After five minutes of tossing and turning, I give up on sleep. I grab my phone, open Instagram, and kill time by scrolling through the latest posts. Both Bianca Santos and Liam Fisher have shared albums celebrating their six-month anniversary. I wonder if the other three-hundred-and-nineteen people who liked Bianca's post noticed how unhappy she looks in the pictures. Even her caption—6 mos. and a thumbs up emoji—is a stark contrast to Liam's lovey-dovey paragraph.

Before I met @biancasantos15 my life felt empty. But once you stepped into my life, everything came alive and I realized that it was you I needed all along. You are the sun to my moon; the day to my night; the—

"Give me a break," I mumble and continue scrolling without bothering to read the rest.

Lou has uploaded an image to her Finsta of her curled up on

her beanbag chair with a mug of hot chocolate in her hands. Her eyes are half-shut, and her lips are pursed in a scowl. *the groundhog lied,* her caption says.

you got something on your shirt, I reply in the comment section, referring to the conspicuous brown stain below her collar. I force myself to laugh, because I know if I don't, the memories will overwhelm me with sadness—or worse: nostalgia.

I was at Southview for Groundhog Day this year. Since it fell on a Saturday, we were allowed to watch the ceremony. We gathered around the television before breakfast, crossing our fingers that Punxsutawney Phil wouldn't see his shadow. To our collective surprise, he didn't.

Liv's response to this news was nearly the same as Lou's. "I don't trust that lying motherfucker for a second," she grumbled, to which Bridget replied, "Language, Liv."

Later that day, Bridget let us watch *Groundhog Day,* the movie, in lieu of Cognitive Behavioral Therapy. Alexa and I sat next to each other, sharing a wool blanket and laughing at Bill Murray's shenanigans. For the first time since I was admitted to Southview, I felt a small glimmer of hope that maybe—just maybe—everything would be okay.

And then it was over. As the screen darkened and the credits rolled, another feeling replaced my short-lived contentment: disappointment. Bridget ejected the disc, and we followed her to the dining room for dinner. I remember that we had pizza that night. It was too cheesy.

I wish there was a way to permanently forget these uncomfortable memories, but until I figure out how, sleep will have to continue to be my temporary escape. Shutting off my phone, I pull my blanket over my head and try to clear my cluttered mind once again.

It must work, because the next thing I know, Mom is shaking my shoulders. "Let's go! We're going to be late!"

"Huh?"

Mom points at my clock. "It's almost eleven. You promised you'd be up ten minutes ago!"

I groan. "Okay, okay. I'm coming."

It turns out that the one thing I hadn't remembered was to set my alarm.

"Dude, you'll never guess what time I woke up today."

"Uh . . . one o'clock?" I guess.

Lou shakes her head, causing her braided ponytail to slap against her dark skin. "Seven thirty! Can you believe it?"

"Why did you get up so early?"

"My stupid parents. Ma was unloading the dishwasher and accidently cut herself on a broken plate. And then Pa flipped out because she's not supposed to lose blood. It's a cancer thing."

Cancer. The word sends a chill down my spine. Between Mom's job as an oncology nurse and Mrs. Jackson's sixteen-month battle with breast cancer, I've grown pretty familiar with the horrific disease.

"Is she okay?" I ask.

"She's fine. They were just overreacting—as usual."

"And where are they now?"

"Mass."

"Right. I forgot they still go."

"Still? They never stopped."

"Did you used to go too? Like, when you were younger?"

Lou wrinkles her nose. "Ma made me. I hated it so much."

"Every kid hates church."

"No shit. Wait . . . have you even been in a church?"

"Uh . . . no, I haven't." I laugh. "Actually, now that I think about it, when I was six, my family went to Italy over the summer, and we visited this really neat cathedral in Milan. We didn't go to a service or anything, but that counts, right?"

Lou rolls her eyes. "No, idiot. That doesn't count."

"Okay, okay. You don't have to be mean about it."

"Sorry. You know how I get when I'm sleep deprived."

"It's cool," I assure her. "If I were you, I'd be pissed too."

"Yeah, well, at least they don't force me to come with them anymore. Want some chips?"

She waves a bag of barbecue potato chips in my face, but I shake my head. "I'm not hungry."

"Your loss." She stuffs a handful in her mouth, chewing as she asks, "So, what's the latest with you and Isaac?"

"Not much. We hang out every now and then, but we mostly text."

"Let me see your phone."

"No!"

"Why? What are you sending him that you don't want me to see?"

"Nothing. I just don't want you snooping through my phone, okay?"

"Secretive much?" she asks. "You know, you're starting to

sound like my girlfriend."

"What do you mean?"

Lou frowns. "Cassie's been distant lately. I don't know what's going on, and she won't talk to me about it. She says everything is fine; that she's worried about college or whatever."

"Maybe she is."

"She got into her number one school. If anything, she should be happy."

"Well, is something going on with her brother? He's not back in juvie, is he?"

"I have no clue. Like I said; she doesn't tell me shit. I can't even ask how her day was without her getting all defensive. It's driving me crazy."

"She probably just needs some space."

"Space? What does she need space for?" Lou sighs. "Oh well. It's not like there's anything I can do to make her snap out of—whatever the fuck she's going through. By the way, did you get your midterm grades yet? I've been meaning to ask you."

I shake my head. "Still waiting. I'm super stressed about math. I feel like I did so badly."

"You always feel that way."

"That's what my mom said."

"My mom says I don't try hard enough," Lou grumbles. "She's always telling me that if I don't get better grades or take more challenging classes, I'll never get anywhere in life. It's hypocritical, you know? I mean, she didn't even go to college, and now she's married to a fucking entrepreneur and drives a Maserati."

"I forgot she didn't go to college," I say.

"She never even applied."

"Why is that?"

Lou shrugs. "No idea. I guess if worse comes to worse, I'll be like her and marry into wealth."

"You'd better start studying then," I joke, but she doesn't crack a smile.

"It's like nothing I do is ever enough for her. It sucks knowing your own mother isn't proud of you."

"You don't know that."

"Yeah, Grace. I do." Lou sighs again. "Christ! Why does everything always come back to my stupid mom?"

"We can talk about something else," I say. "Like, um . . ."

"What are you doing Friday night?"

"Nothing. Why?"

"Cassie's friend Sam invited Becca and me to a sleepover at her house, and she said you can come too. I know you're usually tired after your program—"

"No, I'll come," I interrupt. "I'm stepping down to IOP on Thursday, so I'll only be at CADE for three hours—not six."

"IOP?"

"Intensive Outpatient Program. It's like a Partial Hospital Program, just shorter since I'm doing better with food. The downside is that I'll have to come back to school now. I'm starting one week from Monday."

"Bummer. And your mom will be cool with you staying over?"

"I think so. She wants me to be more social."

"Ma says the same—" Lou stops mid-sentence and shakes her head. "No, I'm not talking about her. From now on, the m-word is officially off-limits."

I laugh. "I'm down with that."

Lou polishes off her final handful of chips and crinkles the bag into a ball. "I'm gonna get more food. You coming?"

"You're still hungry?" I ask.

"I'm on my period. Don't judge me."

"I wasn't judging."

I follow her out of her room and downstairs. In her kitchen, she opens the refrigerator, scanning the unusually empty shelves for something to eat.

"Nothing," she declares, closing the door. "I guess Ma didn't go shopping again."

"You could check your pantry."

"There's no point. All that's there are energy bars and these disgusting protein shakes. Fuck it, I'm going to Noodles and Company. Do you mind hanging here? I'm not allowed to drive friends yet."

"How long will you be?" I ask.

"Fifteen minutes, twenty at most. Want me to get you anything?"

I shake my head. "I'm good."

"Suit yourself. Oh, and if you want to watch TV, my remote needs new batteries, so you can use the one in my parents' room. It should work since we both have Xfinity."

"Okay. I'll see you soon."

While she bundles up in a white down jacket and beige Timberlands, I return upstairs and find the remote on Mrs. Jackson's nightstand next to a stack of *Bon Appétit* magazines. As I'm leaving their room, I pass the bathroom and pause to peek inside. The digital scale under the sink catches my eye, and a feeling I've fought so hard to resist encompasses me like an unwelcome hug.

Temptation.

Moving as if I'm in a trance, I drag the scale to the center of the bathroom and begin to unbuckle my jeans. It isn't until I'm standing in my navy boyshorts that the realization of what I'm about to do dawns on me.

"Stop it!" I say out loud, not sure who or what I'm talking to. Placing my hands on the marble countertop, I stare into the circular mirror above the sink. My face is pale, and my eyes are as wide as quarters. I don't look like someone who's in control. I look desperate. Helpless. Hopeless.

I force myself to breathe deeply. *In . . . out . . . in . . . out . . .* "You don't have to do this." *In . . . out . . .* "You're better than this."

My body is shaking as I wriggle into my pants and shove the scale back under the sink. In the safety of Lou's room, I lie on her bed and blankly stare at the teal ceiling, trying to make sense of how I feel. Part of me is disappointed, while another part, the part committed to recovery, applauds me for walking away.

It's like I'm caught between two worlds, and I can't decide which I'd rather live in. It shouldn't be a hard decision—after all, I'm not supposed to want to stay sick—yet it is. Sickness is familiar; sickness is safe; sickness is expectable. Living, on the other hand, is scary as hell.

The sound of a door opening interrupts my thoughts. I turn on the television, load Netflix, and hastily click on the first show under *Top Picks for Louisiana*: a Netflix Original called *Elite*. Three minutes later, Lou, a bowl of Pasta Fresca in her hands, plops down next to me and peers curiously at the television.

"*Yo fui uno de los afortunados,*" the protagonist says. At the top of the screen, *I was one of the lucky ones* appears in subtitles.

"I didn't know you liked foreign shows."

"Of course," I say casually. "Don't you?"

"I dunno. Subtitles are kind of a hassle."

"We can watch something else if you want."

"Don't bother. Now that I'm caught up with *Orange is the New Black*, I'm gonna need a new show. Can you start it over?"

"Sure. I'm only a few minutes in anyway."

"A few minutes? What were you doing the whole time I was gone?"

"Texting Isaac," I lie. "This is where it starts. Is the volume good?"

"A little louder?"

"How 'bout now?"

"No, no. Give me that." She snatches the remote from me and raises the volume from eighteen to a deafening thirty-seven. When I wince, she explains, "I'm chewing. It's harder to hear."

Rolling my eyes, I rest my head on her shoulder and inhale the pleasant scents of tomato sauce and roasted garlic wafting from her pasta until I can almost taste them on my tongue. In the show, the screen darkens on police surrounding the bloody protagonist, followed by the word *Elite* in red capital letters.

"I bet this could help me raise my Spanish grade," Lou says. "I mean, technically a C is passing, but some people just don't see it that way."

"Like your mom?"

She elbows me. "No m-word, remember?"

"Right," I respond as *Elite* transitions to a shot of a group of adults playing cards. "How could I forget?"

5

When I wake up to my six thirty alarm on Wednesday, I'm sad. I can't figure out why I'm feeling this way, so I stay in my bed, waiting for the sadness to pass, and when it doesn't, I hit the Snooze button and fall back asleep.

Ten minutes later, Mom barges into my room. "Grace, what's going on? Why aren't you up?"

"I don't feel well," I mumble. Even my voice sounds unusually weak. "I think I'm sick."

Mom places the back of her hand against my forehead. "You don't have a fever."

"That doesn't prove anything."

"Well, I leave for work in fifteen minutes," she says. "At least come downstairs so we can have breakfast. You can go back to sleep after that."

"I'll eat on my own."

"Do you really think that's in your best interest?" When I refuse to budge, she sighs. "All right, it's your choice. Jamie finished the Cheerios, so you'll have to make-do with cornflakes. Or you can have a bagel. Just be generous with the cream cheese." She walks away without another word, shutting the door behind her.

I stare at my ceiling for what seems like an eternity, hopelessly willing myself to get out of bed and face the day. It's not breakfast I'm worried about; it's Mom. I don't want her to be upset with me. I'm already enough of a burden to her—of a disappointment.

BEEP! BEEP! BEEP!

"Shut up," I grumble.

This time, I make sure that my alarm is completely off before I reclose my eyes. The last thing I remember hearing is the sound of my mother's noisy engine fading into the distance.

THE HOUSE IS QUIET WHEN I FINALLY EMERGE FROM MY bed at ten to nine. I pull on fuzzy socks and a fleece jacket and trudge downstairs. In the kitchen, I pour a glass of water and glumly stare out the window at the dirty snowbanks and bare trees. I wish they would disappear already. I'm so sick of this miserable weather.

I stick a slice of potato bread in the toaster oven and turn the dial. When the oven dings, I place the bread on a plate, smear a thin layer of jam on top, and head into the TV room. I spend ninety minutes watching *Queer Eye* on Netflix, then another twenty on social media: Twitter, Instagram, Snapchat—I'm so bored that I even check my Facebook feed. I briefly consider texting Mom, but I don't know what I would write.

hey mom. sorry for letting u down again. xoxo ur pathetic daughter.

On the coffee table, to the left of the remote, is my untouched slice of bread. I pick it up to take a bite, but upon realizing that a good third of it is burnt, place it back down and reach for the remote instead.

"Netflix," I mumble into the voice control. *Sorry, I didn't get that* appears at the top of the screen, and I groan. "Netflix!"

Around eleven thirty, as I finish my third episode of *Queer Eye,* I feel another bout of fatigue set in. Turning off the television, I wrap a thick blanket around me to combat the cold, curl on my side, and drift into oblivion.

I awaken a short while later for no particular reason. My phone is dead, but the digital clock under the television reads twelve-o-two, which means that Mom will be home any minute to have lunch with me. I fold the blanket into a sloppy bundle and return to the kitchen. At the counter, I pour a couple cornflakes and a drop of milk into a bowl, mash them together with a spoon, and place the bowl in the sink so Mom will think that I've eaten a sufficient breakfast. I've just stuffed my toast down the garbage disposal when the side door opens, and she bustles in, bringing a gust of freezing wind with her.

"Hi," I say.

"Hi." She shimmies out of her navy down jacket and hangs it in the hall closet. "What time did you get up?"

"Around nine. I had cornflakes."

Mom glances at the bowl. "You could have put it in the dishwasher, you know."

"I'm sorry," I apologize. "It completely slipped my mind. I'm still not feeling so great."

"You are very pale," she observes. "Are you ready for lunch or do you need more time?"

"Now is good. Can I have a sandwich?"

"Sure. Let me change my clothes, and then we'll start. I bought potato chips yesterday. I hope you'll have them with me."

"Where are they?"

"In the snack cabinet."

While she heads upstairs, I find the chips and study the Nutrition Facts on the back of the bag. "Serving size: twelve chips," I quietly read. "Calories: one sixty. No, thank you."

I'm slicing a tomato into thin slivers when Mom returns to the kitchen. She takes a pack of soy deli meat out of the refrigerator and sets aside four slices.

"I'm having a sandwich too," she explains when she sees the concerned look on my face. "So, do you want the potato chips?"

I shake my head. "I'll have popcorn."

"Are you sure?"

"Yes, Mom. I'm sure."

"It was worth a try," she says, not bothering to hide her discouragement. "Where's the bread?"

I toss her the half-empty bag next to my cutting board. "I already took mine."

Once we've assembled our lunches, we sit down at the table to eat. I nibble around the crust of my sandwich while Mom munches on her chips and sips from her mug of coffee. After several minutes of silence—minus the sound of chewing—she clears her throat.

"Grace, did you have snack this morning?"

"I had yogurt." I'm surprised at how easy it is to lie to her. "I know I usually have a bar, but it was at least a cup, so you don't have to worry."

"I do that a lot, don't I?"

"You think?"

"How about this?" she says. "I'll try not to worry so much if you promise to be more open with me. Deal?"

After briefly considering her proposal, I nod. "Deal."

Worry, however, is in abundance when I arrive at CADE at three o'clock. Brooklyn was unable to go shopping, so the kitchen is lacking many of our staple foods, including peanut butter, Nutella, pretzels, apples, and bananas. Even Maggie's cookie butter is out.

While we take turns getting weighed in the office, Teagan walks to a 7-Eleven across the street and comes back with individual bags of popcorn and a king-size box of Junior Mints that we divide among us.

"I haven't had Junior Mints in forever," Maggie says, wiping her cheesy fingers on her black leggings. "I used to get them when I'd go to the movies."

"My favorite movie snack was Raisinets," Kimmy says.

Maggie wrinkles her nose. "Why? Junior Mints are so much better!"

To Maggie's left, Brenda stares intensely at her small pile of candy. "I don't like minty things," she mumbles.

"Then you'll have to supplement with a shake," Teagan responds. "You can drink it in Process Group." She glances at her watch. "Speaking of which, we should get started shortly. Your parents will be here in an hour, and we're very behind."

"Oh my god, I totally forgot it's Wednesday!" Mia exclaims.

"I wish it wasn't Wednesday," Maggie gripes. "I hate Multi-Family."

"At least your parents actually come," Kimmy says. "Mine live too far away, and my aunt and uncle are always too busy."

Maggie shrugs. "It's not like they're missing out on much."

Maggie is right: of all the pointless groups at CADE, Multi-Family Therapy is, without a doubt, the most gratuitous. Every Wednesday, our families are invited to join us an hour before dinner for, as Brooklyn puts it, "an empowering, collaborative discussion." More often than not, there is no "discussion" but rather awkward silence occasionally interrupted by an offhanded comment or needless drama. Last week, Miriam's divorced parents spent five minutes arguing with each other about her weight, while she quietly sat in between them, snapping a rubber band against her wrist. The week before, Maggie's younger sister threw a cherry Slurpee at her, but she missed and wound up breaking a porcelain vase.

Even Art Therapy is more productive in comparison.

After my chaotic morning, I'd also forgotten what day it is. I take out my phone and send Mom a text: *ur coming to MF right?*

Mom: yes. im bringing pasta. i hope thats ok.

Grace: pasta is fine. sorry again for earlier.

Mom: its ok. it happens to the best of us.

Rolling my eyes at her cliché response, I pocket my phone and return my attention to the group. Maggie is still bitching about Multi-Family, while across the table, Brenda has finally begun to eat her Junior Mints—four bites per mint. Teagan watches her with a disapproving look on her narrow face. Every so often, she clears her throat as if she's about to say something. But she never does.

"I can't believe you're already in IOP," Miriam, who's sitting next to me, says. "It's not fair. I've been here longer than you, and I still have no idea when I'll get to transition."

"If it makes you feel better, I'm not sure I'm ready," I admit. I quickly glance at Teagan. She's talking to Mia about the Oscars, paying zero attention to Miriam and me. "I can't even eat breakfast by myself. I was supposed to this morning, but I just couldn't do it."

"Are you going to tell Emilia?"

"I don't think so."

"Good. I wouldn't if I were you." She sighs. "But what do I know? I'm a mess. At the rate I'm going, I'm beginning to think I'll always be."

I take a moment to process this. "You were at Mistlyn, right?"

"Uh-huh."

"Then you know you have to change. If you don't, you'll end up like those skinny women in the adult unit with the empty eyes."

"So will you, you know," she says, and there's a slight bitterness in her voice. "Don't go around giving out advice until you can practice what you preach." She slips her last mint in the pocket of her baggy jeans and stands up. "T, I'm going to the bathroom."

Teagan nods. "All right."

I'm somewhat surprised when Teagan doesn't ask her to do a "pocket check." If it were anyone other than Miriam, I wonder if she would be so lenient.

CHLOE IS BACK. SHE'S SITTING ON A FAUX-LEATHER COUCH
outside of the office with her eyes glued to her phone when I
arrive at Program on Friday.

"Hey, Chloe."

Without glancing up, she nods her head in acknowledg-
ment. "Hey."

"Chloe!" Maggie dives onto the couch and throws her arms
around Chloe's shoulders. "Girl, I missed you so much!"

"You know each other?" I ask.

"Maggie was at Northview when I was admitted," Chloe
explains. "We were, like, practically inseparable."

"I know, right? Everyone thought we were lifelong friends!"
Maggie laughs. "Oh, by the way, Mia was bummed that she
couldn't see you. She discharged two days ago."

"That's all right. I'll InstaMessage her later."

"You know Mia too?"

"Northview," they respond at the same time.

"So, what happened anyway?" Maggie asks Chloe. "Was it
cheerleading?"

"Uh-huh. There was this girl, Hannah, who was obsessed
with dieting. It was, like, all she ever talked about. And then my
team went to the gym one day, and we all got on the scale, and,
oh my god, I was fat af! I was, like, the second heaviest flyer!"

"Careful, Chloe." Teagan, clutching a thick stack of papers
in her hands, walks into the room and places them neatly on the
table. "No body shaming, remember?"

"Sorry, T."

"Where's everyone else?" Teagan asks.

"Kimmy is in the bathroom, I'm not sure where Miriam is, and Brenda texted me that she'll be late," Maggie informs her. "The roads apparently suck."

"So, what else is new?" Teagan responds sarcastically. "All right, you three can get started on your snacks. FYI, Maggie, Brooklyn couldn't find cookie butter at the grocery store. The cashier said it's a seasonal item."

"It's cool. I'll ask my mom to order some online." Grinning smugly, Maggie takes off towards the kitchen with Chloe and I following in her footsteps. She snatches a banana from the fruit basket and begins to unpeel it. "Chloe, can you pass me the Nutella?"

Chloe reaches into the cabinet above the sink and tosses the jar to Maggie. "Give it back when you're done."

"Sure thing."

While they talk, I fill a small bowl with lightly salted popcorn and sprinkle chocolate chips on top. Kimmy emerges from the bathroom as we're finishing up. She unwraps a Chocolate Brownie Clif Bar, pours a glass of milk, and sits next to Maggie. Then she notices Chloe.

"I didn't know you were coming back," she says.

"Yeah, well, here I am." Chloe breaks a pretzel in half and dips it in her Nutella. "I just couldn't stay away."

"At least you live close. If my local CHL hadn't been full, I'd still be in Miami." Kimmy sighs. "I was on the phone with my dad last night, and he says it's going to be in the seventies all week. Do you know how much I'd kill to be at the beach right now?"

"My boyfriend used to live in Miami," I say.

Maggie's green eyes widen with surprise. "You have a

boyfriend?"

I nod. "We've been together for a couple months. His name is—"

"Isaac," Chloe finishes. "That's who it is, right?"

"How did you know?"

"I sensed there was something between you two," she says with a suggestive smile.

"Wait . . . you met him in treatment?" Maggie asks. "Isn't that, like, not a good idea?"

"God, it's cold out there." Miriam, her cheeks as red as a tomato, rubs her wool gloves together for warmth. She stomps her damp boots on the carpeted floor, then closes the door. "Chloe? Is that you?"

"Hey, Mir. Did you do something to your hair?"

"I got bangs." Miriam smiles shyly. "You noticed."

"Yeah, they look good."

"Would you say they're . . ." Maggie pauses for dramatic effect. "Bangin'?"

Chloe cringes. "I'm gonna pretend you didn't just say that."

Teagan takes a seat at the head of the table with her snack: a Tupperware container with celery, carrots, and a smear of hummus. "Good, you're here," she says to Miriam. "Now all we're missing is—"

"Mom, I told you I don't like that brand," Brenda snaps. "Just bring something else, okay? I've gotta go. Later." She slips her phone in the pocket of her fleece-lined hoodie with a deep sigh.

"Now we're all here," Teagan finishes.

Behind her boxy glasses, Brenda rolls her eyes. "Yay."

Despite my shorter IOP schedule, I'm still exhausted when

Program finally ends. Nevertheless, I force myself to exhibit as much energy and enthusiasm as I can for the hour-long car ride to Sam Miller's house.

Mom, however, isn't buying it. "Are you sure you're up for a sleepover?" she asks as she turns onto Meadow Avenue.

"I'm fine," I insist. "Anyway, it's just gonna be Lou, Cassie, Sam, and Becca. It'll be chill."

"Yes, but—"

"This is it." I point to a grey Dutch Colonial with a black *Resist* flag that's flapping in the harsh wind above the porch. "I'll see you tomorrow."

"You'll be okay having breakfast without me?"

"Mom! Stop babying me!"

"I'm sorry. I just worry about you—that's all."

"You promised you wouldn't do that." I unbuckle my seatbelt and grab my duffel bag, where I've crammed my pajamas, toiletries, and medications. "I'll text you when I'm ready to leave."

"All right. If you need anything—"

I slam the door without waiting for her to finish and sludge through a pile of melting snow to Sam's driveway. I ring the doorbell, and after ten or so seconds, Cassie lets me in.

"Hey, Grace."

"Hey. Where's everyone?"

"In the basement. You can leave your shoes here."

"Okay." I kick off my damp moccasins next to a pair of black boots and hang my jacket on the back of a folding chair. "Should I bring my bag with me?"

"I'll take it." She tucks my bag under her arm and pushes open a creaky door. "We have snacks if you're hungry," she says as I follow her down a narrow staircase. "Drinks too, but Sam and Lou already drank all the Sprite."

"I think I'm set," I respond. "I had a big dinner."

"Yo, Grace!"

Lou, who's lounging on a saggy green couch, pats the empty seat to her left. I move a crumpled bag of Barbecue Lays and sit down, glancing around me in intrigue. From a flat screen television to two *Dance Dance Revolution* pads to a closet overflowing with board games and packaged junk food, Sam's basement is a teenager's dream. It reeks of marijuana, but as long as I breathe through my mouth, the stench is tolerable.

On the soda-stained coffee table in front of me is an impressive array of snacks: bowls of potato chips, pretzels, and cheese puffs, a plate of mini pizzas, a large bag of chocolate bars, and another smaller bag of jelly beans. There's also a gallon of Arizona Iced Tea and cans of Coke—diet and regular. An empty two-liter bottle of Spite is on the floor next to a wireless Xbox controller.

"Wow," I remark. "That's a lot of food."

"It's not all mine," Sam says. "My cousins came over last weekend and threw a party. Most of these are leftovers. Want some?"

I shake my head. "I'm good."

"How 'bout you, Bec?" Sam holds out a Coke to Becca, who eagerly snatches it from her.

"Oh, good. It's Diet." She opens the tab with her thumb and the soda gushes all over her white t-shirt. "What the fuck! Did you do this?"

Sam erupts in giggles. Next to her, Cassie and Lou unsuccessfully attempt to stifle their smiles.

"I hate you so much!" Becca exclaims. Shooting Sam a scathing glare, she stands up and storms towards the staircase.

"Where are you going?" Sam calls.

"To find another shirt to wear!"

"Good luck! You're not gonna fit into any of mine!"

"Fuck you!"

She marches upstairs, slamming the door behind her. Cassie and Lou wait until she's gone to burst out laughing.

"Oh my god, Sam," Cassie says. "She's so pissed."

"She'll get over it. She's done worse to me."

"You're not still angry about Craig, are you?"

"Who's Craig?" I ask.

"My ex," Sam says. "We were dating until Becca got drunk and hooked up with him. And no, Cass, I'm not still mad. He was an asshole anyway."

"Oh." To Lou, I quietly ask, "When did that happen?"

"Sometime in October. I don't think you were in school."

Becca returns wearing a pink shirt that barely covers her midriff. She seems calmer than when she left, playfully whacking Sam's head as she walks past her.

"Cute crop top," Sam jokes.

Becca rolls her eyes. "You're dead to me. So, what were you all talking about?"

"College," Cassie lies.

"Boring. We should play a game."

"Like what?"

"Hmm . . ." Becca taps her finger against her chin. "I've got it; let's play Never Have I Ever."

"Seriously?" Sam asks. "Bec, Never Have I Ever is a shitty game. We thought it was boring when we were thirteen."

"C'mon, it'll be fun," Becca insists. "Anyway, you owe me for fucking up my shirt."

Sam groans. "Fine. We'll play Never Have I Ever."

"Great, I'll start. Oh, and whoever loses has to do a punishment."

"My mom bought anchovies yesterday," Sam says. "I think that the loser should have to eat an entire can."

"I'm a vegetarian," I say.

"Don't worry," Lou responds. "You won't lose—trust me."

It doesn't take long for me to realize that Lou is right. Immediately off the bat, Becca declares that she's never had a threesome. Both Cassie and Sam put a finger down.

"Never have I ever done coke," Sam says.

This time, even Lou loses a finger. I try not to act surprised, but it isn't easy to learn something, especially of this caliber, about a person I assumed I knew everything about. It makes me wonder what else she hasn't told me.

By the end of the second round, Lou has six fingers left, Cassie has five, Becca and Sam have three, and I have nine. I was beginning to feel like such a loser, I was actually relieved when Becca said that she'd never kissed someone of the same sex, and I could participate in their stupid game. I want it to be over already, so we can watch Netflix or paint our nails or play DDR, like when we were younger. Even a homemade facial would be better than this ridiculousness.

"Never have I ever . . ." Sam's lips curl into a devious smirk. "Done it in a car."

I sigh. It's going to be a long night.

6

By Monday morning, I'd almost forgotten all about Sam's disastrous sleepover . . . that is, until I wake up to a text from Lou.

Lou: u forgot ur toothbrush at sams. she says she can give it to u at school. ur coming back today right?

Grace: yes but she can throw it out. its gross.

Lou: ok. ill let her know.

Tossing my phone aside, I throw on a navy sweatshirt and grey jeans and head downstairs. In the kitchen, Mom is stirring a small pot of oatmeal at the stove. I notice that her blue argyle sweater is inside out.

"You should fix your shirt," I say.

"What do you—ah, dammit."

She sets down her stirring spoon and pulls her sweater over her head, revealing a lace push-up bra that looks like it came straight out of a Victoria's Secret catalog. Mortified, I quickly avert my gaze.

"Thanks for the head's up." She yawns. "It's been a long morning."

"Mom, it's not even seven," I say. "How early did you get up?"

"Oh, around four thirty," she responds casually. "Is this the right consistency?"

I peer into the bubbling pot. "A little thicker."

"All right. You can pack your bag while you're waiting. I bought more Clif Bars the other day. If you get sick of Chocolate Chip, let me know."

"Okay."

I open the snack cabinet and find the new box behind an unopened bag of peanuts. I rip into it and stuff a bar in my bookbag with a bottle of water and my school supplies. My homework folder is a mess, but I tell myself I'll deal with it later.

By the time I'm done, Mom has begun spooning the oatmeal into three bowls. Afterwards, she adds a sprinkle of brown sugar and several banana slices on top. I snatch the bowl with presumably the least amount of oatmeal, pour a glass of cranberry juice, and sit down while she places the pot in the sink. The faint *beep beep beep* of Jamie's alarm clock going off sounds from upstairs.

"If he's not up by seven, I'll wake him," Mom says. "He's been very fond of the Snooze button lately."

I methodically divide the banana slices in half with the side of my spoon. "Who isn't? Well, I guess you aren't. Why were you up at four thirty anyway?"

"I couldn't sleep. On the bright side, I was able to get quite a lot of work done. It's nice to have some peace and quiet around here."

"Are you calling me noisy?"

She laughs. "Needy is more like it."

As Mom predicted, at seven-o-three, Jamie is still in bed. She waits until I finish my oatmeal and juice to charge upstairs. "Jamie, it's time to get up," I hear her say. "I have to take your sister to school." He must not budge, because she raises her voice. "Now, Jamie!"

A couple minutes later, she returns downstairs with my brother in tow. I'm lacing up my shoes by the door when they enter the kitchen.

"Ready?"

"Yeah." To Jamie, she says, "Your oatmeal is in the microwave. I'll see you later." Kissing his cheek, she grabs her purse and jacket, and the two of us head outside into the blustery late-February weather.

As we drive to school, I hum along to catchy pop songs on the radio and try not to think about everything that could go wrong on my (second) first day back at Chuckles. But when we pass the blue-and-white *Welcome to Chuck L. Everett High School* sign, anxious thoughts invade my mind. I chew on my thumbnail, while my right foot rapidly taps against the floor mat.

"Is everything okay?" Mom asks. She navigates around a Kia with a faded *Student of the Month* bumper sticker and eases into the crowded drop-off lane.

"Fine." I glance at the clock on the dashboard: seven twenty-eight. Outside my window, we're nearing the flagpole. Two students stand at the base struggling to raise the massive American flag in the brutal wind. "Here is good."

"You sure?"

"Uh-huh."

She stops the car, and after saying a quick goodbye, I hurry inside so I won't be late to English. Mrs. Perkenson's wrinkly face breaks into a smile when I speed walk through the door.

"Hello, Grace. How are you?"

"I'm okay. I saw my midterm grade."

Her smile broadens. "I meant to tell you; your grade was the second highest in the class."

"Really? I, um, I didn't expect that." I wonder how badly she must feel knowing that eighteen of her twenty students scored below an eighty-six. "But where do I sit? There's a girl at my desk."

"Oh, I completely forgot. Martina is an exchange student who joined us last week. You can sit next to Matthew. Is that all right?"

"It's fine." Weakly returning her smile, I navigate through the first two rows of desks and claim the one to Matt's left. He raises his head long enough to shoot me a confused look.

"What are you doing? That's Tommy's seat."

"I, uh—"

"Grace will be sitting there from now on," Mrs. Perkenson interjects. "I was going to split you and Tommy up anyway. You two might just be the chattiest duo I've had in my thirty-six years of teaching."

"Thirty-six? I thought you were, like, forty."

Mrs. Perkenson rolls her eyes. "Nice try."

With a sigh, Matt returns his head to his desk, his wavy brown hair flopping in his face. Several seconds later, as Mrs. Perkenson directs a reluctant Tommy to a seat near the front of the room, he begins to snore.

Now it's my turn to sigh.

"Class, listen up." Mrs. Perkenson claps her hands to catch our attention. "Before we review last night's homework, we need to talk about the essay portion of your midterms. You cannot use text talk in expository pieces or any writing assignments I give you for that matter. This is not the first time I've told you this, yet many of you continue to do it anyway." She's so flustered, her face has adopted the shade of a purple plum. "In the future, if I see any text talk—and yes, that includes slang —I will deduct ten points from your grade. Understand?"

A third of the class obediently nods, while the rest could clearly care less. Heather Maiden has even put in her AirPods and is nodding her head to the beat of a song. When I glance at my hands, I'm alarmed to discover a thin stream of blood trickling down my ring finger. Lost in my thoughts, I hadn't noticed that I was picking at my cuticles again.

"Dammit," I mumble. I stick my finger in my mouth to stop the bleeding . . . without realizing that Matt is watching me out of the corner of his eye.

He makes a face. "Gross. What's wrong with you?"

I don't respond. I could write an entire novel describing everything that's wrong with me, and he still wouldn't have a clue. No one would.

WE'RE HAVING WAFFLES FOR BREAKFAST. THE SECOND I enter the kitchen and see Mom spooning a thick beige batter into the waffle iron, butterflies swarm my stomach.

"Uh, Mom? What are you doing?"

"Making waffles," she says simply.

"But it's Thursday. We always have cereal on Thursday."

"We have cereal every day," she points out. "It's good to shake things up now and then. Variety is the spice of life."

I scoff. "Did you read that in one of your books?"

Mom closes the iron and faces me. "Grace, you're going to have a waffle. It won't be so bad—I promise."

Groaning in exasperation, I kick the counter with my bare foot. Bad idea. Immediately, a sharp pain shoots through my big toe.

She arches an eyebrow. "Well, that was mature."

"I don't want a waffle," I insist. "What am I supposed to put on it? You know how I feel about syrup."

"I'm cutting fruit," she responds, "and we have honey and something called agave nectar that was on sale at ShopRite. I've heard it's pretty good."

"Agave nectar? You find the weirdest shit, Mom."

She frowns. "Watch your mouth."

"Sensitive much?" I mumble.

"What was that?"

"Never mind." I open the cabinet above the toaster oven and take out a small bowl. "I'm having cereal. Enjoy your waffle."

Mom watches in silence as I fill three-quarters of the bowl with Cheerios. I top it off with some of the fruit on her cutting board and sit down at the table. Two seconds later, I'm back on my feet.

"Forgot the milk."

Mom opens the refrigerator and hands me a half-gallon of one percent. "Do you need anything else?" Her voice is flat, devoid of emotion. "Juice maybe?"

"I'll have water." I wait a moment for her to protest, and

when she doesn't, I grab a plastic cup out of the drying rack and fill it with tap water. I have to turn my back when I pour the milk so she won't notice that my hands are shaking. "How soon will your waffle be ready?"

Beep! Beep! Beep!

"Now." Mom uses a spatula to transfer the golden-brown waffle from the steaming iron to her plate. "It's not too late, you know," she says. "I have enough batter to make one for you."

"I already started my cereal. I know you don't like it when I'm wasteful."

"I'll make an exception this time. How does that sound?"

I shake my head. "Thanks, but I'm good."

She saws off a piece of the waffle with her fork and stuffs it in her mouth. "It's your recovery."

"Ooh, waffles!" Jamie, wearing a maroon cardigan and skinny jeans, skips into the kitchen. He grabs the plate Mom left for him on the stove and joins us at the table. "What's agave nectar?"

"Try it. It tastes a lot like honey."

"Cool." Jamie adds two massive squirts to his waffle and digs in. "Mmm, this is good," he says as he's chewing. Bits of mushy waffle spray across the table at me.

"Jamie, gross."

"Sorry."

"It's fine." I down my last spoonful of cereal and tilt my empty bowl towards Mom. "I'm done. I'm gonna get dressed."

Mom glances at the clock. "Can we leave a few minutes early? I have a meeting at seven forty-five."

"Whatever."

Discarding my dishes in the sink, I retreat to my room. I

swap my pajamas with black leggings and a grey hoodie paired with my fleece jacket. In the bathroom, I brush my teeth and add a couple strokes of mascara to my stubby lashes. As I'm putting away the makeup, I feel bloated, so I chew two Tums before I return downstairs. Mom is waiting by the door.

"Do you have your snack?"

I reach into the snack cabinet and grab a Clif Bar. "I don't understand why you still make me eat these things," I grumble. "It's not like I need the calories."

"Come on," she responds. "I'm going to be late."

The drive to Chuckles is uncomfortably quiet. In the drop-off lane, Mom stops behind a large van and hands me my book-bag. "I'll see you at noon, okay?"

"Uh-huh." Without saying goodbye, I slam the door shut and join the crowd of students surging through the entrance. I arrive at English a couple minutes early and fool around on my phone until the bell rings.

"Settle down, students," Mrs. Perkenson says. She waits until she has our attention to continue. "I hope you all studied for your vocabulary quiz. Take out a piece of paper so we can—"

"Good morning," Curtis, this year's designated morning announcer, says into the loudspeaker. Mrs. Perkenson frowns—usually Curtis doesn't come on until second period. "We have a special announcement from Jenny Shoe. Jenny?"

"Did you know that approximately eleven percent of the world's population is hungry?" Jenny, an annoyingly upbeat sophomore in my Algebra class, asks. "Well, on February 27th, you can join me in raising awareness by participating in Everett's annual twenty-four-hour famine. For every signup, we'll donate five dollars to the Fight Hunger Foundation. You can register online or meet me in E-131 after school for more information. Let's work together to end world hunger!"

Click!

"Not this again," Matt gripes.

"I think it's nice," Aisha says. "It's about time we did something to help those poor people."

"Do you seriously think that starving ourselves for a day will change anything?" he asks. "Just because you do it for Ramen doesn't mean everyone else should too."

"It's *Ramadan*," Aisha snaps. "You're such a dumbass."

Mrs. Perkenson clears her throat. "That's enough! We have a quiz now, so please quiet down, okay?"

"Yes, Mrs. P," Aisha mumbles, whereas Matt merely rolls his eyes.

Although I hate to admit it, I agree with Matt—not about Ramadan but about the twenty-four-hour famine. Even last year when I wasn't sick, the constant complaining from the participants—never mind the concept in of itself—made me uncomfortable. I can only imagine how much worse it will be this time. Maybe I'll ask Mom if I can skip school that day. She shouldn't have a problem with it, I don't think.

When the bell rings, I drop my finished quiz on Mrs. Perkenson's desk and head to the Nurse's Office for snack. While Nurse Belinda browses plus size tops on walmart.com, I slouch in a plastic chair behind her and subtly sneak chunks of my Clif Bar into the right pocket of my jacket.

"Excuse me? Miss?" A petite girl stands in the doorway. She clutches a green pass in one hand, while the other is placed on her abdomen. "My stomach hurts."

"What's your name?" Nurse Belinda asks.

"Ella Sawyer."

Nurse Belinda types Ella's name into her computer. "Okay, Ella, where does it hurt?"

Ella points to her bellybutton. "There."

"Do you mind if I feel?"

"I don't mind."

The last hunk of my bar disappears into my pocket. "Nurse Belinda?"

"Why don't you lie down?" Nurse Belinda says to Ella. "Do you have class right now?"

"Bio. My teacher is Ms. Williams."

"I'll let her know you're here." As Ella walks into a dark room adjacent to her office, she turns to me. "Yes, Grace?"

"I'm finished." I hand her the empty wrapper, so she can dispose of it in the trashcan under her desk. "I'm going to use the bathroom."

"Oh, Grace?" she calls after me. "One more thing?"

With my hand on the knob, I turn my head. "Yes?"

"May I see your pockets?"

"What?"

"Your pockets. Your mom asked me to check them."

It takes me a moment to process what is happening, and when I do, I feel myself begin to panic. I wipe my sweaty palms on my leggings, racking my brain for a way out of this predicament. "I'll show you after I use the bathroom. I, um, I'm on my period, so I really have to go."

Nurse Belinda stands up, fixes her ill-fitting blouse, and calmly approaches me. "Grace, I need to see your pockets now."

"But—"

"Now!"

My entire body is trembling as I reach into my pocket and reveal the chunks of the bar. Several have bits of fleece adhering to their sticky surface. When I look up, Nurse Belinda's wide eyes are filled with dismay. "I'm sorry."

"Stay here," she instructs. "I'm going to call your mother."

I retreat to the chair and watch her dial Mom's number into the landline phone. "Hello, is this Ms. Sinclair?" she asks in a shaky voice.

She's also ashamed, I realize.

"Um, I have Grace with me right now. I checked her pockets like you asked, and—" She sighs. "Exactly." She pauses. "Uh-huh." Another pause, this one longer than the first. "Of course. Thank you." Nurse Belinda hangs up the phone and returns her attention to me. "Your mother wants you to see Miss Dixon. Do you need a pass?"

I shake my head. Averting my eyes to the floor, I grab my bookbag and head to Guidance with my heart pounding furiously. Mrs. Hawkins informs me that Miss Dixon is meeting with a student, so I sit in a cushioned arm chair across from her office and compose an apology text to Mom.

Grace: hi mom. im really sorry about hiding my snack. im having a bad day. i know that doesnt make it ok but i swear it will never happen again. i love u <3

I reread my text, then press backspace until all that remains is *hi mom. im really sorry.* I send the message, anxiously picking at my damaged cuticles as I wait for her to respond.

She doesn't.

"If you have any questions, shoot me an email." Miss Dixon's door opens, and a small brown-haired boy scurries out. He mumbles "thanks" and disappears into the hall, while she watches with an amused look on her face. Then she sees me. "Come on in, Grace."

The second she closes her door, the actor inside me takes the stage. "I'm so sorry," I tearfully apologize. "I was having bad body image, and I—I couldn't think straight. Please don't be angry."

"Grace, breathe." She waits until I've shakily inhaled to continue. "No one is angry at you. We all understand that mistakes happen. The important thing is how we recover from them."

"I know. It's just that sometimes—"

Ding!

"Sorry," I say.

"It's fine. You can check."

I pull my phone out of my bookbag, enter my passcode, and open iMessage. My stomach drops when I read my mother's text: *we will talk about this when u get home.*

"Shit," I say under my breath.

I'm so screwed.

7

For the first time since I've lived in Connecticut, I don't want to leave school. Waiting outside for Mom after history, my stomach is coiled in knots. I try to practice the deep breathing techniques I learned at CADE to subdue my nerves, but they don't work. If anything, the knots merely tighten.

Mom doesn't say a word to me for the entire ride home. When we arrive at the house, she has me carry in a bag of groceries, and then she takes a seat at the table and stares intensely at me until I sit across from her.

"I don't know where to begin," she says. "You promised me you were doing better, yet you've been in school for four days, and you're already acting on anorexic behaviors again."

"You know I don't like that word," I mumble.

"What else am I supposed to call it, Grace? Disordered habits? Urges? Either way, you lied to me, and quite frankly, I'm not okay with that."

"I only did it because I'm having really bad body image," I

say. "I also didn't sleep great, and my stomach hurt, and then there was this triggering announcement, and I got overwhelmed. I didn't know what else to do."

"There will be days like that for the rest of your life," she responds, "but you have to learn how to work through them. You have so much to look forward to, but you can't just default to restricting every time you have a bad day. If that's the case, you won't be able to go away to college."

This is the first time she's mentioned college, and I don't know what to say other than, "I have time."

"You have a little over a year. That's not very long."

"I'm going to get better," I insist. "Really, I am. I won't skip snacks anymore."

"You won't have a choice. I talked to Miss Dixon, and we agreed that you should eat with her instead of Nurse Belinda. You'll stop by her office every day at the beginning of your free period. If she's busy, you'll wait."

"Okay, but I usually have homework, and the library is the only place that has computers, so I can't wait too long or else—"

"You'll wait for however long it takes," Mom interrupts. "Your health is more important than your schoolwork."

"You know, if I don't do well in school, I won't be able to go to college either," I say, surprising myself with my audacity.

Mom scowls. "You'll go to a state school then. You do want independence, don't you?"

"Of course I do. You don't think I want to get out of this house? I hate it here. I hate everything about this stupid place."

"Then prove it. Prove that you can make it on your own, and you'll never have to come back."

"I will!" I retaliate. "I'm going to get out of this town, and

I'm going to go somewhere warm, and I'm going to start a family —my own family. And we'll be so much happier than we are now."

Mom is quiet for a couple seconds. When she finally speaks again, her voice is different; softer, sadder. "I'm sorry I make you unhappy."

I'm about to respond when her watch beeps.

"It's noon. We should get started on lunch."

"Did you buy more potato bread?" I ask.

"Yes. It's a different brand though. Martin's wasn't on sale."

I find the bread in a grocery bag with red grapes and pita chips and flip it over, so I can analyze the Nutrition Facts. To my dismay, this new brand has twenty more calories per slice than Martin's does. I'm about to broach this to Mom when I remember what she said.

You do want independence, don't you?

Biting my lip, I take out two slices and stick them in the toaster oven. I wasn't exaggerating; I want to get out of here, now more than ever before. But I know that to do so, I have to be compliant. I have to be better.

So, I say nothing at all.

———

"Do you want to talk about it?"

In response to Emilia's question, I shake my head. "Not really."

"How come?"

"Because I've already had, like, five conversations about it with Mom. She says I have to eat snack with my guidance counselor now."

"And what do you think about that?"

"I think that sucks. I eat during my free period, and then I go to the library to do my homework. But Miss Dixon meets with a lot of students, and sometimes those meetings run over. I don't want to wait for ten, fifteen, sometimes twenty minutes just so she can supervise me eating a stupid bar."

"Have you told your mother that?"

"I tried to, but she didn't listen. She never listens to me."

"What's going on with you two anyway?" Emilia asks.

I sigh. "We got in a fight today. Well, two fights actually. It's just . . . she's so . . . god, I don't know how to describe it. We're just different."

"Many families are different, yet they still manage to get along with each other. It really comes down to communication. If you can't communicate, then you won't be able to effectively convey your wants and needs, and you'll end up fighting."

"How am I supposed to communicate with her if she never takes anything I say seriously?"

"How do you know she doesn't?"

"Because she's convinced I'm being manipulative or that my eating disorder is dictating what I'm saying. And yeah, that's sometimes the case, but not always. I have my own feelings, feelings that have nothing to do with my disorder, but of course she doesn't believe me. She thinks I don't want to get better."

"Do you?"

"Obviously. You think I like all this therapy crap?"

"I never said that. However, from my experience working here, I know that it can be difficult to let go of your eating disorder. It's almost like saying goodbye to a friend—a bad friend, but still someone you were close to."

"I know, and for a while that was my reality, but I don't want it to be that way anymore. I want to move on. It's just . . ." I sigh again. "There's so much conflict. When I was in the hospital, Dr. Bennett told me that recovery was a marathon and not a sprint. I didn't understand what he meant at the time, but now I think I do."

"I used to run marathons in college," Emilia says. "No matter how many hours I trained, I often worried that I wouldn't make it to the finish line. But every time I did, I realized that although getting there was a long and exhausting process, it was worth it. I think recovery is a lot like that."

"My mom brought up college today," I say.

"She did?"

"Uh-huh. We've never talked about it before, but I guess it makes sense since I'll be applying in the fall."

"When you think about going to college, how do you feel?"

"Scared," I admit. "At Southview, there was this girl named Dakota. She was two years older than me, and she said that until she went to college, she was doing better. But once she was away from home, she stopped eating and had to be readmitted. I don't want that to happen to me."

"I understand that it's a difficult transition," Emilia says, "however, there are a number of ways to help young adults who struggle with eating disorders prepare for college."

"Like what?"

"Choosing a college that's close to home is a good place to start." When I make a face, she says, "California will be there when you're ready. You said it yourself; this is a marathon. You have your whole life ahead of you, Grace. You don't have to rush."

"I know."

Emilia reaches across the table and pats my hand. "I promise you'll get there. In the meantime, though, we need to get you back in your range. You know what that means."

I wrinkle my nose. "I was hoping you'd forget."

"As if! So, which flavor would you prefer?"

"Do you have chocolate?"

"I believe so. I'll check with Teagan when our session is over." She glances at her watch. "We have a few minutes left. Is there anything else you want to talk about?"

"What was your fastest time?"

"Huh?"

"When you ran marathons, I mean."

"Three-forty."

"Three-forty?" I repeat. "Holy crap. That's good!"

She smiles. "Thank you. I was pretty proud of that."

"I once finished the mile in under six minutes," I say. "I know it's not the same as a marathon, but I was proud too. I used to be in really good shape because of all the running I did for soccer. I was even signed up for an indoor league this winter."

"Do you miss soccer?"

"More than you'd know."

"Well, if you're in a decent place by next fall, maybe you'll be able to play again."

I remember what Mom said this morning. "I've just gotta eat enough."

She nods. "Exactly."

To my surprise, Maggie, Chloe, and Mia also have shakes accompanying their dinner. Unlike me, however, they don't seem to have a problem with them. Maggie even finishes hers within two minutes, then tosses her Styrofoam cup at a nearby trash can, missing by inches.

"Damn. So close."

"Maggie . . ." Teagan warns.

"Sorry, T. I'll pick it up later."

"Is the strawberry good?" I ask.

Maggie wipes a light-pink stain off her upper lip. "It's all right. The butter pecan is my favorite, but they don't have that here."

"Butter pecan?"

"Uh-huh. The color is a little weird but it tastes pretty good."

"Let's talk about something else," Teagan says. She points at a sheet of paper taped to the wall with NO FOOD TALK AT THE TABLE printed on it in all caps. "You know the rules. Now, who did something fun over the weekend?"

"I went to a party," Maggie says. "This girl in my bio class was celebrating her Sweet Sixteen, and invited me and some other girls over to her house. It was sick! She even has an indoor pool!"

"Don't you have an indoor pool too?" Kimmy asks.

"Just a jacuzzi." Maggie shovels a forkful of beef tortellini in her mouth. "The jets are broken though, so it's more like a big bathtub."

"What are you girls talking about?" Emilia sits down next to Kimmy with her dinner: a massive Greek salad with four stuffed grape leaves on top.

"Maggie's bathtub," Chloe says. She points at Emilia's meal. "Is that from Tapas?"

Emilia nods. "My husband works there. He's always bringing home leftovers."

"I love Tapas!" Maggie exclaims. "The flatbread pizzas are literally to die for."

"Have you tried the garlic shrimp?" Chloe asks.

"No, but I want to. I've heard the falafel is super delish too. I mean, I could never live without meat but—"

"Maggie! Chloe! That's enough!" Teagan interrupts. "If you continue to talk about food, you'll have to finish your dinners somewhere else."

Maggie rolls her eyes. "Whatevs. So, what's up with the new girl?"

"New girl?" I ask.

"Yeah, she came in about an hour ago. You were in your session. I'm surprised you didn't hear her. She was pretty upset."

"She was?"

"Big time." Maggie cringes. "There was a girl like that at Northview. For weeks, all she'd do was scream and cry. Like, I felt badly for her, but it got annoying real quick."

I remain quiet, thinking about how brutal my first week at Southview was. Not knowing what to expect caused a lot of anxiety, and with that anxiety came loneliness and fear. I cried myself to sleep for three nights straight, and when we made our evening phone calls, I'd tearfully beg Mom to take me home.

Her response was the same every time: "I'm sorry, Grace, but this is where you need to be."

It wasn't until my second week that I realized she was right.

I couldn't be at home, not when I was still having urges to hurt myself. One time when I was recording my Exchanges, I stole a pen cap from Chanelle. The next morning, I stood in the shower, the hot water rushing over my body, and stared down at the sharp metal as if I was in a trance. I wanted to numb myself from the guilt, the disappointment, the denial, the regret. I wanted to stop feeling—even for a moment.

But I refrained, and when Jackie knocked on the door to let me know that my ten minutes were almost up, I wrapped the cap in toilet paper and discarded it in the trash can. I never told anyone—not even Karoline. I was too ashamed.

Now, as I take small sips of my shake, I feel the shame returning. In my mind, I compose a list of all the people I've disappointed today: Mom, Nurse Belinda, Miss Dixon, Emilia. Then another person pops into my head; a person who, until this moment, I'd neglected to even consider.

That person is me.

8

One vocabulary sheet, one graded homework assignment, one set of reading notes, and two tests to study for. That's my workload for the weekend—not including everything I have to catch up on from missing so much school. While I wait for Isaac to come over (we'd planned to hang out at ten thirty today), I sit at the kitchen table and listlessly skim through *Chapter 9: The Age of Process* in my history textbook. Around ten, I break for snack with Mom, and afterwards, I move on to the vocab. I'm jotting down dictionary.com's definition of *prerequisite* when the doorbell rings.

"Hey!" I greet Isaac, holding open the door so he can come in.

"Hey." He kicks off his dirty sneakers next to my Uggs and hands me his jacket, which I hang in our closet. "How's it going?"

I gesture to the pile of worksheets on the table. "How do you think?"

He grimaces. "I know the feeling. I was up until eleven finishing an essay."

"Hi, Isaac." Mom walks into the kitchen wearing baggy jeans and an oversized Fleetwood Mac shirt. Her hair is piled into a messy bun, and her socks are mismatched—one brown and one blue.

"Hi, Ms. Sinclair."

"Mom, Isaac and I are going upstairs, okay?"

"Okay. I'll be in my office if you need anything."

While she turns on the electric tea kettle, Isaac and I leave the kitchen and head to my room. I perch on the edge of my bed, and he sits next to me. Running his fingers across the green comforter, he asks, "So, what's it like being back in school?"

"Honestly? It's pretty boring." I reach across him for my pillow and place it on my lap, so I'm not tempted to stare at my gross thighs. "I'm glad I only have to be there for half the day."

"I miss that," he says. "If I wasn't taking so many classes, I could pull off a half-day schedule too, like I did when I was in Program."

"Well, I took eight classes in ninth grade and seven in tenth, so I'm doing all right with credits. My grades, meanwhile, are another story." I make a face. "I've never had a C in my life, and now I'm ending the quarter with two. Do you know what that's going to do to my GPA?"

"You've been out of school since October," Isaac reminds me, "and if there's one thing I know about hospitals, it's that they suck big time when it comes to education. Most people wouldn't be able to keep up if they were in your situation—much less get by with okay grades. But you already know that, don't you?"

I listlessly toy with a loose thread on the pillowcase until it comes undone. Then I move on to another one. When I look up, Isaac's clear blue eyes are trained on my face. "Oh, do you want me to answer? 'Cause I thought that was a rhetorical question."

He shakes his head. "Never mind. Will you do a half-day next year?"

"Maybe. I have my Planning and Placement Team meeting in May, so I'm sure we'll talk about it then. I'm definitely considering it."

"What's there to consider?" he asks. "That's a pretty sweet deal, Grace. Anyone in their right mind would be stupid to turn it down."

"I know that. It's just—I don't want to feel like—" I sigh. "It's complicated."

"Grace, have you seen my—" Jamie barges into my room without invitation. He trails off when he notices Isaac on my bed. "Oh. I didn't know you had someone over."

"Do you need something, Jamie?" I ask.

"Yeah, have you seen my headphones? I can't find them anywhere."

"You can borrow mine," I offer. "They're in the TV room, I think."

"Thanks." To Isaac, he says, "I'm sorry if I bothered you."

"It's cool, bro," Isaac assures him. "No worries."

Jamie smiles shyly. "Thanks . . . bro."

"I love your brother," Isaac says once Jamie is out of earshot. "I'm telling you; Ashley's kid is a nightmare. The little shithead is spoiled rotten."

"How do you really feel about him?" I joke. "No, but I get it. I've never met Kevin's daughters in person, but I imagine they aren't much better. I mean, their names are McKenzie and McKayla. That's already saying something, you know?"

"McKenzie and McKayla?" he repeats. "You've got to be kidding me."

"It could be worse. This girl at my program has twin sisters named Heaven and Nevaeh."

"Nevaeh?"

"Heaven spelled backwards."

"You're right; that is worse." Isaac wrinkles his nose in disgust. "By the way, how is Program going? You said Chloe came back, right?"

"Yeah. She was readmitted on Friday."

"How is she?"

"Talkative. She's even chattier this time because she knows most of the girls from Northview. One girl was there for twelve weeks, but the way she says it, it's almost like she's proud, like she's better than everyone else because she was the thinnest or whatever."

"She talks about her weight?"

I nod. "All the Northview girls do."

"You should tell Emilia," he says in a serious voice. "It's shit like that that makes relapsing so easy. I learned that from my roommate at CTC. She was a lot like you."

I briefly consider asking what he means by "a lot like you," but I don't want him to think I'm being insecure. So instead, I nod. "Okay. I'll talk to Emilia tomorrow."

"You promise?"

"Uh-huh."

"I'm serious, Grace. I don't want you to get hurt."

"I won't get hurt." Placing my hand on top of his, I plant a kiss on his lips. "Do you trust me?"

"I trust you," he says quietly, brushing his nose against mine.

"Good," I whisper. Our faces are so close that I can smell his cherry Chapstick. "Then you have nothing to worry about."

THERE'S A NEW COUNSELOR AT CADE. LIKE MY therapist, her name is Emilia, but she goes by Emmy. She's dressed in all black, wears her dark red hair in a pixie cut, and has a massive tattoo of a skull and rose on her left collarbone.

She's also morbidly obese.

As she sits at the head of the table leading a discussion about body acceptance, I can't tear my gaze away from her massive arms. And when she stands up to distribute worksheets, I have to pull my chair all the way in so she can squeeze past me.

I know I shouldn't judge her, but at the same time, I don't understand why CADE would hire this woman to teach us about self-care and balanced eating when she clearly doesn't practice either.

As Mom drives me home later that evening, my stomach chock-full of spaghetti and soy balls, I ask, "Did you see the new counselor?"

"Emmy?" Mom nods. "She seems nice."

"Still, don't you think it's weird that someone like her would work at CADE?"

"What do you mean?"

"I mean, she's just so . . . large. She was sitting next to Teagan, and she's, like, triple her size."

"Grace, I—"

"That's a little weird too," I continue. "Teagan's tiny, Mom. The first time I saw her, I thought she was a patient—not a counselor!"

"Teagan can't control being small," Mom responds, "just like Emmy can't control being big."

"Of course they can. Teagan can eat more, and Emmy can eat less."

"What good would that do? I thought CADE was all about body positivity."

"Yeah, but there's a difference between liking your body and being healthy."

"And who's to say they aren't? Everyone comes in different shapes and sizes."

"But—"

"Grace, you're overthinking this. Emmy and Teagan work long and hard to help teens like you get better. Isn't that more important than how big or little they are?"

"You don't get it," I say.

"You're right. I don't."

When we arrive at home, Kevin's car is parked in the drive-way. "I didn't know he was coming over."

"I invited him last night. I thought I told you."

I shake my head. "You must have forgotten."

"Well, he's here now, so let's make the best of it. Can you do that for me?"

"Whatevs." Snatching the keys, I hurry to our side door, eager to escape the cold. Inside, I hear rowdy laughter and a clean version of Britney Spears' *Work Bitch* coming from the basement.

"I win!" Jamie exclaims.

"You're just too good," Kevin breathlessly responds.

"Do you want to play again?"

"Maybe later. I think Kira and Grace are home."

"Okay. Let me just shut this thing off."

One minute later, as Mom is scrubbing two sauce-stained plates that were in the sink and I'm washing down an ibuprofen with a glass of water, they stagger into the kitchen. Jamie's cheeks are red, while Kevin's white undershirt is drenched in sweat. For a middle-aged man who works in an office all day, he's surprisingly fit.

When she sees them, Mom laughs. "What on earth were you doing?"

"Playing *Just Dance*," Kevin says. "Jamie kicked my ass."

Jamie grins. "Mom, did you buy ice cream?"

"Yes. Save the vanilla for Grace. You can have whatever else is in there."

"All right." Jamie opens the freezer and rummages through soy products and frozen vegetables until he finds an unopened carton of mint chocolate chip. "Yum. Want some, Kevin?"

"Sure."

Jamie scoops heaping spoonfuls into two bowls and hands one to Kevin, while I serve myself a smaller portion of the vanilla. He lathers his in caramel sauce; I sprinkle shredded coconut onto mine. He downs his quickly; ten minutes later, I'm still nibbling on my dessert, which is now the consistency of a creamy soup.

"I'm getting seconds," Jamie declares. He returns to the freezer, this time without any trouble finding the carton. As he sinks the scooper into the ice cream, he begins to hum *Work Bitch* under his breath.

"Well, I know what's gonna be stuck in my head all week." When he turns around to shoot me a scowl, I wiggle my shoulders and sing, "*You want a hot body? You want a Bugatti? You want a Maserati? You better work bitch.*"

"You should play with me some time," he says. "We don't hang out anymore, not like we used to at least."

"We don't?"

He shakes his head. "It's not your fault. It's just that, well, since the hospital, things have been different. You have your program, and when you're not there, you're always with Lou or Isaac. I miss you."

I polish off the last spoonful of my melted ice cream and place my bowl in the sink. After I've rinsed my sticky hands, I lean against the counter while he sits on top of it, swinging his legs back and forth.

"Listen, I wasn't going to tell you yet," I say, "but I feel badly for missing your birthday, so I was thinking that since CADE is in Manhattan, you could come with Mom and me on Friday, and we could stay overnight in a hotel, and in the morning go skating at Bryant Park. Then we could get hot chocolate or something—just the two of us. That should give us a chance to have some fun together, right?"

Jamie cracks a small smile. "Will Mom be okay with it?"

"I don't see why not," I respond. "So, what do you think?"

To my delight, his smile broadens. "I think it's a great idea. Thanks, Grace."

"You're welcome." I stand on my tiptoes and plant a kiss on his sweaty forehead. "It's the least I can do."

9

On the last Wednesday of the month, and my second back at school, I'm late to morning advisory. It shouldn't be a big deal, since advisory is basically a twenty-minute study hall, but Mademoiselle Rousseau, who's notorious for blowing everything out of proportion, naturally has to make a stink about it in front of the class.

"I'm sorry," I say. "My mom's car wouldn't start. What was I supposed to do?"

This is a lie, but I know if I tell her the truth—that I cried myself to sleep over a chocolate chip brownie and was subsequently too depressed to get out of bed to my alarm—she'll send me straight to Guidance.

Mademoiselle sighs. "Find your seat, Miss Edwards."

"*Merci.*"

I hurry to the back of the room and claim the empty desk next to Liam. When he sees me, he removes his AirPods and runs his fingers through his dark hair. He must have gotten it cut recently, as it's shorter than it was the last time I saw him. It looks good—not that I'd ever tell him.

"Hey. I heard you were back."

"Did Bianca tell you that?" I ask.

He shakes his head. "Bianca and I broke up."

Even though I could care less, I do my best to feign sympathy. "That sucks."

"*Silence, classe*," Mademoiselle orders. She turns on the Smartboard with a grey remote, logs onto Gmail, and opens an email titled *Advisory*. "It appears that we're doing a guided meditation today. Now if this link would work . . ." She repeatedly clicks on a URL at the bottom of the email, which directs her to a YouTube video. "I'll turn off the lights while we listen. You don't have to close your eyes if you'd prefer not to, however if I see phones out, they will be confiscated." She presses PLAY, and a man's gentle voice fills the dark room.

"You are about to embark on a guided meditation journey."

To my left, Liam's eyes are closed, his hands folded neatly on his desk. In front of me, Matt's body is trembling with silent laughter. Mademoiselle raises her index finger to her lips.

"Mr. Durham," she hisses. "*C'est assez.*"

"Over the next few minutes, I will guide you into a deep state of relaxation," the man continues, "where you will experience a wonderful calmness and meditative state of mind."

At Mistlyn, an elderly woman named Sue led a meditation group on Monday mornings. It was one of the few occasions that the adolescent patients interacted with the adult patients, so naturally, it was uncomfortable. I'll never forget the first time I participated; I sat on a blue yoga mat next to an emaciated woman who looked at least fifty, even though Alexa claimed that she was only thirty-five.

"You are completely in control," the man says.

Control. That's all any of us wanted, wasn't it? To have control over our chaotic lives? But then we became obsessed, desperate, ravenous for power. Innocent diets quickly turned destructive, and before long, we'd been reduced to fragile shells of the persons we used to be.

Even worse than Sue's meditation groups were the weigh-ins. Every Tuesday and Friday at six in the morning, patients would wander around the ward in cloth gowns while nurses ushered us in and out of two small rooms. Some were barely strong enough to stand. Others were accompanied by feeding tubes. And all of them had a hollow, glazed-over look in their eyes, like they were more dead than alive. *I* was more dead than alive.

"Breathe in deeply."

Per his instructions, I shakily inhale. *It's in the past,* I remind myself. *You're okay now. You're safe.* But no matter how hard I try to ignore the bad thoughts, they continue to circulate my mind. I don't know how to make them stop. I don't know how to escape this vicious cycle.

I'm still trembling as I stand up and approach Mademoiselle. She's on her computer, entering grades into PowerSchool. "Can I use the bathroom?"

She glances at her Fitbit Smartwatch. "Can you wait? Class is almost over."

"Please, Mademoiselle," I plead. "It's an emergency."

"All right. I'll see you in two weeks."

"Thank you. I promise I'll be on time."

When she doesn't respond, I leave the classroom, closing the door behind me, and hurry to the nearest bathroom. A blonde girl applying mascara at the sink glances my way, then returns to her task while I lock myself in a stall and collapse onto the toilet. I'm not sure what to do; if I should text Mom, go talk to Miss Dixon, or simply wait for the feeling to pass. The last thing I want is for them to have another reason to worry about me. It's not a secret that they already think I'm weak.

So I remain in the stall, imprisoned in my own mind, until the bell rings. The hallway is even busier than when Mom dropped me off, but I try not to let the commotion bother me as I navigate to Guidance. In Miss Dixon's office, I sit in a black swivel chair across from her desk and unwrap my Clif Bar.

"I'm glad you're not participating in the fast," Miss Dixon says. She takes her snack—apple slices and peanut butter—out of her polka dot purse and places them next to her computer. "If you ask me, I think it's a bit ridiculous."

"My mom said the same thing when she got the PTO newsletter. She wanted to call Principal Meyers, but I told her not to get involved. She has enough on her plate as it is."

Miss Dixon uses a plastic knife to smear peanut butter on an apple slice. "How are things with your mom?"

"They've been better," I respond honestly. "It's pretty unpredictable with her. Sometimes, we get along fine; other times, we can't be in the same room without fighting. She did agree to let me take Jamie to Bryant Park though. This Friday, we're renting a hotel room after my program, and then we're going skating in the morning."

Miss Dixon smiles. "That sounds like fun. Hopefully, it won't be too warm."

I glance out the small window next to her desk, where sleet falls from the grey sky. Filthy piles of snow from last week's snowfall surround the crowded parking lot. "I don't think I have to worry about that."

"What's the temperature?"

"Um . . ." I check my phone. "Forty-three degrees. It says it's windy too."

"Good thing you packed layers, huh?" Mom remarks. Whereas Jamie and I are already dressed for the day, she's still wearing her pajamas. A steaming mug of coffee is clutched in her hands.

"No kidding." I pull my silver parka over my UConn sweatshirt and zip it up to my chin, while Jamie wriggles into his red ski jacket. "Can I have the money?"

Mom hands me a fifty-dollar bill: forty to cover the price of the skates and ten for hot chocolate. "If you need anything, text me. I'll probably go on a walk later this morning. I might as well have some fun while we're here."

"Do you still remember how to do that?" I ask.

"Haha," she responds dryly. "Very funny. Do you need a snack or—"

"The hot chocolate will be plenty," I interrupt. "You've been to Starbucks. Even the shorts are massive there."

Her eyes drift to my empty cereal bowl on the dusty countertop. "I know, but you didn't have a lot for breakfast, and between the walking and the skating—"

Once again, I cut her off. "Oh my god, Mom! I'll be fine!"

"I'm ready." Jamie stands in the doorway bundled up in a baby blue pompom hat, a plaid scarf, fleece gloves, and black snow boots in addition to his jacket.

I laugh. "You know it's March, right?"

"You said it was windy."

"You're right, I did." I tuck my straight-legged jeans into my Uggs and adjust my purple beanie so it covers both of my ears. "We'll see you later, Mom."

"Be safe!" she calls after us.

Simultaneously rolling our eyes, Jamie and I leave our tiny hotel room and take the elevator to the lobby. Two middle-aged women are chatting by the fireplace while another woman stands outside the bathroom loudly talking on her phone. The bellhop, a cheerful young man named Chris, courteously holds open the door when he sees us approaching.

"Thank you," I say.

Chris smiles kindly. "Have a good morning."

"Oh, we will," Jamie assures him. "Grace, do you know where we're going?"

"It's only a couple blocks from here. Let's walk fast. I'm cold!"

"You know it's March, right?" he teases.

"You don't have to rub it in," I say, even though I'd probably do the same if I was in his shoes. "At least it's warmer than last week. You know how it was below thirty on Thursday?"

"Oh yeah." Jamie makes a face. "I forgot my key and had to wait in the garage until Kevin got home. What about it?"

"One of the counselors at CADE made us go outside."

After an exceptionally boring Process Group, Teagan, insisting that the fresh air would "clear out the cobwebs," had us bundle up for a thirty-minute walk through Central Park. Chloe brought a knitted blanket from the Group Room, while Maggie, who'd left her jacket in her mother's car, borrowed Emmy's massive fur-lined parka. And yet, they still spent the entire time whining about the cold.

"It was miserable," I continue. "I thought my ears would freeze."

"Thirty minutes isn't that bad," he says. "I was in the garage for two hours!"

"We should have a spare key. I used to lock myself out all the time too." The Walk Sign turns on, and we cross the street, approaching the elegant fountain terrace. A pigeon perches on the top left tier. "This is Bryant Park. It looks different without all the decorations."

Jamie glances around him in intrigue. Unlike me, this is his first time visiting the city. "I guess we'll have to come back around the holidays then."

I nod. "I like that plan."

Bryant Park's skating rink is quieter than I'd expected, especially since it will close in a couple days. Once I've rented two pairs of skates from a bored-looking woman at the rental desk, Jamie and I head to the locker room. We lace up our skates quickly and follow a young couple onto the ice. The second my feet touch the frozen ground, I stumble and grab hold of the wall.

"You all right?" Jamie asks.

"I'm fine," I lie. Whereas he took lessons at our local rink for four years, I can't recall the last time I went skating. It was probably sometime in middle school with Lou or Liam. "You go ahead. I'll catch up."

"Okay."

Flashing me two thumbs up, Jamie disappears behind a woman and a little girl. I, on the other hand, am hopeless. Every time I let go of the wall, three seconds later, fear or lack of balance send me right back.

I pull the hood of my sweatshirt over my beanie to combat the blustery wind. Why did I think this was a good idea?

To my surprise, it isn't much longer until my muscle memory kicks in. I cautiously release my hands and allow my feet to guide me around the rink. I move slowly at first, then as my confidence builds, so does my pace.

"Looking good!" Jamie exclaims as he laps me for the umpteenth time.

"You're not so bad yourself!" I respond.

"Watch this!"

He loops around behind me and snatches my beanie. I reach for his hat, but I miss and grab the back of his jacket instead. The next thing I know, we're lying on the ice, him on top of me, laughing uncontrollably.

"Are you hurt?" I ask once I've managed to catch my breath.

"No. Are you?"

"I don't think so." When I try to stand up, however, a sharp pain shoots through my right knee. I wince. "Ouch!"

"Here, I'll help you."

Jamie extends his hand, and I grab hold, using my uninjured leg to push off the ice. "Thanks."

"No problem."

"Listen, I think I'm done, but if you want to stay—"

"That's all right. My feet are pretty sore anyway."

So, after finishing our lap, we walk—or in my case limp—off

the rink. Jamie sits on the bench while I untie his skates. The second I remove them, a huge sigh of relief escapes his lips.

"You might need a bigger size next time," I say.

Jamie rubs his toes. "No kidding. So, where now?"

"One sec." I place my skates on the floor and adjust my wool socks, which are bunched around my ankles. "We have to return these, and then we'll find somewhere to get hot chocolate."

"Awesome," he responds with a toothy grin.

At the rental desk, I hand our skates to the woman. "Do you know where the closest Starbucks is?"

"There's one on 43rd and 6th," she says. "It's next to McDonalds."

Following her directions, Jamie and I leave Bryant Park and navigate through the busy city to 6th Avenue. We spot Starbucks across the street and hurry to the crosswalk, making the Walk Light by seconds. Inside the crowded shop, we wait behind a woman and her Maltese to place our order. A knitted pink jacket is wrapped around the dog's furry body.

Jamie nudges me. "Isn't it cute?" he whispers.

"Very. Did you see the dog on 5th Avenue with the red boots?"

"The Beagle?" Jamie nods. "I wish we could get another dog."

"I know," I say. "So do I."

"What can I get for you?" a perky cashier with curly hair and neon blue eyeshadow asks.

"Grande hot chocolate with whipped cream," Jamie says.

"And you?"

"Uh . . ." My foot nervously taps against the floor as I scan the overhead menu. I'd looked up the calories yesterday, yet with so much noise and commotion around me, I'm having a hard time thinking clearly. "Short hot chocolate. No toppings."

"That'll be six ninety-one." I give her a ten-dollar bill and receive three ones, a nickel, and four pennies in return. "Your name?"

"Grace."

"Okay, Grace. Your order will be ready shortly. Can I help who's next?"

While an older man places his order, Jamie and I wait by the milk dispensers with the woman and her Maltese. "How's your kn—" he begins to ask when my phone buzzes.

"Is that Mom?"

I nod. "She's just checking in. Hold these."

I hand him my gloves so I can reply to Mom's message: *at starbucks. skating was fun.* I press the blue arrow, then repocket my phone as another barista—a man with braided blonde hair—calls my name.

"I'll get them," Jamie offers. He picks up our hot chocolates and follows me to the back of the shop, where an employee is wiping down a booth. We patiently wait for him to finish to sit across from each other. Jamie takes a sip and exclaims, "That's hot!"

I laugh. "What were you expecting?"

"Good point." He blows on his drink, then tries again. "Nope, still too hot."

"Slow down," I say. "We don't have to rush."

Jamie studies his cup. Beneath the Starbucks logo, *I Love New York* is printed in a neoclassical font. "I wish we could stay here. Not forever of course, but at least for another day or two. It's nice to get away from home, you know?"

"I do," I say. "It's not that I dislike home; I just feel . . . stuck, if that makes sense. Every day it's the same thing. School, food, therapy, Mom."

"Are you and Mom okay?"

"We're fine. We're just working things out."

"Oh."

"But let's not talk about Mom. Tell me something about you. That's why we're here after all, isn't it?"

"Something about me . . ." Jamie taps his finger against his chin. "Well, there is one thing."

I dip a stir stick into my cup, swirl it around for several seconds, then lick the chocolate-coated wood. When I glance up, Jamie is watching me with a skeptical look on his face. "You were saying . . ." I prompt.

"Right. I think I have a friend."

"What do you mean 'you think'?"

"I mean, we've never hung out outside of school, but she's super nice to me, and we have a lot in common. We like the same TV shows and food and—"

"What's her name?"

"Sara Fisher."

"Liam's sister?"

"Oh, yeah. I forgot you're friends with Liam."

"Liam and I aren't friends anymore," I say.

"You aren't? What happened?"

As I have countless times before, I painstakingly recall our fallout in my mind: thirteen-year-old Liam, wearing an old soccer jersey and penguin-patterned lacrosse shorts, sitting across from me on my bed. I watch his demeanor shift from confused to dismayed as I swallow my fear and confess my love for him. I hear his devastating words: *I'm sorry, Grace. I just don't like you that way.*

"Nothing," I lie. "We just don't talk anymore."

"Well, Sara and I do. We sit together at lunch and talk about . . . everything. On Thursday, we spent most of the period predicting what will happen on the next season of *Stranger Things*." He laughs. "I want to ask her if she'd like to come over sometime. Do you think I should?"

"I think that's a great idea. Just make sure you clean your room. No offense, but it's kind of a nightmare in there."

"It's not *that* bad," he insists.

"Oh, really? You've had the same dirty socks on your floor for weeks—and don't even get me started on your closet."

"Whatever. Are you gonna finish your hot chocolate?"

"No, I've had enough. Do you want the rest?"

"Um . . ."

"It's okay, Jamie. Mom doesn't have to know. Anyway, I'm full, so it'll just go to waste."

Jamie reaches across the table and snatches my cup. "Hell no."

Watching him guzzle down my drink, I smile sadly. "We should probably head out. I told Mom we'd be back around eleven."

Jamie uses his glove to wipe a brown stain off his upper lip. "Fifteen more minutes."

"Ten," I negotiate. "Then we go back. Deal?"

Jamie extends his pinky towards me. The nail is encrusted with dried blood and chipped purple polish, and the skin surrounding it is inflamed. Before he can resist, I grab his hand and pry open his fist, revealing the rest of his fingers. All of them look the same, if not worse, as his pinky.

"What happened to your nails?"

Jamie quickly retracts his hand. "Nothing!"

"You're biting them, aren't you?" When he doesn't respond, I remove my right glove and show him my own damaged cuticles. "Look, I do it too. Mom says it's an anxious habit."

"I'm not anxious," he mumbles. "I'm fine."

"There's nothing wrong with having anxiety," I say. "It's just a matter of knowing how to deal with it. When I was in treatment, I learned a lot of coping skills that are actually pretty use—"

"I said I'm fine!"

"Okay, okay. You don't have to be so sensitive."

Jamie is quiet for several seconds. "I want to leave now," he says finally.

"What about the ten minutes?" I ask, but by then, he's already on his feet.

With a sigh, I push back my chair and follow him towards the door. He's a couple paces ahead of me, nearing the woman with the Maltese, who's talking on her phone while the dog lies next to her black boots. The dog's curious eyes hone in on my brother when he approaches them, although this time, Jamie doesn't smile. He doesn't even look its way.

10

"Are you done with the salt?"

"Yeah. Where do you want me to put it?"

"Leave it on the counter," Lou says. "So, how was skating?"

I shrug. "It was okay."

"Just okay?"

"I mean, I enjoyed being with Jamie and all, but at the same time, everything felt kind of forced, like we were trying too hard to get along. It's never been that way with him."

"Oh." Lou frowns. "Did you at least take pictures?"

"Of course. I'll show you them when my hands aren't covered in flour."

"Good idea." She glances around her kitchen, where baking ingredients, measuring cups, and other cooking utensils are scattered all over the place. "I'm so not looking forward to cleaning this up."

"You said this is for your church, right?"

"Uh-huh. Every March, my church does a bake sale to raise money for a mission trip. Ma isn't feeling well, so she asked if I could make lemon cupcakes. They're her specialty."

"And why are we helping her? I thought you hated your church."

"Because she promised she'd bring home leftovers. And let me tell you, those women who run the bake sale make some hella good food."

I laugh. "Now I understand."

"Where did you put the recipe?"

"Um . . . oh, it's behind the sugar. Here."

I hand Lou the recipe we'd printed off the internet, and she skims through the instructions with her thick brows furrowed. We've been working for twenty minutes, and so far, all we've managed to accomplish is assembling the dry ingredients.

"It says we need to beat the butter and sugar together with an electric mixer until they're light and fluffy. I think the mixer is in the cabinet under the sink. Can you check?"

I open the cabinet and lug the heavy mixer onto the counter. Lou places a stick of butter and a cup of sugar in the bowl and flips the ON switch. But it doesn't start.

"What the hell?"

"Did you plug it in?"

"Of course I . . . oh, never mind." She untangles the cord from around the mixer and wedges it into an outlet. The whisk immediately kicks into gear. "Okay. Now we have to add the eggs one at a time. Here, you do it. I always mix in the shells by accident."

I take the carton from her and crack an egg on the side of the metal bowl, waiting until the yolk has integrated with the sugar and butter to move on to the next. By the time I've added all four, as well a teaspoon of vanilla extract and two tablespoons of lemon zest, the batter is a liquidy yellow consistency.

"It looks too thin," I remark.

"That's because we haven't put in the dry ingredients yet." Lou grabs the glass bowl containing flour, salt, and baking soda, dumps it in the mixer, and raises the switch to full speed. Flour goes everywhere.

I reach around her and turn off the mixer. "Slow down, okay? You're supposed to gently mix it in—not all at once. Also, how many cups of sugar did you add?"

"One, I think."

I sigh. "The recipe calls for two, dumbass."

"Oops. Do you think we should start over?"

"Don't bother. I'm sure it'll be fine once you put in the right amount of sugar."

"Why are we so bad at this?" she asks as she dips a measuring cup into the bag of granulated sugar.

"Because our moms do all the cooking for us," I say. "Not to mention that every time I try to help Mom in the kitchen, she gets annoyed with me, and we end up fighting."

"Dude, same. It's, like, give me a break. I'm doing my best."

"Right? And then when I say I don't want to help, she accuses me of being lazy. I can't win."

"You know what?" Lou taps her index finger against her chin, a mischievous look on her face. "Fuck it!" She opens the spice cabinet, takes out a plastic bottle labeled *Onion Powder*, and before I can stop her, shakes a substantial amount into the cake batter. "Now that's more like it!"

"What the hell are you doing?" I ask.

"I'm just having a little fun. What's the harm in that? Hmm." She scours the cabinet for more savory spices. "How about ground mustard?"

I have to bite my lip to keep from laughing. "Go for it."

"Ranch Dressing Mix?"

"Oh, yes. We can't forget that."

"Um . . . cayenne pepper?"

"No, no. That'll mess up the color."

"Good point." Lou shuts the cabinet and hands me the mustard and the dressing mix. "You do the honors."

"Your mom is going to kill us," I say, but I take them from her nevertheless.

"What can I say? Payback is a bitch," Lou responds smugly. "Maybe I'll even go to church so I can see the look on her face."

"You might as well. There's no way she's bringing you left-overs now."

"Dammit!" Lou smacks her forehead. "I completely forgot about that!"

"You sure you want to go through with it?" I ask.

Without even hesitating, she nods. "Let's do this."

I'm sitting in a small room—alone. The walls are grey, the furnishings are sparse, and the concrete floor beneath my yellow gripper socks is spotless. I've been here before, though I can't remember when. I can't remember much of anything come to think of it. It's like I've been drugged; numbed; stripped from reality and banished to Zombie Land.

It wouldn't be the first time I've been there either.

I rest my heavy head against the table in front of me and close my eyes to the familiar tune of *Sweet Child O' Mine* that's playing somewhere nearby. When I reopen my eyes, a plump woman in turquoise scrubs has claimed the chair on the other side of the table. Her face is blurry, as though it's pixelated.

Above the woman's head, the clock is frozen at ten twenty-six, same as the date printed on my wristband. The paper is loosely looped around my scarred arm. I bet it would slide off effortlessly if I tried.

The blurry-faced woman clears her throat. She's speaking to me, but the music has become so loud that I can only catch certain words: *food . . . eat . . . hospital . . . sick . . .*

"I'm fine," I insist in a weak voice. "I just want to go home."

"Eat," the woman repeats.

She places something on the table and slides it towards me. It's a paper plate, about the size of my hand, with a swirly blue trim. And on it is a single lemon cupcake.

I wake up to my six thirty alarm feeling both confused and unsettled. Rubbing my eyes, I force myself out of bed and go downstairs. In the kitchen, Mom is standing at the stove spooning a thick beige batter into a pan.

"What are you making?" I ask.

"Pancakes. I hope that's okay."

"You know that pancakes are basically waffles, right?"

"I'm not going to fight with you," she says. "If you want cereal, that's your choice. You're old enough to make those decisions."

I instinctively begin to open the cereal cabinet, but I pause with my hand on the knob and look at Mom. She's watching me in her peripheral vision, while she continues to monitor the pancakes. Wisps of steam rise off the golden-brown surface. The sight alone is making my mouth water.

I clear my throat. "Fine. I'll have the stupid pancakes."

Her lips twitch into a faint smile. "Thank you."

"Whatever. Is there anything I can help with?"

"No, I'm all set."

"Oh. Okay."

"But perhaps we can make something together later," she offers. "I heard you baked cupcakes yesterday."

I'm suddenly reminded of my distressing dream. "Yeah, uh, Lou's church was having a bake sale, and her mom wanted her to help."

"That's nice. How did it go?"

"We did our best," I lie. "I don't think they were very good though."

"Well, if you're ever interested in learning how to cook, I'd be happy to teach you."

"I'll think about it. How soon will breakfast be ready?"

Mom uses a spatula to lift one of the fluffy pancakes. "Now."

She slides three pancakes and a small pile of mixed fruit onto a plate and hands it to me. I take a seat at the table while she wipes spilled batter off the counter with a sponge.

"Honey or syrup?"

"Honey."

She retrieves a bear-shaped bottle from the cabinet above the stove. Crystalized sugar coats the cap as I drizzle a modest amount of honey onto my pancakes. I wait until she's sitting next to me to saw off a piece and tentatively take a bite.

"Not bad, huh?" she asks. When I don't respond, she tries again. "So, how's your knee?"

I make a face. "It's still pretty sore."

"If it isn't better by this weekend, I'll contact an orthopedic surgeon. Hopefully you didn't tear anything."

"God, I hope not."

Mom stabs a banana with her fork and pops it in her mouth. "At least you're not playing soccer anymore."

For some reason, her comment really strikes a nerve. "Anymore? You know, just because I'm off the team now doesn't mean I'm done forever. I'm definitely trying out next year—that much I know."

"As long as you're eating enough, I have no problem with that."

I groan. "It's all about the food with you, isn't it? It's never about what I want."

"Grace, what are you talking about? Everything I do is for you. My entire life revolves around your well-being."

"Stop doing that!" I exclaim.

"Doing what?"

"Turning the tables on me. Making me feel like a failure. Psychoanalyzing everything I do."

"I'm just looking out for you. I'm sorry if you can't understand that."

I avert my gaze to the two untouched pancakes on my plate, then to the sticky fork clutched in my hand. My grip is so tight around the metal handle that my knuckles have started to turn white. "It's not like you understand me either," I say softly.

"How can I when you never tell me anything?"

"I'm trying."

"I know," she says, and her voice, as well, is notably quieter than usual. "So am I."

11

I never imagined that there would be a subject I'd find more unbearable than math, but the longer Mr. Duffy drones on about European Nationalism, I'm beginning to question whether that is still true. I'm not the only one bored out of my mind, as all my classmates are either on their phones or asleep. In front of me, Jess and Tiffany are talking about a party they went to over the weekend.

"Did you hear that Liam hooked up with another girl?" Jess whispers. She opens a Tupperware container containing an undressed salad and begins to push around the vegetables with her fork.

"Yes! Do you know who she was?"

"Some sophomore on the basketball team. Don't tell Bianca though. You know how she gets." Now Jess is using the tines to methodically remove shredded carrots from the lettuce. She's already divided the tomatoes, cucumbers, and peppers into three uniform piles.

"What are you doing?" Tiffany asks.

Jess shrugs. "Just sorting my salad."

"In 1929, a treaty that recognized the Vatican City as an independent state was passed," Mr. Duffy informs us in his usual monotone. "Does anyone know what this treaty was called?"

Laura Mulroney raises her hand. "The Lateran Treaty."

Mr. Duffy scribbles *Lateran Treaty* on the whiteboard with a red EXPO marker. "Can someone else explain how this relates to European Nationalism?" When no one volunteers, his bushy brows furrow disapprovingly. "Did anybody do their homework? Yes—thank you, Mr. Flaherty."

While Michael Flaherty responds to Mr. Duffy's question, I stare out the window overlooking the teachers' parking lot. Two students—a boy and a girl—are chatting next to Mrs. Perkenson's Subaru. As I watch, the boy leans in for a kiss, pressing the girl's back against the car as she drags her fingers through his curly hair.

"Grace?" Jess shakes a stack of papers in my face.

"Huh?"

"Homework," she impatiently explains.

"Oh, thanks." I take the stack from her, select the packet on top, and pass the rest to Heather Maiden, who sits behind me. *Chapter 12 Reading Notes: The Rise of Fascism* the header reads.

I sigh. This, in addition to my English reading chart and the Spanish vocabulary sheet I planned to do during my free period (but couldn't because Miss Dixon was in a meeting), means I'll have at least an hour of homework tonight—if not more.

In the parking lot, the couple is still kissing. Now the boy's hand is up the girl's skintight shirt. Another sigh escapes my lips. Some days, I really hate this school.

When history ends, I head to the office to wait for Mom to pick me up. As I'm standing at the front door, deleting Classroom updates on my school email, someone tugs on my ponytail. "Lou, what the hell?"

Lou smirks. "How's my bestie doing?"

"Bestie?" I repeat, half-serious, half-teasing. "What are we in second grade?"

"I wish. Maybe then I wouldn't have my mom up my ass twenty-four seven."

"Are you talking about the bake sale? Because I knew we shouldn't have—"

"It's not the bake sale," Lou interrupts. "She threw a fit about that too, but it was actually about college this time."

"College?"

Lou nods. "I told her I want to tour Vassar over break, and she said I'd never get in; that I don't take school seriously, I slack off—stuff like that. I mean, it's not a secret that she thinks I'm stupid, but she doesn't have to rub it in all the time."

"That was really shitty of her," I say.

"Right? I'm still gonna apply though. She doesn't get to tell me how to live my life. I'm not a kid anymore, and the sooner she understands that, the better. You feel me?"

I'm about to respond when my phone buzzes. Mom texts: here. where r u?

"I have to go," I say. "Mom's taking me to CTC. She wants to get my knee checked out since it's still sore."

"Yikes. Let me know how that goes."

"I will. I hope you can work things out with your mom."

Lou rolls her eyes. "Don't hold your breath."

When I join Mom in the car, she hands me my Subway order: a six-inch wheat flatbread with provolone cheese, lettuce, tomatoes, cucumbers, pickles, and honey mustard and a bottle of one percent milk. Her six-inch Italian is in one cup holder, while the other contains a large iced coffee. Since we don't have time to eat lunch at home, we decided this morning that Subway was the next best option.

"How was school?" she asks.

"Fine." I unwrap my sandwich, and the uncomfortable silence that has dominated our car rides for the last two weeks resumes.

We arrive at Connecticut Treatment Center ten minutes later. As we follow a faded sign to the Department of Ortho-pedic Surgery, we pass the Emergency Room, where two EMTs are wheeling a stretcher through the entrance. And in a split-second, I see her: the scared little girl wrapped in a blanket to combat the brisk October air as a paramedic reassures her that *everything will be okay.*

It's as if I'm riding Disney's Tower of Terror; plummeting into sheer darkness with my heart in my throat. I quickly avert my gaze, afraid that if I look any longer, the memories will over-whelm me.

Keeping her left hand firmly on the wheel, Mom pats my thigh with her right. "It's in the past," she says. "Just like every-thing else is."

I'm not sure how to respond, so I continue to stare out the window. "You missed the turn."

"Did I?" Glancing over her shoulder, Mom cautiously reverses into a crowded parking lot. She finds a spot between a

Honda Civic and a Mini Cooper and quiets her engine. "Sorry about that."

"No worries."

I leave my bookbag in the car and follow her inside the modern two-story building, discarding my sandwich wrappers in a trashcan on my way. Mom checks me in at the receptionist's desk, and afterwards, we sit in the waiting area and take out our phones to pass the time until it's my turn.

"Grace?" A stony-faced technician with thick black hair beckons me through a door. She leads me down a hallway to a white room with an elevated X-Ray machine in the corner. There, I sit on an examination table while she takes my blood pressure. "How are you today?"

"I'm okay."

"I understand you're here because you hurt your knee?"

"Yeah. I was skating with my brother a couple weeks ago, and I fell. It's a little swollen, but I can walk fine for the most part."

"Well, I'll take an X-Ray to be sure. Which knee is it?"

"Right. Do I have to take my pants off?"

"You're wearing sweats, so as long as you roll them up, it shouldn't be a problem." She waits until I've complied, stopping mid-thigh, to continue. "I need you to swing your leg onto the table. You can lie down if it makes you more comfortable."

"I'll sit."

I watch her pull the X-Ray machine over my knee. One minute later, I hear her yell "hold still," followed by three muffled buzzing sounds. The next thing I know, she's switched off the machine and is lugging it back to its resting position.

"Come with me," she says.

"What happens next?" I ask as I carefully step off the table and limp into the hallway.

"Dr. Wilson needs to examine your X-Rays." She stops at Room Six and nudges the door open with her hip. "You'll wait here."

Unlike the previous room, the walls are a pleasant shade of blue, and three identical cabinets overlooking a white counter have replaced the bulky X-Ray machine. A box of tissues, glass jars containing Q-tips and cotton balls, and a multiline telephone crowd the countertop.

"The doctor will be in shortly," the technician says and leaves without another word.

Once she's gone, I casually lean against the examination table, squinting to read a poster about osteoporosis that's taped to the second cabinet. Under *What Is Osteoporosis?* a simple explanation states: *Osteoporosis is a condition that weakens the bones and increases the risk of fractures. It is a "silent disease" because bone loss occurs without symptoms.* The explanation is accompanied by an image of two cartoon women. The first stands up straight, while the second is hunched over, her transparent spine shaped like a sideways U.

Isaac has osteoporosis. He was diagnosed in the hospital as a result of malnutrition. He doesn't talk about it often—in fact, the one time I remember him mentioning his condition was on our first date. Whereas I'll be able to play soccer again someday, he never will. It's no wonder he redid his room. If I was in his shoes, I wouldn't want the constant reminders either.

A knock on the door makes me jump. I glance away from the poster as the orthopedic surgeon, a middle-aged woman with oval glasses and short brown hair, enters the room. She sets down her computer and gives me a firm handshake.

"It's a pleasure to meet you, Grace. I'm Dr. Wilson."

"Hi." I shake her hand. "So, what's up with my knee?"

"The X-Rays look good, so I'm thinking you probably sprained it. I'll do an examination to be sure." Rolling up my pant leg, she begins to prod and bend my knee with her ice-cold hands. "Does it hurt here?" she asks several times. "How about here?"

"No . . . no . . . no . . ." She presses on a spot below my patella, and I wince. "Yes."

"Okay. It looks like you do have a minor sprain. I'll give you a brace—you should wear it for one month, as well as ice your knee on a daily basis. Do you play sports?"

Once again, my eyes hone in on the osteoporosis poster. "Not right now."

"Good. Try to avoid any physical activity for the time being. Too much pressure on your knee could make the sprain worse. If it's not better in six weeks, have your mom call me, and I'll take another look."

"All right." After a beat of silence, I ask, "So . . . are we done?"

"We are." Dr. Wilson glances at her watch. "It must be nice to get out of school early, huh?"

I don't bother trying to explain my half-day schedule to her. "Yeah."

"You're a . . ."

"Junior. At Everett."

"So is my son. He goes to private school though."

"Cool." I step down from the table and slide on my moccasins, anxious to leave before she can ask me about—

"Have you started looking at colleges?"

Dammit. "No," I respond curtly.

"Oh. Okay."

And just like that, the conversation is over.

WALKING INTO CADE ON MY LAST DAY OF PROGRAM IS A strange feeling—and not only because of my knee brace. As Mom and I take the elevator to the third floor, I try not to dwell on the fact that if all goes well with my recovery, I'll never step foot in this facility again. I'll never shock myself on the entry door with the staticky knob or pass the bizarre Elizabethan painting across from the phlebotomist's office or stumble on the miniature staircase leading up to the Adolescent Services Department. No matter how many times I make that mistake, I always forget they are there.

In the kitchen, I prepare my snack—Spicy Buffalo-flavored Wheat Thins and an apple—and then I join the others at the table. They chat about boys, television shows, and their weekend plans, and I try to pay attention even though my mind is in a million different places.

After snack, while Teagan passes out worksheets for today's Dialectical Behavioral Therapy lesson, I follow Emilia into her office. I perch on the edge of the couch and nervously tap my foot against the off-white rug as she takes a seat at her desk.

She must sense my trepidation because she says, "You'll be all right, Grace. I know change is scary, but you're not alone.

You'll have your mother and your guidance counselor and your new therapist to help you navigate recovery outside of a treatment facility."

"I don't want to disappoint them," I admit quietly.

"You won't. Everyone understands that this is a process, and that just because you don't require a treatment program anymore doesn't mean you're fully recovered."

"And college?"

"What about college?"

"It's all anyone talks about at school, and I still have no idea what I'm going to do. Even Lou knows more than me."

"Have you thought about what major you want to pursue?"

"No."

"Well, how about the size of the school?"

"Small. I'd probably get overwhelmed if there were too many people."

"That's a good start. Maybe over spring break—if you don't have other plans of course—you and your mother could tour local small colleges so you can get a better idea of what you're looking for. Boston is close. There are a number of schools there that might interest you."

"I guess. I just . . ." I sigh. "I just feel like everything is happening too fast. I knew I'd have to leave CADE eventually, but I didn't think it would be this soon."

"You can do this," she reiterates. "One minute at a time, right?"

I take a deep breath, then slowly exhale. "One minute at a time."

When my session ends, Emilia and I hug. I wonder if she can feel how fast my heart is beating inside my chest.

"It's time to take control of your life," she whispers. "It's time to break free."

"Thank you," I mumble into her soft ivory sweater. "I'll miss you, Emilia."

Emilia pats my back. "I'll miss you too, Grace."

In the dining room, Maggie, Kimmy, and Chloe are raving about a Netflix Original that they're hooked on, while Miriam and the new girl Rylee prepare their dinners in the kitchen. When they're finished, they switch places with Kimmy and me. Once Kimmy has dished out her cheese ravioli and I've microwaved my soy burger and sweet potato fries, I sit between Miriam and Maggie to begin eating.

I drag a fry through a dollop of ketchup as Miriam nibbles on an asparagus stalk and Maggie chows down on a corn dog. On the other side of the table, Rylee spreads her marinara sauce around her plate with her fork. The sound of the metal utensil scraping against the ceramic is very grating, but nobody, not even Teagan or Emilia, bothers to point it out to her. So neither do I.

"This is it, huh?" Miriam says. Behind her reddish bangs, her eyes dart back and forth between the thick slice of vegetarian lasagna on her plate and me.

"It doesn't have to be," I respond. "You have my number. If you need anything—"

"No, if *you* need anything."

I laugh. "We can be like—what's the opposite of pro-ana?"

"Pro-recovery?" she suggests.

"Yeah. Pro-recovery buddies."

Now Miriam is laughing as well. She picks up her fork and

finally digs into her lasagna, starting with the slightly burnt edges. "I like that plan."

Whereas Miriam is able to polish off her lasagna in twenty minutes, it takes Rylee nearly twice as long to finish her spaghetti and chocolate protein shake. Once her plastic cup is empty, we clear our dishes and follow Teagan into the Group Room for my Goodbye Group.

"Have you chosen your Goodbye Song?" Teagan asks. She and the other girls recline onto the surrounding couches, while I sit upright on the beige ottoman in the center of the room.

"*Shake It Out*," I respond. "It's by Florence & the Machine."

Teagan unlocks her phone and opens Spotify. "Ah, found it."

Regrets collect like old friends

Here to relive your darkest moments

As Florence Welch's haunting voice fills the cramped room, I close my eyes and nod along to the familiar beat. I force myself to stay in the present, because I know if I don't, my crippling fears will overwhelm me.

This is a good thing, I remind myself. *This is me taking control of my life*. A soft sigh escapes my lips, followed by another seconds later. *This is me breaking free*.

12

"In eight hundred feet, the destination is on your left."

"You can turn that off now," Mom says.

"Okay."

I pick up her phone and press *End Route* on Maps as Mom pulls into a crowded parking lot. She finds an empty *Visitor Parking* spot near two dumpster bins and quiets the engine. Peering at the building—a broad, three-story estate with a red brick exterior—she remarks, "This reminds me of my old therapist's office."

"I didn't know you had a therapist," I say as I follow her through a set of automatic doors into the lobby. To our right is a wooden bench and a directory; to our left, an elevator and the door to an emergency staircase.

"Yes, when I was your age. His name was Dr. Wojciechowski, but everyone knew him as Dr. Wojo." Mom peers at the directory. "221. Stairs or elevator?"

I gesture to my knee brace. "Elevator."

When we reach the second floor, we walk down a lengthy carpeted hallway, scanning the room numbers in the process. Anna David's suite is located at the end, next to the men's restroom. Mom holds open the door, and I enter a well-lit waiting room. Eerie meditation music quietly plays from a speaker on a black coffee table, while inside Anna's office, I hear muffled talking.

Next to the speaker is a colorful stack of pamphlets. As Mom reads this week's edition of *Time*, I pick up a green brochure titled *Teens and Eating Disorders* and skim through statistics, resources, and inspirational quotes such as "today is a fresh start" and "this too shall pass." If I had ten dollars for every time I've heard something along those lines, I'd be set for life.

By the time I'm finished reading, it's nine past three. I place the pamphlet on top of an outdated flyer for a Sports Nutrition Workshop and nudge Mom's arm. "She's late."

"She's probably wrapping up."

"For ten minutes?" I groan. "This is so stupid!"

"First of all, it's not stupid," Mom responds firmly, "and second of all, if you're so bored, why don't you tell me about school? I know you had a chemistry test today. How was that?"

"It was fi—" I begin to say when Anna's door opens. A muscular boy in a football jersey says a few parting words to Anna, then disappears into the hallway.

"You must be Grace." Anna's hazel eyes peer at me from behind her rectangular glasses. She's wearing a multicolor striped blouse and white ankle pants. "I'm Anna. It's nice to meet you."

"Same," I lie. "This is my mom by the way."

"Kira." Mom shakes Anna's hand. "Do you want me to come in or should I wait here?"

"Wait here," Anna responds. "I'll invite you in at the end of our session."

So while Mom returns to her magazine, I follow Anna into a roomy office that's furnished with a desk, a black task chair, a filing cabinet, and a maroon couch. In the corner, under a window that overlooks a vacant courtyard, I notice a digital scale. I place a massive decorative pillow onto the blue shag rug and take a seat on the couch.

"Don't get comfy just yet," Anna says. "I have to weigh you first."

"Right."

I kick off my shoes and join her in the corner, waiting until 0.00 shows up on the scale's display to step on backwards. Once she has recorded my number, I return to the couch and prop my injured leg on an ottoman, while she sits across from me in the chair.

"Is this your first time seeing a nutritionist?"

I shake my head. "There was a woman at my residential, Nikki. I'd meet with her once a week to talk about my meal plan."

"You're on Exchanges, yes?"

"Yeah. Here, this is from yesterday." I hand her a crumpled Exchange sheet that I'd stuffed in my pocket before Mom and I left.

Anna studies the chart. "Is this about what you eat every day?"

"Pretty much. I eat different foods obviously. Like for dinner, I'll have hot dogs, soy burgers, soup—stuff like that. I'll sometimes have a frittata, but only when Mom buys the good cheese."

"How about pizza?"

I shake my head. "I don't like pizza. It makes my stomach hurt."

"It does?"

"Uh-huh. A lot of foods do."

"Like what?"

"Waffles, cake, muffins," I list. "Most desserts actually. Mom makes okay cookies, but I don't like the stuff she gets at the store. Also, she keeps buying ice cream even though I've told her, like, one hundred times that I prefer fro-yo. Oh, and I hate dough-nuts. They're gross."

"When was the last time you had a doughnut?"

"Uh . . . a couple years ago, maybe. I don't really remember."

"A couple years, huh?" Anna considers this. "You know, it's good to challenge yourself to eat foods that intimidate you."

"They don't intimidate me," I say. "I just don't like them."

"Did you like them before you had an eating disorder?" When I don't respond, she says, "It's common for people strug-gling with eating disorders to develop fears of certain foods that they may perceive as bad or unhealthy."

"But they *are* unhealthy," I point out.

"It's okay to indulge sometimes. Food is meant to be fun."

"At residential, we'd do this thing called Fun Foods," I say, "and it was when every Monday, Nikki would choose a dessert that we'd have to eat. Sometimes we would make it too. A lot of the kids were really anxious about that, but not me. It was never anything too bad, like chocolate cake or brownies or—"

"Doughnuts?"

"Yeah. No doughnuts."

Anna taps her index finger against her chin. "When you were younger, what was your favorite kind of doughnut?"

"Jelly, I guess. Powdered—not glazed."

"That's my favorite too," she says with a smile. "If you're up for it, I'd like you to go out and get a doughnut this week. There's a new bakery on Main Street that I've heard great things about—The Sweet Spot, I believe it's called."

"I don't know . . ."

"At least think about. The only way you'll be able to over-come your fear is by facing it head-on."

"I'm not afraid," I mumble.

"Then you shouldn't have a problem, yes?" When I don't respond, she changes the subject. "Is there anything else you want to talk about with me?"

"Not that I can think of."

"Let's see . . ." Anna opens a manila folder titled *Grace E*, removes a stapled packet, and flips to the second page. "According to Emilia's notes, you're doing well physically. But when was the last time you got your period?"

"Uh . . . September, I think."

"So, you haven't gotten it since you started refeeding?"

I shake my head. "Nope."

Anna continues flipping through the packet. "Are you sexually active?"

"No!" I exclaim. Lowering my voice, I add, "I mean, I'm not. Not yet."

"Okay, well, we'll keep an eye on your period. If you still haven't had it in another month, we can reevaluate your meal plan. Perhaps you aren't eating enough fats."

"I'm eating the same amount of food that I did at residential. It's not my fault if I have a slow cycle."

"Of course it's not your fault. That said, a normal cycle is indicative of good health. It's a sign that your body is functioning properly."

"My body is fine. Even when I was eating less, it was fine."

"How do you figure?"

"I used to play soccer," I explain. "Before I was admitted to the hospital, my team was training for playoffs. We'd run two miles at the start of practice, and I was able to keep up with everyone else. I was actually one of the fastest runners."

"Do you miss soccer?"

"Of course. The problem is that everyone says in order to play again, I have to eat more. I don't know if I can do that. I mean, I already feel like I eat too much, and the only exercise I'm allowed to do is take walks around my block."

"If you'd like to increase your amount of exercise, I'd be happy to help you adjust your intake."

"I'll think about it."

"All right." Anna checks her watch. "We're almost out of time. I'm going to invite your mother in for the last few minutes, okay?"

"Okay, but can you not tell her about the doughnut thing?"

"Why not?"

"I just . . ." I sigh. "Never mind. You can tell her if you really want to."

"I'll leave that up to you," Anna says. "After all, this is your recovery."

"I know," I respond. "Everyone says that too."

THE SWEET SPOT IS A SMALL, RETRO BAKERY NEAR MAX Burger and a fitness center Mom briefly belonged to. The fluorescent ceiling lights casts a rainbowlike shimmer against the checkered floor, and the booths are bright red. There's even a jukebox in the seating area. I watch as a young woman inserts a quarter into the coin drop and pushes a yellow button. Rick Astley's *Never Gonna Give You Up* begins to play.

Another young woman, presumably her friend, buries her face in her hands. "You've got to be kidding me, Allie."

I'm also fighting frustration—only for a much different reason. And as I stand at the counter, overwhelmed by the sugary aroma, the noisy chatter from the three boys behind us in line, and the abundance of calorific baked goods in the display case, I'm having second thoughts about agreeing to come here.

"You're looking," Mom says.

"I don't know what you're talking about," I lie.

She sighs. "You know ten or twenty calories won't make a difference, right?"

"I know."

"So choose what *you* want—not what your disorder wants."

I glance behind us, where one of the boys is watching us out of the corner of his eye. "Can you keep it down, Mom?"

"I'm sorry. I didn't realize I was embarrassing you."

"I'm not embarrassed. I'm—"

"What can I get for you?" the chipper cashier asks.

"I'll have an Old Fashioned," Mom says. "Grace?"

"Uh, Jelly. Powdered."

"That'll be three seventy-five."

While the cashier bags our doughnuts, Mom places her credit card in the chip reader. "How do you feel about getting a debit card, Grace?"

Her question takes me by surprise. "I don't think it's necessary. I mean, it's not like I buy a lot of stuff."

"Yes, but it's important to learn how to handle your money. We could set up your own bank account and—"

"Okay, fine," I interrupt. "If it matters so much to you, I'll get one."

"I want it to matter to you too. You're almost seventeen. Before long, you'll be an adult, and then you'll have many more responsibilities."

"You can't expect me to act like an adult when you treat me like a kid," I say. "That's not how it works."

"I don't treat you like a kid."

The cashier hands Mom a brown paper bag. "Would you like your receipt?"

"No, thank you," Mom responds. "We can take them home if you prefer," she says to me. "It's noisy here, and, well, I know that can be overwhelming for you."

I roll my eyes. "Sure, Mom. You don't treat me like a kid at all."

"Grace, I—"

"That booth in the back is empty. Let's sit there."

We take a seat across from each other on the soft red seats, and Mom distributes our doughnuts. I tear off a chunk and hold it between my index finger and thumb, feeling the sticky powder adhere to my skin. Then, ignoring the obtrusive thoughts racing through my mind, I pop it in my mouth.

"When was the last time we went out for doughnuts?" Mom asks.

"Not sure. It's been a few years."

"They're pretty good, huh?"

"They're all right." I take another bite, this time out of the center. A drop of the gooey raspberry jelly misses my mouth and spills onto my chin. I sigh. "Great."

"Smooth, Grace," Mom says.

"I'd like to see you do better," I retort. "These things are literally a recipe for disaster!"

"When did you get to be so funny?"

"Well, it's obviously not genetics."

She chuckles. "Touché."

As I'm cleaning my face with a napkin, I say, "Just so you know, I wasn't scared of doing this. I know you think I don't want to get better, but I do—I swear."

"Hey. Look at me." Mom sets down her doughnut and reaches for my hands. "I never thought that about you, okay? I know you want this; I see you fighting for it every day, and you have come so far, but sometimes when things don't go as planned, I forget that, and I'm only able to focus on the bad. And that's not fair, because there is so much more good."

"You're just saying that."

"I'm not," she insists. She retracts her hands and wipes them on her jeans, wrinkling her nose when the powdered sugar from my doughnut smudges the dark denim. "Now go wash your hands. They're disgusting."

"Thanks a lot."

I polish off the last bite of my doughnut and stand up. In the bathroom, I scrub my hands with lemon-scented soap until they're no longer covered in sugar and grease and swish my mouth with sink water. When I return to the booth, Mom's eyes are glued to her phone.

"You're worse than me," I joke.

"Jamie's PE teacher emailed me," she responds in a serious voice. "He hasn't gone to gym all week."

"What?"

Mom sighs. "I'll call him when we get home. Come on, let's get out of here."

Zipping up my grey hoodie, I follow Mom outside. For the first time in months, the temperature is warm and mild—fifty-eight degrees, according to my phone. Spring will be here in less than a week, and I can't wait. I'm ready to put this dreadful winter behind me once and for all. I'm ready to move on.

13

On the first day of spring, my brother comes down with a dreadful cold—or so he claims. Although he doesn't have a fever, nor any other cold-like symptoms, Mom excuses him from school for two days. By the third day, however, she's not so lenient.

"Jamie, you have to get up," I hear her insist as I prepare my breakfast—cornflakes and a glass of orange juice—in the kitchen. Jamie says something that I can't make out, and she groans. "I'm not playing this game anymore. Get out of bed."

Two minutes later, she returns downstairs visibly upset. "I can't win with him. He isn't sick—that much I know."

"Maybe he has a test," I suggest. "In middle school, I'd always pretend to be sick when I hadn't studied. How are his grades?"

"He has a C in math, and he has a couple missing assign-ments that I've been meaning to talk to him about, but other than that, he's doing well. Speaking of which, your report card came in the mail yesterday."

"Crap." I'd received my report card last week in advisory, however after seeing my GPA, I've been purposely avoiding telling Mom. I forgot that the school mails them out as well. "I'm sorry. I know it's not great."

"You don't need to apologize," she responds. "You're smart. I'm confident that you'll get your grades up by the end of the semester."

"I hope you're right. The SATs, on the other hand . . ." I make a face. "They're next week, and I feel like I'm going to do so badly."

"First of all, I doubt that's true," she responds, "and also, if you aren't pleased with your score, you can always retake it. But until that happens, I wouldn't overthink it. Many colleges don't even require you to submit scores anymore."

"That's what Emilia said. I don't know if she told you, but we talked about college when I was at CADE."

"She did. She said you were thinking about touring colleges in Boston over spring break."

"That was her idea. But I know you'll probably be too busy with work."

"I could take a couple days off," Mom says. "My boss shouldn't have a problem with that."

"You have a nice boss."

"Her son was in rehab when he was your age. She gets it."

"You told her about me?"

"I had to. I couldn't significantly reduce my hours without giving her a legitimate reason. You understand that, right?"

I stick a heaping spoonful of cereal in my mouth so I won't have to respond.

Mom sighs. "I'll talk to her today and figure out what fits with her schedule. Would you rather go towards the beginning or end of break?"

"Beginning."

"Great. I'll see what I can do."

"Okay . . ."

Sensing my apprehension, Mom says, "I promise it will be fun. Think of it as your reward for getting through the SATs."

"So, from one school thing to another. Sounds really rewarding."

"You'll be surprised. Boston is great. There's so much to do, so much to see—"

"So many people," I grumble.

Mom, who's rinsing her bowl in the sink, flicks water at me. "That's enough negativity for one morning, thank you."

I flinch. "On that note, I'm going to get dressed."

Handing her my empty dishes, I head upstairs to my room. I rummage through my pants drawer for my grey skinny jeans, and when I can't find them, settle for black leggings. Because it's almost sixty degrees, I pair the leggings with a loose off-the-shoulder top that I bought at Marshall's.

Jamie's door is ajar when I pass his room, so I pause to peek inside. He's face-first on his bed with a pillow over his head. On the other end, his feet—one bare, one half-covered in a dirty white sock—poke out from his thick comforter.

"Jamie?" I whisper.

No response.

"Jamie, I'll see you later. Feel better." I close the door and tiptoe away without another word.

Whether or not he's actually asleep, I don't know. What I do know, however, is that something is not right. I wish there was a way that I could help him, but then again, it's hard to help someone else when you still haven't figured out how to help yourself.

Mr. Duffy's narrow eyes dart around the classroom. He's sitting behind his desk, stopwatch in his hand, supervising every junior whose last name falls between Ch and Fo as we plod through the SATs.

"Pencils down," he orders flatly. "Close your booklet. You may now take a five-minute break. When the break is over, we will move on to the final section."

I follow my classmates into the hallway, where they vanish into the bathroom or meet up with friends from other testing rooms. Lou is sitting outside of A-107 with a sour look on her face.

"I hate math," she grumbles. "It's, like, the second dumbest thing ever."

"What's the first?"

"Religion." She sighs. "I can't wait to get out of here, so I won't have to listen to Ma grill me for not going to church or sit through another bullshit dinnertime prayer. That's why I have to do well on the SATs—or at least okay."

"And how do you think you've done so far?"

"Bad. I should have taken the prep course."

"I know the feeling."

"At least you have extra time, right? Because of your special needs?"

"It's called an Individualized Education Plan, and that's only if I request it ahead of time."

"Why didn't you?"

"I'm not dumb," I say. "Just because I have issues doesn't mean I should be treated differently than everyone else."

"Nobody thinks you're dumb," Lou responds, "but if I were you, I'd totally take advantage of that stuff. Hell, I'll gladly take your extra time any day of the week."

"Miss Jackson!" Ms. Lloyd emerges from A-107 and scowls at Lou. "What are you doing out here? Break ended two minutes ago!"

Lou groans. "Okay, okay. I'm coming." To me, she says, "I'll text you later. Good luck."

"Thanks," I respond. "I'm gonna need it."

But luck is not on my side, as the final section—math with a calculator—is even harder than I expected. Time is almost up by the time I reach the grid-in questions, so I hastily attempt to solve the first two and make educated guesses on the rest.

After Mr. Duffy has collected our packets, we grab our phones from the box on his desk and head outside, where our rides are waiting bumper-to-bumper in the pickup lane. I scan the colorful lineup for Mom's car, but it's nowhere to be seen.

"Grace!" Kevin pokes his head out the window of his Kia. "Over here!"

Confused, I tentatively approach him. "Where's Mom?"

"She had to meet with a patient, so she asked me if I could pick you up."

"But don't you work too?"

"My twelve o'clock meeting was cancelled. Come on, get in."

He unlocks the door, and I climb in, feeling the sticky vinyl of the seat cover rub against my bare legs. Between this and Mr. Duffy's excessively air-conditioned room, I'm regretting wearing shorts—even if it is sixty-four and sunny.

"You look tired," Kevin observes. He flicks on his left turn signal and follows a black Toyota onto East Main Street.

"I just spent four hours taking the SATs. Of course I'm tired."

"I remember those days. The ACTs were worse—are you signed up for those too?"

"No." I turn on the radio and adjust the dial to my favorite alternative station. Third Eye Blind's *Semi-Charmed Life* blasts through the speakers.

"I love this song," Kevin remarks.

"You do?" For some reason, I hadn't pegged him as an alt-rock type.

He nods. "The first concert I went to was Third Eye Blind. They were playing near my college, so my friends and I ditched psychology to see them. It was definitely worth the F."

"My friend's girlfriend missed school to go to a Metallica concert," I respond. "She said they're even better live than on the radio."

"I was never into hard rock," Kevin says. "My sister, however, used to listen to it all the time. She must have owned at least one hundred hair metal albums when we were growing up."

"I didn't know you have a sister."

"Aurora. She's a year older than me."

"What's she like?"

Kevin smiles. "Amazing. She's the strongest person I know. She's been through a lot, but she never gave up—no matter how tough things were. She said it's the hard times that build character, and that without them, she wouldn't be who she is today. And she's right."

"I know. I sometimes feel that way too." I regret my words the second they leave my lips. The last person I want to be vulnerable with is my mom's four-month boyfriend. "So, uh, does she live around here?"

"No, she lives in San Francisco."

"Lucky."

"You really miss California, huh?"

"More than you'd know," I say. "But I'm going to move back there someday. I want to live by the ocean. I want a dog too."

"Why can't you have a dog here?"

"You're allergic."

"So? It's not my house."

"Still, I wouldn't want to walk it in the winter. I don't know why anyone would. I mean, I see people walking their dogs when it's, like, twelve degrees outside, and they look miserable."

"When you love someone, you'll do just about anything to make them happy," Kevin says. "I learned that when I had my daughters."

"I wish my dad felt that way about me." Dammit! Once

again, my big mouth has a mind of its own. "I'm sorry. I know he's probably the last person you want to talk about."

"It's okay. My father left me too."

"I didn't know that."

"It was a while ago. I've moved on."

I want to ask him more questions: *how old were you? How did you move on? Do you ever think about him? Do you still miss him?*

But I don't. Instead, I raise the volume on the radio, hug my sweaty legs to my chest, and stare out the window in silence until I'm home.

———

"W<small>HY IS MY PASTA GREEN</small>?" J<small>AMIE ASKS, STARING AT THE</small> mound of colored penne on his plate in disdain.

"It has spinach in it," Mom responds. "It was on sale, so I thought I'd give it a try. I'm sure it tastes fine." She stabs two pieces with her fork and pops them in her mouth. "See? I don't notice a difference."

"I hate spinach," Jamie grumbles, but he digs in nevertheless, shoveling pasta in his mouth so quickly, I'm surprised he doesn't choke.

I can tell Mom is dying to comment on my brother's uncouth eating, but she holds her tongue. "So, Grace, how were the SATs?" she asks instead.

"They sucked. I still have a headache from all the math."

"Well, no one ever said standardized testing was easy."

"No kidding. Hopefully, I'll do well enough so I don't have to retake it."

"What are you thinking?"

"1150, 1100 minimum."

"You're smart. I wouldn't be surprised if you get at least a 1200."

"Yeah, right. This girl in my English class, Lizzie, has a 4.3 GPA, and she only scored an 1180 on the PSATs."

"I didn't do so well on the SATs," Kevin says, "and I still got into my top college. Most schools look at more than your scores. They want a diverse demographic with students who are skilled in a variety of areas—not only academics."

"Then why do my teachers care so much?" I ask.

"Your scores reflect how well they're doing their job," he explains. "If everyone in your math class scores below average on the math portion of the SATs, what do you think that says about your teacher?"

"That he sucks." I finish my last forkful of saucy penne, then wash down the garlicky aftertaste with a sip of water. "Which he does."

"I take it you don't like math?"

"I hate it."

"She calls her teacher Mr. Dipshit," Mom pipes in.

"Well, yeah. What does he expect with a last name like Lipschitz?"

"My tenth grade English teacher was Mr. Booth," Kevin says. "He was bald, so everyone called him Smoothy Boothy."

For the first time since we sat down to dinner, Jamie cracks a small smile. "Smoothy Boothy. That's funny."

"Believe it or not, he thought so too."

"Not Mr. Lipschitz," I say. "One time, this girl accidentally called him Mr. Dipshit to his face, and he gave her detention for a month. That was the last time anyone made that mistake."

"You live and you learn," Mom says.

Jamie and I look at each other and roll our eyes at her cliché response. Then, when Mom turns to Kevin to ask him about his day, Jamie opens his mouth, exposing the mushy green pasta on his tongue. I try to suppress my laugher, and in doing so, choke on my milk.

"Are you all right?" Mom asks once I've caught my breath.

Across the table, Jamie is biting his lip; he, too, is on the verge of laughter. I roll my eyes again—this time at his expense.

"Don't worry, Mom. I'm fine."

After dinner, I head upstairs to finish an English essay that's due in three days. I've just opened the document on Google Drive when my phone lights up with a text from Isaac.

Isaac: hey. havent seen u in a while.

Grace: i know. ive been crazy busy.

Isaac: oh ok. wanna facetime?

I check the time—seven-o-two—before responding: *sure. ill call u.*

Propping my phone against my computer, I open Facetime, type his name into the search bar, and select his number. While I wait for him to answer, I fix my hair in the reflection of the screen and run my tongue over my teeth to make sure that I don't have food in them.

"Hey." Isaac's grinning face comes into focus. He's in his room—I can tell by the new Weezer poster behind him—and he's wearing a UCF sweatshirt. A backwards baseball cap is shoved over his messy blonde hair.

"Hey," I say.

"How are you?"

"I'm okay. I just finished dinner. We had green pasta."

His brows crinkle in confusion. "Huh?"

"It was spinach flavored," I explain. "Mom bought it on some sale."

"That's not too bad. My mom has gotten way worse things on sale."

"Like what?"

"Well, this one time, she brought home three cartons of hemp milk because she had a buy one get two free coupon."

"Hemp milk?" I repeat. "As in the same hemp that's in marijuana?"

"Uh-huh. It was gross though, so if you want to get high, I'd stick with the real deal."

"Thanks for the heads-up, but I'll pass. You do know it's dangerous to do drugs on medication, right?"

Isaac groans. "Now you sound like Evan."

"Evan?"

"My friend. The guy is a total sissy. He never does anything fun. It's pathetic."

I take a moment to process this. "So, you're saying I'm pathetic?"

"No, no, no. Of course not. You're just . . . smart, like you said."

"And pathetic."

"Come on, Grace. I didn't mean it that way." Isaac rubs his forehead, visibly frustrated. "You don't have to be so sensitive."

"I'm not sensitive," I say. "I'm tired—that's all. I took the SATs today, and it was a nightmare. Not to mention that break is totally gonna suck because Mom is making me tour colleges in

Boston. We're only going for a couple days though, so we can hang out when I get back."

"I can't," he says. "I'm going to London with my dad."

"Oh." I don't bother trying to hide my disappointment. "That sounds like fun."

"So does Boston. I went there on a field trip in eighth grade. It's pretty sweet."

"I guess." He's about to respond when someone knocks on my door. I hold my index finger to my lips. "Shh."

"Grace? Can I come in?"

"That's my mom. I gotta go."

"All right. I'll talk to you—"

I end our call without waiting for him to finish and turn off my phone. Slipping it in my pocket, I power on my computer to pretend that I've been writing my essay this entire time. "Come in!"

Mom enters my room. "I heard voices. Were you talking to someone?"

"I was watching a video for school," I lie. "What's up?"

"I just want to make sure you weren't upset that Kevin picked you up today." She perches on the edge of my bed and clasps her hands together, twiddling her thumbs as she speaks. "I meant to text you, but I was with a patient."

"Why would I be upset?"

"Because I know how you feel about him. I know you think he's just another guy who's going to leave sooner or later, and maybe you're right." She stares at my wall with a longing expression on her face. "But maybe this time will be different."

I'm quiet for several seconds. "I'm not getting my hopes up," I say finally.

"I know," she responds in an uncharacteristically soft voice. "I wouldn't expect you to. All I'm asking is that you give him a chance. Can you do that? For me?"

After another beat of silence, I nod. "Sure."

Mom kisses my forehead. "Thanks, hon. I love you."

I rest my head against her shoulder and gaze out the window. The sky reminds me of the stage curtain in Chuckle's auditorium: black and velvety, not a star in sight. "Love you too, Mom."

14

On my first day of spring break, all I want to do is relax. So, after eating a bowl of Special K and strawberries at nine thirty, I spend the rest of the morning in my room watching *How to Get Away with Murder* on my computer.

Around twelve o'clock, Mom knocks on my door. "What time do you want to make lunch, Grace?"

I pause the show long enough to say, "I'll be down in five minutes."

"Okay."

She walks away while I resume my episode. I watch the last few scenes with bated breath, and when I'm finished, I shut down my computer and head downstairs. Mom is shredding mozzarella cheese at the counter. A package of flour tortillas is to her left; to her right, containers of salsa and guacamole.

"Would you like a quesadilla?" she asks. "I could make one for you too."

I shake my head. "I'll have soup."

I open a can of tomato soup and dump the contents into a bowl. Sealing the edges with plastic wrap, I place it in the microwave and set the cook time for ninety seconds. As my soup is warming up, I sprinkle some of Mom's shredded cheese on an English Muffin and put it in the toaster oven to melt.

"Do you want to split a grapefruit with me?" Mom asks. She holds up a mesh bag containing four massive pink grapefruits.

I hesitate. "I don't know. They look kind of bruised."

"Well, they taste delicious. I believe these ones are from . . ." she checks the label, "California. You should like them then."

"If you insist . . ." I watch her slice the fruit down the middle with a knife. When she hands me my half, a drop of juice spills onto my index finger. I wince as the acid stings my damaged cuticle. "Ouch!"

She raises her eyebrows. "Are you ever going to stop torturing your nails?"

"I'm trying. Some habits are really hard to break." The microwave beeps, and I carry my soup to the table. "Is your quesadilla almost done?"

Mom peeks into the oven. "It needs another minute. Are you all packed for Boston?"

"Yeah. My bag is in my room."

"Good. We should leave in a couple hours so we don't get stuck in traffic."

"How long will it take to get there?"

"About ninety minutes."

"Oh, that's not too bad. I'll probably sleep anyway."

"Bring your earplugs. I want to listen to the news."

I sigh. "And you say *I* torture myself."

Despite leaving early to avoid rush hour, the drive to Boston takes longer than we'd anticipated due to a gnarly accident on the highway. I try not to look as we inch past two totaled cars and their injured drivers, but my eyes have a mind of their own.

"Thank God that's not us," Mom says. "That would really mess up break, huh?"

"No kidding." I shudder at the thought. "Driving seems scary."

"It's all right once you get used to it. Have you considered taking a class? I could sign you up for a course over the summer."

Wee-woo . . . wee-woo . . . wee-woo . . . A wailing ambulance joins the two police cars that are already at the scene. One officer uses a crowbar to pry open a door, while another comforts a woman sitting on the side of the road and two EMTS wheel a stretcher out of the back of their vehicle.

"I'll think about it," I say.

"You should decide sooner than later. I've heard that they fill up quickly."

Now that we're finally past the accident, the traffic is smoother. In the near distance, I notice a green *Welcome to Boston* sign. "I said I'll think about it."

I spend the remainder of the drive to our hotel staring out the window. The city is bustling with people—most of them college students wrapping up their final weeks of school. A group of girls sit outside of a Starbucks, laughing over coffee and scones. Another girl carrying a thick textbook hurries after a boy wearing earphones. When he sees her, he removes his left earbud and greets her enthusiastically.

I continue to watch them in my periphery until they disappear into a brick building with Harry Potter decals on the windows. I quickly pull out my phone and snap a picture for Jamie. Ever since he read *The Sorcerer's Stone* in second grade, he's been a diehard Potterhead. He stills wears his grey *I Solemnly Swear That I Am Up To No Good* t-shirt even though he outgrew it years ago.

Mom leaves the car in the back lot of a grocery store across from the hotel so she won't have to pay for parking. Inside the lobby, we wait for our room key behind a man with two rowdy boys.

"Second floor, turn right when you get off the elevator," the receptionist tells us. "Do you need help with your luggage?"

Mom shakes her head. "We're fine. Thank you."

Handing me the key, she picks up our bags and briskly walks towards the elevator. Our room—number two sixty-eight—is located across from a vending machine. Two queen-sized beds, a desk, a bathroom, and a flat screen television welcome us when we push open the heavy door.

While Mom uses the bathroom, I collapse onto one of the beds and gaze at the off-grey ceiling with my hands behind my head. Being here is a surreal feeling when I remember how different my life was mere months ago. And while the idea of preparing for a future that once seemed hopeless is intimidating, it's also incredibly exciting.

If only Dr. Bennett could see me now, I think with a smug grin on my face.

Two hours later, however, when Mom declares that she's found the perfect place for dinner—a four-star pizzeria three blocks from our hotel—my excitement dwindles.

"Can't we go somewhere else?" I ask. "There has to be a Panera nearby."

"We always go to Panera," she responds. "I want to try something new."

Sensing that she won't change her mind, I reluctantly concede. "Fine. When are we leaving?"

"How about now? It'll be impossible to find parking at this time of day, so we'll have to walk."

"Okay." I shove my sneakers over my blue ankle socks and double-knot the tattered laces in a matter of seconds. "I'm ready."

She slips the room key into her purse. "Then let's go."

The city is even busier now that it's late afternoon with pedestrians wandering around in search of somewhere to have dinner. Mom and I squeeze past a group of young adults loudly conversing outside of a tavern. I can still hear their obnoxious laughter as we round the corner.

"Where did you say this place was?" I ask.

"It should be coming up soon. Ah, there it is." Mom points at a small pizzeria across the street with a blue-and-white striped awning. I begin to step off the curb when she grabs my arm. "Careful, Grace," she says as a taxi speeds past us.

I impatiently wait with my hands on my hips for the traffic to let up. "Can we go? There aren't any cars."

Mom checks both directions before nodding her head. "Lead the way."

The inside of La Migliore Pizza is surprisingly charming compared to its shabby exterior. On a polished countertop, three display cases with cheese, pepperoni, and vegetable pizza slices rotate next to a salad bar. Beneath the cases is a glass cooler containing drinks ranging from classic beers to cream sodas to elegant liquors with names I can't pronounce.

"I can help whoever is next." An overweight man with a thick Italian accent beckons Mom and me to the counter.

"I'll have a slice of cheese," I say, "and a chopped salad, dressing on the side."

Mom nudges me. "You should have a drink too."

I pretend I don't hear her. "That's all."

"And for you?" he asks Mom.

"Slice of vegetable and a farmhouse salad. No pepperoni."

The man enters our order into the register. "That will be sixteen forty-one. Cash or card?"

"Card."

Mom places her card in the chip reader while another man, a scrawny twenty-something-year-old, prepares our food in front of us. I watch him open the rotating cheese case and cross my fingers that he'll select one of the smaller slices, which he thankfully does. Once he's plated our pizza and salad, he hands us two trays. Mom thanks him, and we head to a booth in the back of the pizzeria to eat.

"That's a lot of vegetables," I remark as I drizzle balsamic vinaigrette over my salad.

Mom holds up her finger until she's finished chewing. "You should try it. It's good."

I wrinkle my nose. "You know how I feel about mushrooms."

"Yes, I do." She takes another bite of her pizza while I shovel a forkful of salad in my mouth. "Grace, do you really think that's enough for dinner?"

"It's a big slice," I insist, "and anyway, shouldn't you be happy that I agreed to go out for pizza at all? It's not like this was my first choice."

"Of course I'm happy. That said, one slice of pizza and a salad seems like a pretty small dinner if you ask me."

I shrug. "It's a good thing I wasn't asking."

"Grace—"

"I know how to feed myself!" I interrupt. "Stop micromanaging me!"

With her lips pursed in disapproval, Mom finishes her pizza —except for her crust, which she leaves on her plate—and moves on to her robust salad. Across the table, I scrape a glob of cheese off my pizza with my plastic fork and try to think of something to say to break the awkward silence.

But when nothing comes to my mind, I remain quiet. We both do.

───────

My first tour is scheduled for nine o'clock. Mom wakes me up an hour before, and we head to the hotel lobby, where other guests are enjoying the continental breakfast. She serves herself a plate of scrambled eggs, toast, and a fruit medley, while I fill a bowl with Rice Krispies. I grab a banana and a carton of one percent milk and follow Mom to a table near the entrance. Every time someone walks in or out of the automatic doors, the crisp morning breeze causes goosebumps to surface on my bare arms.

"Do you want my shirt?" Mom gestures to the plaid button-up she's layered over her white t-shirt.

"I'm fine," I grumble. "I just wish you'd booked a later tour."

"The only other time was at four thirty, and that's when

your second tour begins," she responds. "You already knew that, so I don't understand why you're agitated."

"I'm not agitated. I mean, I'm a little frustrated, but that's only because I know I'm gonna get tired. Ninety minutes is a long time for a tour."

"I know it's overwhelming, but once you get started, you'll feel better about everything. Trust me; I've been in your shoes."

"You have?"

She nods. "I might not have struggled with a mental illness, but I was a troubled kid. It wasn't until I went to college that I was able to turn my life around. I had no idea what I was going to do with my future, and then I took a pre-med class and fell in love with it."

"Isn't that where you met Dad?" I ask.

"It is. Although falling in love with him took quite a while longer."

"Why is that?"

"I thought we were too different. He was wealthy, he was popular—not to mention that he was very intelligent. Meanwhile, I was the socially awkward girl on financial aid. My grades were all right, but they were nothing compared to his."

"Isaac and I are different too," I say.

"How so?"

"He's a lot more confident than I am. He also knows more about himself."

"No one expects you to have it all figured out at sixteen," Mom responds. "Heck, I know many adults who still haven't got a clue."

"Like you?" I say.

She rolls her eyes. "Haha. You're hilarious."

"I know." I use my spoon to scoop up the soggy Rice Krispies at the bottom of my bowl. Then, before she can pester me, I guzzle down the rest of the milk in the carton.

Mom pats my arm. "Well done," she says as the man with the two rowdy boys leaves the hotel, sending another gust of wind our way.

"I'm gonna get my sweatshirt," I respond.

The campus of Southern Boston University is a lot different than I'd expected. With numerous college pamphlets floating around Chuckles, most of them depicting colorful, outdoorsy campuses, I'd imagined something similar. But this is Boston after all—not some rural town with plenty of open space for a campus. And, as I walk through the revolving doors of Southern's fourteen-story building, I realize that it would be impossible for one city to support over thirty colleges without going vertical.

After checking in with a woman at a circular desk, Mom and I sit on plastic chairs and wait for our tour guide. I stare out the window to my left, where three girls and two boys are talking to each other. The girls wear SBU t-shirts and black leggings, while the boys sport basketball jerseys. Not once during their entire conversation do they stop smiling.

Is this what college is like? I wonder. Between teachers, parents, and high school graduates, I've heard many different perspectives on college. While teachers claim that research writing and weekly tests will prepare us for the challenging workload, students insist that the social experiences are more important than anything else.

My neighbor Alex, who's a freshman at our community college, once told me, "Don't listen to your teachers. College is awesome. As long as you manage your time well and don't party too much, you'll be fine."

Yet despite Alex's reassurance, it isn't time management or parties that I'm worried about; it's food. Yesterday, when we returned to the hotel after our disastrous outing at the pizzeria, I choked down a bag of vending machine popcorn while Mom quietly nibbled on a bran muffin. She didn't have to say a word for me to understand that she was disappointed.

And she wasn't the only one. I was disappointed in myself too.

Outside the window, the students are gone; in their place, a woman in too-tight jeans is passing by with a Black Labrador. I watch as the dog pauses to lap up a small puddle of filthy rain water.

"How cute," Mom remarks.

"She looks like Tiana," I say. "God, I miss her. Remember that time she chased the mail carrier down our block because he forgot to give her a bone? Or how she'd follow Dad around with her tennis ball?"

Mom smiles. "I sure do. It drove him crazy."

"She really liked him. I mean, she liked all of us, but there was something about him—I could never figure out what it was. It's not like he paid her any attention."

"Yes, he did. He just had a funny way of showing it."

"If you say so . . ."

"He was devastated when she died," Mom continues. "I don't know if you know this, but after we came home from the vet, he cried."

"For real?"

"Believe me; I was just as surprised." She briefly glances at the dog and the woman, then back at me. "I hope this doesn't come across as micromanaging, but when we talk about you father, is it hard for you?"

"No," I lie. "It's fine."

"Are you Grace?" A young man with cropped blonde hair stands in front of us. He wears fitted khakis and a grey shirt that reads *Choose Kindness* in a rainbow font. A silver hoop punctures his left earlobe.

"I am."

"I'm Noah, your tour guide. You must be her mother?"

"Kira. It's nice to meet you."

Noah shakes Mom's hand. "It looks like it'll just be the two of you today. Our morning tours tend to be less busy."

"Isn't that nice?" Mom nudges me with her elbow.

I ignore her. "Does that mean it won't be as long?"

Noah's bellowing laugh echoes through the lobby. "I see someone is eager to get out of here," he jokes. "I'll tell you what; I'll do my best to make your tour as speedy as possible. How do you feel about walking and talking?"

"I'm down with that."

"Mom?" Noah asks.

Next to me, Mom is struggling to stifle her grin. She removes her button-up and wraps it around her waist, as it's much warmer inside SBU than it is on the busy city streets. "What the heck? Let's do this."

15

As do most vacations, spring break flies by. On my final afternoon, Mom drops me off at Isaac's house. He texted me two days ago that he was leaving London early, so we could hang out if I still wanted to. Naturally, I agreed.

"I'll see you in two hours," Mom says as she pulls up to the Nielson's property.

"See ya."

I get out of the car and cut across the freshly mowed grass on my brace-free legs. The day after we returned from Boston, Mom and I paid a visit to Dr. Wilson, who confirmed that my knee was healing well.

"Call me if you experience any pain," she said. "And maybe stay off the ice for a little while."

"You don't have to worry about that," I assured her. "I won't be going near ice anytime soon."

At the Nielson's door, I ring the bell and lean against the railing beneath their mailbox while I wait for someone to let me in. A thick college brochure poking out from the metal lid catches my eye. It was only yesterday when I, too, received my first brochure—coincidentally from a school in Southern California.

"Get used to it," Mom said when I showed her the envelope. "You'll be getting a lot of those over the next few months."

"Hi, Grace," Ms. Nielson greets me. She holds open the door so I can come inside. "How was your break?"

"It was good." In the entry, I kick off my sneakers next to muddy hiking boots. I notice a small hole near the heel of my sock and make a mental note to ask Mom for a new pair for my birthday in May. "How was yours?"

She smiles. "Relaxing. Do you want something to eat? I just went shopping."

I shake my head. "Thanks, but I already had snack."

"In that case, Isaac's upstairs. Let me know if you need anything."

After I've thanked her again, I ascend the Nielson's staircase and knock on Isaac's closed door. When he doesn't answer, I twist the knob and poke my head inside. He's lying on his bed with his AirPods in, mumbling the lyrics to Beck's *Loser* as he fools around on his phone.

"Isaac? Hello?" I touch his shoulder, and he flinches.

"Grace! Shit, I totally lost track of time!" He removes his AirPods and adjusts his baggy sweats, so they fully cover his plaid boxers. "I'm still jetlagged from my trip."

I laugh. "It's cool. How was London?"

"Sick! I so want to live there one day."

"Do you have pictures?"

"Uh-huh. I probably took, like, two hundred, but these are

the ones I like the most." He opens the *Favorites* album on his Photos app and hands me his phone. "Check them out. I have to go to the bathroom."

While he's gone, I sit on the edge of his bed and admire pictures of him posing outside of Big Ben, waiting to ride the Coca Cola London Eye, and giving bunny ears to a guard at Buckingham Palace to name a few.

When I'm finished with his London adventures, I continue scrolling through the album. Most of his favorited pictures from last year are of him playing soccer. In them, he's even skinnier than when we met; his baggy uniform hangs on his skeletal frame, and his face is sunken and pale.

Seeing this side of him, a side he hides so well, sends a chill down my spine. I have those kinds of pictures too: live photos of me staggering around the soccer field, reflections of my ribs and hip bones in the bathroom mirror, selfies where I'm wistfully staring into the distance or, worse, faking a smile, my skin stretched across my drawn cheeks.

I don't let myself look at those pictures anymore. But then, I haven't deleted them either.

I'm about to exit Photos when a picture of him and a thin blonde-haired girl catches my eye. It was captured just over a year ago in what looks like a rose garden. His arm is wrapped around her narrow waist, while her hand rests on his chest. Yet despite their overt affection, it's her blue eyes I'm drawn to the most. They're so sad, full of anguish and pain.

"Pretty cool, huh?" Isaac discreetly closes the door and sits next to me, resting his chin on my shoulder. "Whoa! What the hell are you doing?"

I ignore his question. "Is that Holly?"

"Yeah."

"She's pretty."

He takes his phone from me and studies the picture. When he speaks again, his voice is devoid of emotion. "She's miserable."

"What's wrong with her?"

"There were a lot of things that were wrong with Holly. I was with her for seven months, but I never felt like I really knew her. There were times when she was on top of the world and others when she wouldn't leave her room for weeks. She'd tell me she loved me; that without me, her life meant nothing, then the next day, she'd completely avoid me. She wouldn't even answer my texts. She'd run away a lot, make plans that she didn't keep, cut herself—"

"I cut myself," I admit. "I mean, I don't anymore, but I used to."

"I never understood that," he says.

I shrug. "What's there to understand? I was in pain, and I needed a release. It's not any different than restricting."

"But scars don't fade."

"Neither do memories." When he doesn't respond, I ask, "Are you still in touch with her?"

"No. A couple weeks after we broke up, she moved to Arizona, and I never saw her again."

"Why Arizona?"

"Not sure. Maybe she just needed a fresh start. That, and she hated the cold. It made her sad."

"I know the feeling. Winter sucks."

"No shit." Isaac turns off his phone and slips it in his pocket. "Okay, that's enough of that."

"But I didn't see the rest of your photos," I protest.

"That's because you were too busy snooping," he teases. He positions his body so we're facing each other and gently kisses me. "Anyway, I have a better idea."

"Oh, yeah?"

"Mmm-hmm."

He presses his lips against mine again, although this time, his kiss is more intense. I lean closer to him as he caresses my face in his hands. For several seconds, I happily embrace his affection, but then his fingers travel from my cheeks to my arms to my waist, and that happiness is replaced with anxiety and discomfort. When he starts to unzip my jeans, I pull away.

"Don't."

Isaac sighs. "Sorry. I just—" He shakes his head. "Fuck. Never mind."

"I want to," I say.

"It's okay. You don't have to explain."

An awkward silence unfolds between us. He stares out the window with his shoulders slumped in defeat, while I look straight ahead at his cluttered bookshelf and try to think of something to say to break the tension. On the second shelf from the top, between a Rubik's Cube and his psychology textbook, a tattered Stephen King novel catches my eye: *Carrie*.

I clear my throat. "Hey, Isaac?"

"Yeah?"

"So, um, Prom is in a couple weeks, and I wanted to know if you'd maybe like to go with me?"

"I don't know. It's not really my scene."

"Oh," I mumble. "I just thought I'd ask."

Shrugging nonchalantly, he reverts his gaze to the window.

His hand is only inches from mine. If I wanted to, I could reach over and intertwine our fingers; reassure him that just because I'm not ready to be intimate when he is doesn't mean I feel differently about him.

But the longer I think about it, the more I realize that I'm not so sure if that's true. So, my hand remains on my lap, as limp as a dead fish.

YESTERDAY 6:08 PM
Isaac: hey can we talk?
Yesterday 8:21 PM
Isaac: hello? u there?
Yesterday 8:59 PM
Isaac: grace i know ur seeing my texts. why arent u responding? are u mad at me?
Yesterday 10:31 PM
Isaac: i dont understand u.

I stare at my phone, as though I'm in a trance, with my thumb hovering over the keyboard. *i . . . m . . . s . . . o . . . r . . .* Mrs. Perkenson's bright ceiling lights cast a glare against the screen as I carefully compose an apology text to Isaac. Then I stop.

What do I have to be sorry for? I wonder. *I didn't do anything wrong . . . right? Right?*

"I'm so fucking exhausted, man," Matt grumbles to Tommy. "I was up until one working on a fucking essay."

"Dude, same," Tommy responds. He's sitting on Matt's desk googling the answers to our AP Euro homework on his phone.

"I'm already on my second cup of coffee. I'm gonna be so jittery at practice."

"Don't remind me. Coach has been up my ass about everything lately. The dude needs to chill the fuck out."

Tommy props the worksheet against his knee and jots down *The Peace of Augburg*, misspelling *Augsburg*. "I heard he's getting a divorce."

"Who told you that?"

"Some guy who babysits his kids. He seemed like he knew what he was talking about." All of a sudden, the tip of his pencil breaks. He groans. "Dammit!"

"Sorry I'm late."

Mrs. Perkenson bustles through the door holding her purse in one arm and a stack of papers in the other. When he sees her, Tommy snatches his coffee off Matt's desk and scurries to his seat in the front of the classroom.

Matt yawns loudly. "Later, man."

With iMessage still open, I leave my one-sided conversation with Isaac and text Lou: *i need to talk to u. meeting in a-wing bathroom p3?* I send the text, chewing on my thumbnail while I wait for her to respond.

She doesn't.

"Phones away, students," Mrs. Perkenson orders. "For the next fifteen minutes, I'd like you to get in your small groups and review last night's assigned reading for *The Handmaid's Tale*. I'll be walking around the room in case you have questions."

With a sigh, I pocket my phone and join Lizzie Abbot and Julian Surls at Julian's desk. I take my reading chart out of my homework folder, and they do the same. Julian begins copying answers off Lizzie's, who shoots him a disapproving look.

"Again?"

"I had a team dinner," Julian explains, "and an APUSH paper that's due on Friday, and I had to study for a psych quiz, and—"

"Maybe if you weren't taking a million APs, you'd have time to do your homework," Lizzie interrupts. "Now hurry up before Mrs. P. sees you. I don't need to get in trouble because you have shitty time management."

Julian finishes filling in the last question and hands Lizzie her sheet. "Thanks."

Lizzie rolls her eyes. "Whatever."

"How's it going, you three?" Mrs. Perkenson asks. She stands behind Julian and peers over his shoulder, squinting to decipher his barely legible answers.

"Fine, Mrs. P.," Lizzie responds. She nudges Julian.

"Yeah, we were just talking about, uh . . ."

"The Japanese tourists," I finish, "and how they remind Offred of the freedoms she had before the government collapsed, like being able to wear anything she wanted."

Julian nods. "What she said."

"Well, let me know if you have any questions. I understand that this is a challenging text."

"We will." Lizzie waits until our teacher is out of earshot to say, "I started watching the show this weekend, so I think I get it now."

"Thank God for that," Julian says. "I'm confused as hell."

"Don't you have Hulu?"

"No."

"I don't have Hulu either," I say.

"You guys are missing out," Lizzie says. "Anyway, about the tourists . . ."

While Lizzie explains the scene to a very bewildered Julian, I steal another glance at my phone. Still nothing from Lou, but Mom has texted me twice: first to say that she bought more soup, then to tell me that she forgot she's seeing her gynecologist at eleven and will be a couple minutes late.

no prob, I respond and press the blue arrow.

"There's still one thing I don't understand," Julian says. "What's up with the names? Offred? Ofwarren? Those aren't their real names, right? So how did they get them?"

Lizzie looks at me. I shrug. "No clue."

"This is a weird-ass book."

"I like it," Lizzie says. "Maybe if you did your homework for once, you would too."

Julian ignores her. His eyes are trained on his phone, his thumbs flying across the screen. "Oh, shit."

"What's up?"

"SAT scores just came out."

"For real?" Lizzie takes out her phone and enters her four-digit passcode. "Oh, shit!"

I glance around the room, where sure enough, all of my classmates are on their phones. Mrs. Perkenson stands at the Smartboard with a sour look on her face. Nevertheless, she remains quiet. She knows better than anyone that at this point, it would be futile to try to regain our attention.

Taking a deep breath, I log onto my CollegeBoard account and click on *My SAT*. My heart is pounding as I select *School Day SAT – March 24th* from under *My Test Registrations*. I know it's irrational to be this nervous considering the number of people who have reassured me that colleges aren't only interested in scores, but how I could not after years of teachers stressing the importance of this test?

The page finally loads: 650 on Evidence-Based Reading and Writing. 540 on Math. 1190 total.

A huge sigh of relief escapes my lips. I did it; I exceeded my goal by forty points. I'm smiling as I text Mom: *got my sat score* . . .

She responds immediately.

Mom: and?

Grace: 1190!

Mom: way to go!

Grace: thanks :)

"Okay, you should all know your scores by now," Mrs. Perkenson says, finally getting back to business. "Put away your phones so we can continue with class or you're all receiving fifties for your participation grade."

"Hell no," Lizzie says. She opens her book and starts flipping through the heavily sticky-noted pages. "Where were we anyway?"

"We were talking about the names," I say.

"Oh, yeah. I'll google it."

The second she notices Lizzie's phone, Mrs. Perkenson zips over to us. "Elizabeth! What did I say?"

"It's about the book," Lizzie explains. "I promise."

Mrs. Perkenson's beady eyes narrow. "I'll allow it."

"What a bitch," Lizzie mumbles as our teacher walks to the back of the room, where Heather is raising her hand.

"I can't wait for this fucking year to be over," Julian gripes.

"Me too," I say.

Lizzie nods in agreement. "Me three."

As usual, the rest of the morning crawls by painfully slowly. When history ends, I head outside to wait for Mom. I climb onto a brick ledge overlooking the sidewalk and open Instagram to pass the time. I've just approved a follower request from Katie Brinkley, a girl I played soccer with in the fall, when Curtis' chipper voice comes on the loudspeaker.

"It's that time of year again," he announces. "In two days, Prom tickets will be on sale outside of the cafeteria. For every purchase, you'll get a complimentary friendship bracelet courtesy of the Feminist Coalition. Also, Vice Principal Goldstein would like to remind everyone to be conscious of the dress code. Remember: too much skin is a sin. Have a great day."

"He realizes that thing is super sexist, right?" a familiar voice says.

When I turn my head, Cassie is standing next to me. Ironically, her outfit—a teal crop top and low-rise jeans—violates the dress code in more ways than not. "What are you doing out here?"

"Free period. You?"

"My mom is picking me up."

"Right. I forgot you leave early. Mind if I sit?"

"Go ahead."

Cassie sets down her backpack and shimmies onto the ledge. "So, what's new? Did you have a good break?"

"It was all right. My mom and I went to Boston to tour colleges."

"Boston is great. I remember looking at colleges there. I even applied to a few."

"SBU?"

She nods. "That was my safety school. Why? Are you thinking of applying?"

"I might. Mom says I should look at other schools too. We've been home for a week, and she's already making a list." I roll my eyes. "What about you? How was your break?"

"It was, um . . . it was rough."

"Why is that?"

"Things aren't so good with my brother. He's sick, and no one is doing anything about it."

"He's bipolar, right?"

"Yeah." Cassie averts her gaze to the sky, blinking tears from her blue eyes. "It's just so fucked up. Sometimes, I feel like Derrick doesn't want to get better, like he's comfortable being sick."

"That makes sense," I say.

"It does?"

I nod. "When I was in the hospital, everything was easier. I didn't have to deal with pressure or judgement or anything like that. I got to be in this safe little bubble where my only responsibility was talking about what got me there. Hell, I didn't even have to brush my teeth."

"Then how come you don't go back?"

"Because it's not real. Out here can be scary, but at least I have independence and privacy and my friends and my phone. It's those things that make staying worthwhile."

Cassie is quiet several seconds. "How can I get him to realize that?" she asks finally.

"You can't. Until he wants to get better, nothing you say or do will make a difference."

"What if he never wants to?"

"Then that's his choice."

She sighs. "Fuck."

"I know it sucks," I say, "but right now, the best thing you can do is be there for him, and the best thing you can do for yourself is let others be there for you."

Cassie doesn't respond.

"Lou misses you like crazy, Cass," I continue. "You're all she ever talks about."

"I know," Cassie says. "I miss her too. I'm thinking about asking her to Prom."

"You are?"

"Uh-huh. But you can't say anything to her, okay? This has to be our secret."

"You have my word." In my peripheral vision, I see Mom pull into the parking lot. "I have to go. I hope things work out with your brother."

Cassie smiles sadly. "Me too."

With my bookbag in one hand and my phone in the other, I jump off the ledge and join Mom in the car. "Who were you talking to?" she asks as I'm buckling my seatbelt.

"Cassie. She was telling me about her spring break."

"Oh. Did she do anything interesting?"

I shake my head. "Nothing to report."

Mom turns onto the main road, navigating around a slow-moving Honda with a *Student Driver* bumper sticker above the license plate. "1190, huh? You must be happy."

"I am. I'll probably take it again, but it's still higher than I expected."

"When are you going to stop doubting yourself?" she asks.

"I don't like to get my hopes up. That way, it's not a huge letdown if things don't turn out how I wanted."

"And if they do?"

"If they do, it's even better because I wasn't expecting it."

"You have a very interesting way of thinking about things."

I grin. "Believe it or not, you're not the first person to tell me that."

Three minutes later, when we arrive at our house, Mom asks, "So, what do you want for lunch? BLTs? Grilled cheese? Soup?"

"Soup."

Hanging my bookbag on the back of my chair, I open the pantry and rummage through boxes of pasta, condiments, and a variety of canned fruits and vegetables until I find a can of minestrone. I spoon half of the soup into a Tupperware container and the rest into a bowl, cover the bowl with plastic wrap, and place it in the microwave for ninety seconds.

"I bought more popcorn while I was out," Mom say. "It's in the snack cabinet."

I find the bag and portion out a reasonable serving while she divides a Macoun apple into eight slices. As I'm putting back the popcorn, the microwave beeps. I wrap a towel around the streaming bowl of soup and carry it to the table.

"Is that all you're having?" I point at Mom's lunch: her apple and a cup of coffee.

"I already ate at work," she explains. "One of my colleagues had a party yesterday and brought in the leftovers for us."

"What did you have?"

"Vegetable Masala. It was delicious."

"That's Indian, right?"

She nods. "I'd love to take you to an Indian restaurant some-time. I think you'd enjoy the food."

"I don't know. I heard it's pretty spicy."

"Depends on what you order," she says.

"We'll see," I respond.

After lunch, I head upstairs to start my homework. I alternate between a logarithms worksheet and Chapter 19 in my AP Euro textbook, which wraps up our unit on World War II, until one forty-five. I finish paraphrasing the author's lengthy explanation of the Manhattan Project, set down my pencil, and return to the kitchen. Even though Anna's appointments almost always run over, Mom still insists on arriving before two o'clock.

Sure enough, Mom is standing at the door in a purple shirt and faded jeans. A novel titled *The Teenage Brain: A Neuroscientist's Survival Guide to Raising Adolescents and Young Adults* is tucked under her arm. I slip my moccasins over my socks and follow her out to the car. Ten minutes later, all of which we spend listening to alternative songs on the radio, she drops me off at Anna's office building.

"I'll see you at two thirty."

"Okay."

I walk through the automatic doors, ascend the stairs to the second floor, and amble down the hallway to Anna's suite. She's still conferencing with her one thirty patient, so I take a seat in the waiting room and recheck my conversation with Lou to see if she has replied yet. She hasn't.

"Grace?"

When I look up, Anna stands in front of me wearing beige capris and a white-and-purple striped sleeveless turtleneck.

Behind her, a father and mother guide their teary daughter into the hallway. Even after the door closes, I can hear the girl's sobs.

Inside Anna's office, I step on the scale and wait for the familiar *beep!* Once she has recorded my number, I recline onto the couch while she logs my weight into my chart.

"How's my weight?" I ask.

"Steady."

"Steady is good, right?"

"It sure is. So, how was your trip to Boston?"

"Better than I expected. Boston is pretty neat."

"Did you have difficulty with food while you were there?"

"Mom and I went to a pizzeria on the first night, so that was challenging, but other than that, I think I did okay."

"What did you get?"

"A slice of cheese. With salad."

"Just one slice?"

"It was really big," I exaggerate. "Like, at least double the size of Mom's homemade pizza."

"Well, I'm glad you had a successful trip. When I met you three months ago, I don't think you would have been able to do that."

"Me neither."

"Is there anything in particular that you'd like to talk about today?"

I think Isaac wants to have sex with me. Those unnerving words hover on the tip of my tongue, ready to spill if I open my mouth. Across from me, Anna patiently waits with her hazel eyes trained on my face.

I clear my throat. "Mom wants to take me out for Indian

food. She says I need to broaden my horizons—whatever that means."

"Perhaps she has a point," Anna says. "Luckily for you, there are a number of excellent Indian restaurants around town. You should pick a day to go to one with her."

"I'll think about it."

"What's holding you back?"

"Nothing is holding me back," I insist. "I just don't want to go, and then not like the food. That happened a lot at Southview when we'd eat out. One time, we went to a fast food joint, and I was nauseous for the rest of the day. I almost threw up."

"You do know that part of recovery is pushing yourself to try new foods, yes?"

"My problem isn't trying new foods; it's being comfortable with food I used to eat before I got sick, like cake and lasagna. Stuff like that."

"I have an idea." Anna opens the top drawer of her filing cabinet and takes out a blue notebook and a pencil. "Let's make a list of food that you want to reincorporate into your diet, and then each week, you can choose three to try."

"How about two?" I negotiate.

Anna nods. "Two it is."

I spend the remainder of our session brainstorming food—from chocolate cake to French fries to macaroni and cheese—that prior to this year, I genuinely enjoyed. Anna jots them down, every so often making suggestions of her own. By two twenty-nine, we've come up with a couple dozen items.

"Here you go," she says and hands me the list.

"Um . . ." I study her messy scrawl, contemplating my

options. "Bread with butter and regular potato chips. We already have that stuff at home, so it shouldn't be too bad."

"Well, I look forward to hearing how it goes."

"Yeah." I quickly glance at my phone. "It's two thirty."

Anna chuckles. "Are you *that* eager to get out of here?"

"No, but I have a lot of homework, and I get tired at night, so I usually try to get it done in the afternoon."

"All right, well, I'll see you next week. Is your mom in the waiting room?"

"I don't think so. She went to the library, so she's probably downstairs."

"Okay. Goodbye, Grace."

"Bye, Anna. Oh, here's your money." I hand her the seventy-dollar check Mom gave me when she dropped me off and leave Anna's clinic. As I'm walking down the hallway, my phone buzzes.

Lou: sorry for not getting back to u. i dont feel good, thats why i wasnt at school. whats up?

Grace: just some drama with isaac. its a long story.

Lou: do u wanna come over tonight? we can talk.

In the lobby, Mom is sitting on the bench across from the elevator. She smiles when I approach her. "Good session?"

I ignore her question. "Can I hang out with Lou later?"

"Do you have homework?"

"Yeah, but I'll do it when we get home."

"Then it's fine."

"Thanks." To Lou, I reply: *see you at 7?*

Lou: yea that works. see ya.

"Is everything all right?" Mom asks.

"Of course. Why wouldn't it be?"

"No reason. Just thought I'd ask."

"Well, everything is fine."

"And your weight? Is that fine too?"

I groan in frustration. "Oh my god, Mom! You said you wouldn't do this!"

Mom scowls. Without saying a word, she unlocks the car and gets in the driver's seat. I sit next to her with my arms folded across my chest. As she backs out of the parking lot, the radiant sunlight accentuates the scars on my wrists. After months of hiding them behind long sleeves, seeing them now, as plain as day, makes me sad. No, not sad: regretful.

"Steady," I say.

"Huh?"

"My weight. Anna said it's steady."

"Thank you for telling me."

"Yeah."

I look away from my scars and stare out the window, where two preteen girls are speeding by on bikes. They remind me of when Lou and I would race each other around our neighborhood: her on her seven-speed fuchsia cruiser, me on the dated yellow road bike Mom found at Savers. We'd pedal at breakneck speed down sidewalks and across lawns, desperate to reach the "finish line"—the faded crosswalk between a community garden and Saint Peter's Preschool—first.

More often than not, I would triumph.

"What are you thinking about?" Mom asks, catching my wistful expression in the reflection of the glass.

With my gaze still trained on the girls, I shrug. "Better times."

16

I wake up on my seventeenth birthday to the sound of raindrops steadily pounding against the roof. Outside my window, thunderclouds loom in the ominous grey sky, but despite the nasty weather, I'm feeling all right. I turn off my nagging alarm and follow the familiar scent of French Toast to the kitchen. Sure enough, Mom is standing at the stove flipping six egg-drenched bread slices with a spatula.

"Hey, birthday girl," she greets me. "Lovely weather, huh?"

I roll my eyes. "Yeah, right."

"It's supposed to lighten up by noon. Do you mind cutting this for me?" She holds out a banana and a serrated knife, which I take from her. "Thanks."

"Want me to do strawberries too?" I ask as I'm unpeeling the banana.

She nods. "That would be great."

While we're working—her monitoring the toast; me dicing

the fruit—she says, "I get off work early today. If you want, you can open your presents when Jamie comes home from school."

"I'm down with that," I say. "So, um, what did you get me?"

"You'll just have to wait and see," she responds with a grin.

For the second time since I woke up, I roll my eyes at her expense. "Typical."

Despite being slightly undercooked, the French Toast isn't half bad. Once I've washed honey off my hands, I head upstairs to prepare for school. I dress in a grey long-sleeved shirt and capri leggings and brush my teeth. In the bathroom mirror, I notice that my forehead is breaking out, but since I don't have time to apply concealer, I simply twist my hair into a loose side braid to hide as much of the acne as I can.

"Do we have Tums?" I ask Mom when I return to the kitchen. "I feel bloated."

"There should be a bottle with the vitamins," she responds.

"Thanks."

I open the cabinet next to the sink and find the Tums behind Jamie's gummy multivitamins. I chew two cherry-flavored tablets, say goodbye to Jamie, and follow Mom out into the downpour.

Ten minutes later, we pull up to Chuckles behind a silver Subaru. I say goodbye and break into a sprint, trying to avoid getting drenched by the incessant rain. Inside, the floor is covered in muddy footprints and small puddles of water. I navigate around them to English and sit beside Matt, who's Snapchatting his girlfriend of the month. I watch him smooth back his damp hair before he takes the picture, pursing his lips in a seductive half-smile. Then he notices me.

"Can I help you?"

I avert my gaze to my lap. "Sorry. I didn't mean—"

"It's fine," he interrupts. "Happy birthday, by the way."

"Huh?"

"It's your birthday, right?"

"Yeah . . . I didn't think you knew."

"Bianca posted something on your Facebook timeline. Didn't you see it?"

I shake my head. "I turned off my notifications. But thank you."

Matt shrugs. "Whatever."

While he responds to another Snap, I open Facebook. On my timeline, Bianca has commented *happy birthday, beautiful* with a red balloon emoji. I wish I had her number to text her, but since I don't, I simply heart her comment and write *@biancasantos thanks! you rock!* With a smile on my face, I press the blue arrow and wait for the school's subpar Wi-Fi to upload my reply. It blows my mind when I remember that this is the same girl who, not too long ago, hated my guts. This is the girl who called me a freak, slept with my childhood crush, and was ultimately responsible for me being admitted to the hospital.

In fact, until Bianca told me about her older sister, who died by suicide when Bianca was ten, I was convinced that it was her mission to ruin my life. I guess Mom was right: people really can change.

School is surprisingly lowkey this morning. Nevertheless, when the bell rings for sixth period, interrupting Mr. Duffy's snoozefest lecture, I'm more than ready to go home. I'm weaving through the crowded halls to the front office when Lou sneaks up behind me. She presses her phone against my ear and blasts the intro to *In Da Club* at top-volume.

Go, shawty, it's your birthday
We gonna party like it's yo birthday

I jump. "Not funny!"

Lou smirks. "You think that's bad? Remember my cousin Aliyah?"

"The bitchy one from Thanksgiving?" I nod. "What about her?"

"It's her birthday too, so this morning, I sent her this." Lou shows me a screenshot of a Grumpy Cat meme. It says: *Thought about wishing you a happy birthday . . . decided against it.*

I roll my eyes. "Go to class, Lou."

"Whatever you say, birthday girl." She plants a kiss on my cheek and takes off in the opposite direction, calling over her shoulder, "Save me some cake!"

"Cake," I repeat under my breath. "Awesome."

The last time I had cake was a couple months ago at CADE. It was Brenda's birthday, and the counselors decided to challenge us with ice cream cake after dinner. To no one's surprise, Brenda refused to eat her slice. She sat in her chair with her arms folded across her chest while the rest of us nibbled on ours. By six forty-five, when we were allowed to go home, she still hadn't budged. The next day, Maggie said she didn't leave until after eight o'clock.

"Did she eat the cake?" Chloe asked.

"I don't know. She wouldn't tell me."

"It wasn't very good, was it?"

Maggie shook her head. "I've had better at Chuck E. Cheese's."

When I met with Anna last week, we spent most of my session deliberating dessert options for my birthday. We eventually decided on vanilla cupcakes and cream cheese frosting—my favorite childhood treat.

Since then, I've tried not to think about how many calories are in the four-point-six-star recipe Mom found on allrecipes.com. But when Jamie returns home from school around three, disrupting a heated Scrabble game between Mom and me, those cupcakes are the only thing on my mind.

While Jamie and I hang out in the TV room, Mom vanishes into the kitchen. Several seconds later, we hear the refrigerator open, followed by a cabinet and the utensils drawer. As planned, she returns with a plate of vanilla cupcakes and a bowl of homemade cream cheese frosting and places them on the coffee table. She wedges a blue-and-red-striped candle into a cupcake, ignites a flame with a match, and hands it to me.

"Make a wish, hon."

I take a deep breath and blow. Mom and Jamie applaud as I remove the candle and set it down on my paper plate.

"Are you one . . . are you two . . ." Jamie begins to chant.

I wait until he reaches "seventeen" to exclaim, "Stop!"

He grins. "Can we eat now?"

"Let Grace go first," Mom says. She passes me the bowl of cream cheese frosting and watches as I spread a thin layer onto the cupcake. "Grace—" Before she can finish, I apply more frosting. Her lips twitch into a faint smile. "I'm sorry."

"It's okay." I wait until both of them have frosted their cupcakes to take a bite. It's even better than I remember; the cake is moist and fluffy, and the frosting is whipped to near-perfection. "This is good, Mom."

Across the table, Jamie nods in agreement. He's already finished three-quarters of his cupcake. "Facts."

Mom's smile broadens. "They were always your favorite when you were younger."

"They were everyone's favorite," I say. "At my parties, they'd be gone in minutes."

"How come we don't have parties anymore?" Jamie asks.

"Downside of growing up, I guess," Mom responds.

"You know, if I were Jewish, I'd be getting ready for my bat mitzvah," he says. "Those parties are so sick!"

"*Bar* mitzvah," Mom corrects. "A bat mitzvah is for girls."

"Oh. My bad." After a beat of silence, he asks, "Can I have another cupcake?"

Mom passes him the plate, and he selects the largest of the four remaining cupcakes. For some reason, as I'm watching him lather on frosting, I'm overcome with sadness. It doesn't make sense; just a few minutes ago, I felt perfectly fine.

"So, do you feel any different?" Mom's voice snaps me back to reality. "Any older?"

"Maybe a little. Anna says I grew half an inch, so I feel taller at least."

"How tall are you now?" Jamie asks.

"Five-seven," I grumble. "She says I'm still growing too."

"There's nothing wrong with being tall," Mom, who's just shy of five-ten, points out.

"I wish I was tall," Jamie says.

"You'll get there, hon." Mom pats his shoulder reassuringly. "Just give it some time."

"Okay." He takes a huge bite from the top of his cupcake. "Maybe I need to eat more," he says as he's chewing.

"Doubt that. Here, you have frosting on your nose." She hands him a napkin. "I think I'm ready for seconds too. Grace?"

I shake my head. "I'm good."

"Let me know if you change your mind." She starts to pull the plastic knife out of the frosting when it suddenly snaps in half. "Dammit! I'll get another one."

While she heads to the kitchen for a replacement knife and Jamie reaches for his third cupcake, I gaze out the window, where the clouds have begun to part. Small beams of sunlight penetrate the sky, casting a pleasant glow onto the flourishing dogwood tree in our front yard. I can't remember the last time I saw something so beautiful, so pure.

Tears well in my eyes, but I quickly brush them away. Still, Jamie notices.

"Are you okay?"

"I'm fine," I whisper. "I'm just a little emotional right now."

"But it's your birthday."

"I know." Another tear slips down my cheek. "I'll be right back."

Setting down my plate, I leave the TV room and lock myself in the bathroom. As I sit on the toilet, I pat my eyes with a tissue until my bladder is empty. That's when I see it; a small brownish stain on the crease of my underwear. I glance into the toilet, and sure enough, several red dots taint the light-yellow water.

Suddenly, everything makes sense.

"Oh shit," I mumble. "I'm healthy."

"KEVIN IS MOVING IN."

I glance up from my computer, where I'm reading a Wikipedia article about 20th century peace treaties for an AP Euro paper. It's due next week, and I'm just beginning my research. "Huh?"

"His apartment has asbestos, so he asked if he could stay with us," Mom explains. She takes a seat across from me with a mug of coffee. "I said yes."

"You should have talked to Jamie and me first," I say. "We live here too."

"I know."

"If you know, why didn't you?"

"It was a spur-of-the-moment thing, and, as you know, I really like him. It felt right. But you're right, Grace; I should have consulted with you. I'm sorry."

"Does this mean his kids are going to visit now?"

"I don't know. Maybe."

"What do you mean 'maybe'? Mom, they won't have anywhere to sleep. I don't know if you've noticed, but we're not exactly living the high life."

"We have air mattresses in the attic, and anyway, they'd only stay for a weekend at most. I'm sure we'll work it out."

"That's what you always say."

"Grace—"

"Forget it, Mom. I have to finish this assignment so . . ."

She takes the hint. "Okay, I'm leaving. We can talk about this later if you want to."

I shrug. "It's not like there's anything to say. You've already made up your mind."

Mom opens her mouth to argue otherwise, but she must decide against it, because all she says is, "New pads are in the bathroom closet. Let me know when you're ready for snack."

She walks away while I return my attention to my paper. *The 20th century was one of the most violent times in European history,* I type. *People were constantly at war with each other because they had different opinions and couldn't compromise. That is why peace treaties were so—*

Buzz . . . buzz . . . buzz . . .

I stop typing mid-sentence and reach for my phone. "Hey, Lou. What's up?"

"You'll never guess what just happened."

"Tell me."

"Cassie asked me to Prom!" Her voice emanates excitement.

"Lou, that's great. I'm so happy for you."

"It was really cute; she bought me a Boston Crème Doughnut, and when I opened the napkin—because those things are messy as fuck—she'd written on it: *Prom? I donut want to go with anyone else.*"

I laugh. "That's so corny."

"Well, it worked. We're shopping for dresses tomorrow, and even though you aren't going, I was hoping you'd come with us. We can get fro-yo for snack, and Cass is eighteen now, so if you want that cartilage piercing you've been talking about, she could totally pretend to be your older sister. Think of it as a belated birthday gift."

"You don't have to do that. You already gave me a gift."

"Gift cards don't count. Please, Grace. Say you'll come."

"Okay, I'll come," I agree, "but I'm not sure about the piercing. Things between Mom and me are a little weird right now, and I don't want to piss her off."

"At least think about it. We're leaving at two, so we'll pick you up around then."

"All right. I'll see you soon." I end the call and turn off my phone. "Hey, Mom?"

"Yes?" Mom calls from her office.

"I'm going shopping with Lou tomorrow, okay?"

"What time?"

"Two. We're getting fro-yo for snack." Silence from her end. "Mom?"

"Sorry, I'm on the phone with our insurance company."

"So . . . I can go, right?"

"Uh-huh."

"I don't need a ride."

"Uh-huh."

"And I'm thinking about getting my cartilage pierced. Is that okay?" I hold my breath, crossing my fingers as I wait for her to respond.

"Uh-huh."

"Sweet!"

Grinning smugly, I open a new tab and type *cool cartilage piercing* into the search bar. I spend the next fifteen minutes—time I know I should put towards my essay—scrolling through pictures on Google Images. In one of them, a woman has the National Eating Disorder Association symbol tattooed behind her ear. Dakota, my former roommate at Southview, had the same symbol on her ankle. She told me that she and her best friend, who was also recovering from anorexia, got them over the summer to celebrate their two years out of treatment.

"It was a big moment for me," she said. "Even though things aren't great now, whenever I look at my tattoo, I remember why I get up every day and fight. It doesn't have to be this way. There is more to life than this disease."

I enlarge the photo on my screen and touch my thumb to the symbol. I wish I could be as strong as Dakota and anyone else who finds the courage to overcome their disorder. Maybe someday, I will be. Maybe someday, I'll finally understand what recovery is all about.

17

"Hold still. It's going to pinch a little."

I take a deep breath, then relax my shoulders. To my left, Lou and Cassie's eyes dart back and forth between the piercer—a young woman with dyed-pink hair and a septum ring—and me. The woman presses her piercing gun against my right cartilage and counts down from three in a husky voice.

"Three . . . two . . . one."

I feel a sharp pinch that lasts for several seconds. Then it's over. The piercer wipes my cartilage with an antiseptic and hands me a mirror, so I can admire my new piercing. It's even better than I'd imagined—that is, aside from the bright red hue surrounding the sterling silver stud.

"You need to clean it with solution three times a day," the piercer says. "Here." She gives me a black business card with a phone number on the front and a list of instructions for proper ear care on the back. "Call us if you have any questions."

"Thank you." Offering her a parting smile, I hop off the chair and follow Lou and Cassie into the lower level of the mall.

"Proud of you, sis," Cassie jokes, whacking me with her Nordstrom bag. Lou is empty-handed; we've been to three department stores so far, and she still hasn't found a dress she likes.

I laugh. "I can't wait until I'm eighteen."

"Eighteen definitely has its perks. I'm psyched that I can vote now."

"And join the army," Lou reminds her.

Cassie dramatically clutches her hand to her heart. "Not in a million years!"

"Guys, look. Pinkberry." Lou points at the frozen yogurt store. A young man stands behind the counter waiting for his next customer. "You down?"

"Totally."

"Grace?"

I shrug. "All right."

Lou speed walks towards the counter with Cassie and I trailing close behind. "I want a medium Black Raspberry with mini M&Ms and whipped cream," she informs the man.

"And you?"

"Small Blood Orange with marshmallows," Cassie says.

I quickly scan the overhead menu. "Small Strawberry. No toppings."

The man prepares our order and rings up the total. "That will be thirteen dollars and sixty-two cents."

"I'll pay." Cassie whips her credit card out of her wallet and places it in the chip reader. While she's waiting for the card to process, she hands us three spoons and a stack of napkins in addition to our frozen yogurts. "Find somewhere to sit. I'll catch up."

"Thanks, babe." Lou plants a kiss on Cassie's cheek and heads to the seating area outside of a Starbucks. She claims a circular table near the middle and drags over a third chair. "Yum! I fucking love this stuff. I can't believe it went out of business in the Center."

"People prefer self-serve," I say. "I think it's a control thing."

"Whatevs. So, what's new with you?"

"Guess who's moving in tomorrow."

"Kevin?"

"Yeah." I make a face. "I'm still pissed at Mom for not telling me sooner."

"Why? I thought you said he was nice."

"He is, but there have been nice guys before, and they always left when things got out of hand."

"What do you mean by out of hand?"

"Mom works a lot, and she has issues, you know? She can be, um, how do I say it . . . stuck in her ways. And then there's Jamie and me. Jamie's been in a funk lately, and it's hard to be around him when he's so emotional all the time. Of course I'm not any easier. If I was her boyfriend, I'd probably leave too."

"You never know. There's someone for everyone."

"I wish she'd hurry up and find that someone. I'm so over her flings."

"Whose flings?" Cassie sits next to Lou and claims her frozen yogurt. The deep orange color reminds me of a sunset; the marshmallows of fluffy clouds.

"My mom's."

"Isn't she dating Devin?"

"Kevin, and it's complicated." I sigh. "Let's talk about something else, okay?"

"Like what?" Lou asks.

"Like when you're finally going to choose a dress," Cassie teases. "You know it's just for one night, right?"

"I know, I know. If I don't find anything at Lord & Taylor, we can go back to Macy's, and I'll get the purple one. I can always cut off the stupid bow."

Cassie laughs. "Whatever tickles your fancy. Can I have a bite of your fro-yo? I've never tried Black Raspberry."

Lou sticks a spoonful of the creamy pink yogurt in Cassie's mouth. "Good, right?"

Cassie waits until she's swallowed to say, "Very. Want to try mine?"

"You know I do."

I've never felt more like a third wheel than I do watching them feed each other. "You guys are too much."

"Aww. Is someone jealous?" Lou teases.

I roll my eyes. "In your dreams."

"Grace, your ear is bleeding." Cassie leans across the table and pats my cartilage with a napkin. "There. That's better."

When Lou sees the blood stain, her dark eyes grow wide. "Not to be a downer, but your mom *is* cool with this . . . right?"

"Of course," I respond casually. "She said so herself."

"A CARTILAGE PIERCING? GRACE, WHAT WERE YOU thinking?"

"You said I could, Mom," I protest.

"Like hell I did." Mom buries her face in her hands. "Did you ever consider, even for a *second*, that this might not be a good idea?"

"Please don't make me take it out," I beg. "I like it a lot, and—and I swear I'll take good care of it so it doesn't get infected."

"You can keep the piercing," she says, "but you're giving me your phone. You've lost it for a week."

"But, Mom—"

"Do you want me to take away your TV privileges too?"

"No," I mumble. She holds out her hand, and I reluctantly give her my phone. "Lou was gonna text me tonight. I'm supposed to help her decide which dress to get online." It turns out that while we were at Pinkberry, someone else had bought the last purple dress in her size.

"That's not my problem," Mom responds. "If you're so worried about it, you can call her on our home phone."

"We have a home phone?"

"It's in my office next to the printer."

"Fine. I'll use the stupid home phone."

Sighing dramatically, I leave the kitchen and trudge down the hallway. Mom's office is a small room packed with a creaky desk, a mesh task chair, a filing cabinet, and various electronic devices. To the right of the printer is a framed photograph of Jamie and me when we were younger; to the left is the home phone. I pick it up to call Lou when a printed email conversation on Mom's desk titled *Re: Grace* catches my eye. Unable to contain my curiosity, I set down the phone and move a ballpoint pen that was blocking the name of the sender. *William S. Edwards.*

"What the hell?" I mumble. I snatch the paper off her desk and peer at the tiny font. Dad writes:

Kira,

I heard that Grace was in the hospital. Why was I not informed of this? She's my daughter too. If there is anything I can do to help, let me know. I'm willing to cover Grace's hospital bills, as well as the cost of any other treatment she receives in the future. Her health is the most important thing to me.

William

My heart is racing as I reread my father's note. According to the date to the right of his address, he sent it six days ago at ten o'clock at night—well, seven o'clock his time. Six days, and I haven't heard a single word from Mom. How can she rightfully accuse me of going behind her back when *she* has been lying to me this entire time?

"Sorry to bother you. I for—" Mom stops mid-sentence when she sees me holding Dad's email. "What are you doing?"

"Were you gonna tell me about this?" I demand. When she doesn't respond, I throw the paper at her and storm out of her office.

Mom follows me as I charge upstairs. "Grace, let me explain."

In my room, I collapse onto my bed and stare at the wall, willing myself not to cry. "Just leave me alone."

"Grace—"

"Mom, I don't want to hear it," I interrupt. "Can you please go?"

"No, I'm not going. I'm worried about you." She sits on my bed and reaches for my hand, but I push her off me.

"Mom! Get the fuck out!"

She refuses to budge. "Yell all you want. I'm staying until you talk to me."

"Fine, stay here on your own." I jump to my feet and leave my room, slamming the door behind me. With my back against the door, I sink to the floor and blink tears from my eyes. On the other side, I hear Mom sniffle a couple times. "Are you sitting there?"

"Yes," she responds quietly.

"Why didn't you tell me?"

She takes a shaky breath. "This is the first time I've heard from him in years, and I didn't know what to do. But I promise you; if he sends me anything else, you'll be the first person I tell."

"Why should I believe you?"

"Don't you trust me?" When I remain quiet, she blubbers, "You're the most important thing in my life. I would never do anything to purposely hurt you, you know that?"

A tear trickles down my cheek. "I know."

"I want you to feel like you can talk to me about anything or tell me when you're going to do things like restrict food or—or get piercings."

"Only if you promise to stop keeping secrets about Dad," I negotiate.

"All right," she says. "No more secrets. What do you want to know?"

"Is this really the first time he's emailed you?"

"It's the first time in a while. He used to email me at least once a week. He would ask how you were and if he could visit you. But I told him that there was no way in hell I'd let him come near you. After that, I never heard from him again—until now."

"And Christmas," I remind her.

I close my eyes and, as I have on countless occasions, think back to late December, when Dad's unexpected holiday card came in the mail. I see his words, so sloppy that they were nearly illegible: *Dearest Gracie and Jameson, I'm sorry I didn't reach out sooner but I needed time to clear my head.*

"I didn't know he was planning to send you a card," Mom says. "I was just as surprised."

This I don't doubt. "And the hospital? How did he find out about that?"

"I'm not sure. Some connection maybe. He has his ways."

"Are you going to take his money?"

"No, I'm not."

"How come?"

"Because I don't want to owe him in any way. That's not fair to you and your brother. Plus our insurance covered just about everything."

"It's not fair to you either, Mom."

"I can handle it."

"You always say that."

"Grace . . ." She sighs. "Forget it. Is there anything else you want to know? Anything at all?"

There are many more questions I'm itching to ask her, but I'm not sure I'm ready to dredge up those painful memories. "Not right now," I lie. "But I'll let you know if there is."

"Okay." After a long beat of silence, she says, "Listen, I'm going to Town Hall this afternoon to help distribute food to a women's shelter. Do you want to come with me?"

"I'll think about it."

"I know that means 'no' in your own private language."

I laugh softly. "I guess you know me pretty well, huh?"

"As I should," she responds, but her voice is no longer as solemn. "Can you at least let me out of here?"

Even though she can't see me, I smile. "I'll think about it."

"You're quiet today," Anna observes.

"I know," I say. "I'm sorry."

"You don't have to apologize. Do you want to talk about what's going on?"

I stare at my sneakers—dark grey Nikes with a neon blue trim—and remember how excited I was when I unwrapped them on my birthday. Once I was certain that they fit, I tore off the twenty-six-dollar Marshall's tag that was looped through the black laces, wrapped my arms around Mom, and proceeded to thank her profusely for the gift. By the time I let go, she was beaming. I couldn't remember the last time I'd seen her smile like that.

"Well, um, there was this . . . thing with my mom."

"What kind of thing?"

"My dad knows about the hospital. I don't know how, but he does. He sent my mom an email saying he wanted to cover the cost of my treatment because my health matters to him or some crap like that. That was over a week ago. I don't think she was going to tell me."

"How did you find out?" Anna asks.

"I was in her office. I saw the email on her desk."

When I look up, Anna's eyes are filled with concern. "Oh, Grace. I imagine this must be very difficult for you."

"The funny thing is I'm not that upset about the note," I say. "I'm upset that she didn't tell me. She's always giving me crap for keeping secrets, and then she goes and does something like this. It's not fair."

"Did you talk to her about it?"

"Yes. Well, yelled at her is more accurate. We got into a fight, and she started to cry. She said she was sorry; that I was the most important thing in her life, and she'd never do anything to hurt me on purpose."

"How did it feel to hear her say that?"

"I'm not sure," I respond honestly. "I never doubted that she cared about me. I mean, she used to drive me to Manhattan every day. Most of the parents at CADE made their kids take a bus, but not Mom. So yeah, it's obvious that she cares. The problem is that she cares to the point where she will do literally anything to protect me—even if it's not right."

"Such as keeping secrets?"

"Exactly." I sigh. "I'm still a kid to her. In her eyes, I'm still this helpless little girl that needs her mommy to save her from the scary world. It doesn't matter how many times I tell her to back off; she never does. I'm starting to think that she doesn't know how."

"Mothers are a pain, huh?"

Above Anna's head on a narrow shelf, my eyes hone in on a framed photograph of two grinning girls that I hadn't noticed before. Both have Anna's hazel eyes and reddish hair, though one wears hers in a high ponytail, while the others is styled in pigtails. The older girl, who looks about eight, has her arm slung around the younger girl's shoulders.

"You have kids?"

Anna nods. "Ella and Zoe. They're everything to me."

"Then I guess you'd also do crazy things to protect them."

"You're probably right," she admits, "but at the same time, I understand why you're frustrated. It's perfectly normal to want independence."

"That's another thing that's not fair," I say. "Other kids my age can drive cars and go to parties and eat out with friends and not have their parents breathing down their necks twenty-four seven. It's like this whole mental illness thing has us frozen in time, and I just want to move on already. I'm so fucking sick of it." I catch myself a second too late. "Sorry for swearing."

"Let it out," Anna encourages. "After everything you've been through, you should be angry."

"Damn right!" I exclaim. "This whole year has been a fucking nightmare! I mean, just a couple months ago, I was refusing food, cutting myself, spending entire afternoons isolating in my room—and don't even get me started on all the pointless fighting. It was like a demon had possessed me, which I know sounds totally crazy, but that's how it felt at the time."

"It doesn't sound crazy. Mental illness is debilitating, and when it's at its worst, it can feel like an out-of-body experience. You lose all control."

"That's ironic."

"How come?"

"The whole reason I stopped eating was so I could have control," I say, "but somehow, things got turned around, and I ended up with none. I couldn't deal with real life. That's why they put me in the hospital."

"The important thing to remember is that you're not in that place anymore," Anna says, "and as hard as it might be, you have to face reality—starting with your mother. So, what are we going to do about her?"

"Put her on a boat and send her to some remote island," I suggest. "Or I could forgive her, but that's a lot less fun."

Anna smiles. "It's also a lot more practical."

"You're right. After all, I've lost count of how many times I lied to her." Even the thought of how manipulative I was—and still sometimes am—makes me cringe. "What does that say about me?"

"That you weren't well."

"I know. I still feel badly though. I mean, I didn't then, but now that things are different, I do." Once again, my eyes drift to my sneakers. "I really want to move on. I don't want this life anymore. I just . . . I just want to feel okay."

Anna is quiet for a couple seconds. "I'm proud of you," she says finally. "You should be too."

"How come?"

"Because what you just said, that's recovery. You're on your way, lady."

Recovery. It's a word I've heard over and over again, yet for reasons I can't explain, this time feels different; this time feels . . . real. "You think?"

Anna's kind smile returns. "No, Grace. I know."

18

Lou has a new television: a thirty-two-inch Samsung flat screen. It's wedged between her dresser and her radiator on top of a cream-colored stand that I remember seeing a while ago in her cluttered basement.

The second I enter her room, I do a double-take. "Whoa. Where did that come from?"

Lou closes the door and stands in front of her full-length mirror to admire her makeup: smoky eyeshadow, curled lashes, and crimson lipstick. Her cousin, a professional cosmetologist, had stopped by earlier this afternoon to help her prepare for Prom.

"Pa bought it for me," she says. "It's my reward for doing well on the SATs."

"That's so unfair," I gripe. "I did better than you, and all I got from Mom was a high-five and pumpkin bread."

"Pumpkin bread?"

"Yeah. It didn't even rise well."

"No surprise. When Ma used to bake sweet breads, they always turned out as flat as bricks!"

"Used to?"

"She's been tired lately," Lou explains. "But she'll get back to it soon."

"She'd better. She makes some damn good food."

Lou arches an eyebrow. "You know, it's been a while since you talked about food like this."

"Like what?"

"Like you enjoy it, like it's a good thing."

"I hadn't noticed," I say, "but I guess between my birthday and Boston and all that, something clicked, and I realized that it's okay to treat myself now and then. I've started eating independently too. Look." I reach into the pocket of my sleeveless hoodie and show her a bag of Tiny Twists. "It was too early to have snack when I left, so I told Mom I'd eat them at your house. I know it's not much, but it's a start." I open the bag and pop a pretzel in my mouth. "Want one?"

She shakes her head. "I'll pass. See, I have the opposite problem when it comes to junk food."

"Pretzels aren't junk food."

"They're carbs. I can't have carbs *and* look good for Prom."

"Lou, it's a school dance. No one is going to care."

"*I* care. Anyway, you're thin, so you're not allowed to have an opinion."

"You think I'm thin?" I ask, unable to help myself.

She rolls her eyes. "Do me a favor, and don't ask stupid questions, okay?"

I grin. "Okay, fine. I'll shut up."

"Thank you." After a beat of silence, she says, "I'm sorry

you aren't going."

"Don't be. I'm not going to force Isaac to do something he doesn't want to."

"What's up with you two anyway?"

"What do you mean?"

"I dunno." She opens the top drawer of her dresser and rummages through her underwear and bras. "You just don't seem as happy as you used to. When was the last time you even saw him?"

"Two weeks ago." When her eyes widen, I quickly add, "At least we've started texting again."

"Again?"

"Well, I mean, after the whole, um . . ."

"Sex thing?"

"Yeah. After that, I felt confused and upset and also guilty, which I know I shouldn't have, but I did anyway, and I—I didn't know what to do."

"So . . . your brilliant solution was to ignore his texts?"

I nod meekly. "Does that make me an awful person?"

"Of course not. What happened wasn't your fault. I'm sure a lot of people would have reacted the same way."

"And now? What the hell am I supposed to do?"

"You have to decide." She swaps her red push-up bra with a white strapless one and tosses the former into her hamper. "Stop giving a fuck about what anyone else thinks. What do *you* want?"

"I, um . . ." I clear my throat. "I'm not sure."

"Well, then that's something you'll have to figure out." She opens her closet, where her dress hangs on a wooden hanger. "Can you zip me up?"

I stand behind Lou and tug on the zipper until it stops below her scapula. The silky coral fabric is a stunning contrast to her dark skin, and the A-Line shape does wonders for her curvy figure. She's definitely lost weight—whether from stress, dieting, or a combination of both, I'm not sure.

"Damn," I say as I'm fixing her straightened hair. "You're beautiful."

She grins. "Can you take a picture?"

"Of course."

Lou hands me her phone and strikes a pose with her lips curled into a broad smile. "Now look silly," I instruct after I've snapped several photos. She sticks out her tongue and raises her right eyebrow while simultaneously furrowing her left. "Perfect!"

Lou retrieves her phone and scrolls through the photos. "I love them. Dude, I can't wait to post these on Instagram!"

Ding!

"Cass is here. You coming?"

"I'm right behind you."

I follow Lou downstairs and out onto her spacious front lawn. Cassie is waiting by a rose bush in a sparkly turquoise dress. Lou greets her with a kiss and slings her arm around Cassie's shoulders while I take more pictures. Once I've finished, they exchange corsages and climb into Cassie's car to head to Prom.

"Later, Grace!" Lou calls out the window.

"Have fun!" I respond enthusiastically. I watch them drive away, and although I'm happy for them, I can't ignore the jealousy bubbling up inside of me. How come Lou was able to work things out with Cassie when my relationship with Isaac is still confusing as hell?

When I return home, Mom is working on tonight's dinner: cheese and black bean quesadillas with a chopped salad. I pour three glasses of water and a cup of milk for Jamie and place them on the table.

"How's Lou?" Mom asks as I'm putting the milk back in the refrigerator.

"Excited. She looks great too."

"Are you disappointed that you're not going with Isaac?"

"Not really," I lie. "You know how I feel about parties."

"Prom's not that great anyway," Mom says. "When I was your age, I was dating the captain of the synchronized swimming team, Emilio."

"You had a synchronized swimming team?"

"My school was strange. As I was saying, Emilio asked me to Prom, and I agreed, and then on Prom night, he shows up at my house—twenty minutes late, might I add—in a convertible. By the time we got there, my perm was ruined, the straps on my dress were all tangled up, and I had bird poop on my shoulder."

I have to bite my lip to suppress my laughter. "Oh my god."

"Let's just say that was the last time I went out with him."

"Was Senior Prom any better?"

"Considering that my date hooked up with my best friend, not really."

No longer able to contain myself, I burst out laughing. "That's it. I'm never going to a school dance!"

"Don't knock it until you've tried it. Many people like them . . . for some reason." Mom slides two quesadillas onto each of the four plates to her right. She adds another half to Jamie and

Kevin's and hands them to me. "Put these on the table. I'll go get the boys."

While Mom disappears into the hall, I place the plates at our designated spots and serve myself a reasonable portion of salad. I push a couple walnuts, a nut I genuinely can't stand, to the side as Jamie prances into the kitchen. Mom and Kevin follow close behind him.

"Ooh, quesadillas!" he exclaims. "Thanks, Mom!"

"You can thank Kevin," Mom responds. "He suggested that we have Mexican."

"When I lived in New York City, one of my roommates was from Mexico," Kevin says. "Every Friday night, she'd make quesadillas. She was partial to corn tortillas, but flour works too."

"I didn't know you lived in New York City," I say.

"I went to grad school there. I grew up in Kansas, so city life was quite an adjustment."

"I can only imagine," Mom says. "Grace, do you remember how many people live there? You looked it up a while ago."

"Um, I think it was something like eight-and-a-half million."

Mom nods. "That sounds about right. When Grace was at her program, it could sometimes take us thirty minutes just to get on the highway. I'm glad we don't have to make that drive anymore, right, hon?"

"Uh-huh."

"Well, we should probably sit down. I'd hate for the food to get cold."

So, we gather around the table and begin eating. I dip my quesadilla into a pile of salsa, while Mom lathers hers with sour cream and Jamie and Kevin skip the condiments altogether and eagerly dig in. Once we've satisfied our hunger, we take turns recapping our days. Kevin pokes fun at a ridiculous political argument between his colleagues. Jamie complains about a reading check that "everyone did bad on." I agree with him that reading checks are the absolute worst.

"Worse than pop quizzes?" he asks.

I hold up my index finger as I finish chewing. "Depends on the class. I don't think I've ever gotten above a C on a pop quiz in math. It's impossible to remember everything."

Mom, who has been uncharacteristically quiet for most of dinner, waits until I'm done speaking to turn her attention to my brother. "Jamie, I scheduled an appointment with the barber tomorrow, so I'm going to pick you up from school a little early, okay?"

Jamie shakes his head. "I don't want to get my hair cut."

"Jamie—"

"I mean it, Mom. Forget it."

"I'm not going to forget it, Jamie. Your hair is too long. You're starting to look like a girl."

Jamie abruptly stands up and pushes his chair back. It wobbles slightly before falling onto the floor with a loud clatter. "You don't know shit," he snaps and storms out of the kitchen.

An exasperated sigh escapes Mom's lips. "Oh, for the love of God. Not this again."

"I'll talk to him." Kevin wipes his hands on his napkin and takes off after my brother. "Jamie?" we hear him say a couple seconds later. "Jamie, open the door. I just want to talk."

Mom picks up Jamie's chair and collapses onto it, burying her face in her hands. "Why do you two have to be so damn defiant?"

"I, uh . . ." Not sure how to respond, I change the subject. "I'm gonna change my clothes. It's, like, really cold in here."

"Finish your salad first."

"I did. I just don't like the walnuts."

"Grace, I'm not screwing around. Finish your damn salad."

"Fine."

I scoop up the small pile of nuts with my fork and pop it in my mouth, making a face as I chew. Once I've swallowed, I discard my dishes in the sink and head upstairs. As I pass Jamie's room, I hear him talking to Kevin in a calmer, yet still defensive voice.

"She thinks she can control me, but I'm not a kid anymore. It's my hair. It's my life."

"She's just looking out for you."

"I mean, I guess so. It's just that sometimes I get the feeling that she's embarrassed by me; that she thinks I'm too girly or sensitive or whatever. I don't wear pink and paint my nails for attention, like everyone says; I do it because I like it. This is who I am, and I get so much crap for it. It's not fair."

Closing my bedroom door, I swap my jean cutoffs with a pair of sweatpants. Jamie and Kevin are still talking when I move to the bathroom to brush the taste of cheddar cheese out of my mouth, though their conversation has taken on a lighter tone. Jamie has even begun to laugh.

In the kitchen, however, the mood is far from upbeat. Mom stands at the sink scrubbing Jamie's dinner plate with her shoulders slumped and her eyes suspiciously wet.

"He seems better," I say.

"That's good," she whispers.

"Why do you care so much about his hair?"

"I don't, not really. I just care about him. You know how he skipped gym a while back?"

"Yeah?"

"It happened again, so I called his teacher to talk about it, and he said he's noticed that Jamie's been withdrawn lately. He doesn't interact with his peers. Most of the time, he doesn't even change his clothes. His grade is a D. Who gets a D in gym?"

"A lot of people think gym is a joke," I say. "When I took gym, some kids would stand around and talk with their friends the entire time. I bet their grades sucked too."

"All I want him to do is try. He doesn't have to be good at it, and he doesn't have to like it, but he has to try. That's it." She sighs. "You don't think I'm being unreasonable, right?"

"No, but I think there are things he's not telling us."

"Fantastic," she mutters sarcastically. "More secrets."

"It seems like all this family does is keep secrets," I say. "We're all so happy here, aren't we?"

"Grace, if this is about your father—"

"Not everything is about Dad," I interrupt.

"I know that," she says. "I just thought you might still be upset about the email. I'd completely understand if you are by the way. I'm sure I'd be upset too."

"I'm not upset," I respond. "I mean, it was a really crappy thing for you to do, but mostly I just want to move on. Can we do that? Please?"

Mom nods. "We can."

"Jamie is working on his homework." Kevin walks into the kitchen. He takes a bottle of beer out of the refrigerator and pops open the cap with his thumb. "Something called a

WebQuest. He's using your computer, Grace. I hope that's okay."

"It's fine. I told him he could while his is getting fixed."

Last Friday, Jamie came home from school in tears. He claimed that he'd banged his computer into a table and shattered the screen, but Mom and I had our doubts. Jamie was never one to break things—even by accident.

"Is he . . . should I apologize?" Mom asks.

"I'd wait until tomorrow," Kevin responds.

"All right. Thank you for, um, handling it."

"Anytime. He's a great kid. He's just going through some stuff."

"You don't say," she mumbles sarcastically.

"It could be worse," I point out. "At least he still likes food."

Ding!

"Excuse me, I have to answer this," Kevin says.

While he responds to the text, Mom turns to me. "And you? How do you feel about food these days, Grace?"

I glance at Kevin. He's leaning against the counter with his eyes glued to his phone. "Better. I ate a quesadilla, didn't I?"

"You sure did."

"And I didn't complain either," I continue, "even though you used way too much cheese."

"I'll keep that in mind for next time. I personally thought they were good—cheese and all."

"What are you girls talking about?" Kevin turns off his phone and slips it in the pocket of his navy dress pants.

"The quesadillas," Mom says. "Grace is insisting that they were too cheesy."

Kevin bites his lip. "I mean, she has a point."

For the first time since Jamie's outburst, Mom cracks a small smile. She grabs a dish towel and whips it against Kevin's thigh. "You're supposed to have my back!"

"Oh, so now you want me to lie too?"

I can't help but laugh at their playful bantering, and when Kevin places his hands on her hips and kisses her, I'm not nearly as bothered as I usually am. Maybe Mom is right, and I should give him a chance. He'll never be my dad, but then again, that might not be such a bad thing after all.

"A CHEESE STICK, HUH? THAT'S DIFFERENT."

"And Veggie Straws," I say. "Mom bought a bunch at Shop-Rite the other day. They're good."

Miss Dixon peers at the bag clutched in my hands. "I'll have to check them out sometime. So, how was your weekend?"

"It was . . . eventful," I respond, choosing my words carefully. "I got my cartilage pierced."

"You did? Can I see?"

I move my hair to the side to expose my ear. The skin surrounding the stud is still red, though it's no longer sore. Mom found the ear care card in my jacket pocket and has been following the instructions down to a T by making me clean it three times a day—with soap *and* alcohol.

"Looks good," Miss Dixon says. "Where did you get it?"

"At the mall. But I didn't tell Mom, so she was pissed."

"Why didn't you tell her?"

"Because I wanted to do something spontaneous, and I knew if I asked her, she'd say no. I feel like my life is like white bread. Not good, not bad—certainly not exciting. For my own sanity, I needed to spice things up."

Miss Dixon takes a moment to process my analogy. "So . . . cinnamon raisin bread?"

"Yes, but without the raisins. Can I go now?" I show her my empty bag. "I finished my snack."

"You may. I'll see you later."

"See you."

I push back my chair and leave her office, discarding my wrappers in the trash on my way out. I still have ten minutes until the period ends, so I head to the library to start my reading homework for *The Handmaid's Tale*. Cassie is standing at the counter, tapping her foot against the floor while Mr. Chadwick talks to another student.

"Hey," I say.

"Hey. I heard your mom was upset about . . ." She gestures to my ear.

"Oh, yeah. She took away my phone."

"Shit. I'm sorry."

"No worries. I got it back."

"How did you do that?"

"I told her I'd mow the lawn after school."

Cassie makes a face. "In that case, I'd let her keep my phone."

"It shouldn't be so bad," I say. "She owes me anyway."

"What does that mean?"

I shake my head. "Nothing. Lou said Prom was fun."

"It was all right. There was too much standing around, and some of the parent chaperones were super annoying, but it was nice to be with her. So thank you for that."

"No problem. You guys deserve to be happy."

Cassie smiles. "So do you, you know."

"Miss Meyers? May I help you?" Mr. Chadwick beckons Cassie to his computer.

"I've had a book on hold for a while," she explains. "Can you check the status?"

"Of course. One moment."

"Bye, Cass," I say.

"Later, Grace."

With five minutes until the bell, I'm only able to read half the chapter. After bookmarking the page, I follow my peers into the busy hall and head to chemistry. Ms. Lloyd is absent, so I spend the first part of the class filling out her assignment—a worksheet on chemical reactions—and the rest completing my reading. By the end of the period, my eyes ache from the tiny print.

Mr. Duffy is in one of his no-nonsense moods. "Quiet down," he orders. "I have an important announcement. As you are all aware, finals are only three weeks away. Now, many teachers require their students to take a test, but I'm not like that. I believe in creativity, in thinking outside the box, in the power of," he pauses for dramatic effect, "imagination!"

"Is that why he gives us quizzes every fucking week?" Jess mumbles to Tiffany.

"For your final," he continues, "you will work in groups of two to create a presentation on one of the topics we've covered this year. I've already assigned groups—" this elicits a groan from the class, which he ignores, "so when I call your name, find your partner. Sam, you'll be working with Heather. Justine, I've paired you with Adam."

Justine exchanges a flirtatious smile with Adam. According to several rumors floating around Chuckles, they hooked up at Prom and have been sleeping together ever since.

"For our third group, I have Grace and Jessica."

I glance at Jess, whose glossy lips are pursed in a scowl. Unsurprisingly, I'm not the only one dissatisfied with Mr. Duffy's pairing. While he continues assigning groups, I take out my phone to text Lou.

Grace: guess who i got paired with in history?

Lou: idk who?

Grace: stupid jess :(

Lou: sorry that sucks. im stuck with Eli.

Grace: at least hes smart.

Lou: true. i miss having history with u tho.

Grace: u can blame my half day scooter.

Grace: *schedule

Lou: lol

Pocketing my phone, I return my attention to the front of the classroom, where Mr. Duffy has just paired the last two students. "All right, get with your partners," he says. "I'll let you brainstorm ideas for the rest of the period."

With my bookbag in one hand and the outline in the other, I wait for Tiffany to move so I can sit next to Jess. "Hey."

Her eyes remain glued to her phone. "Hey."

"So . . . should we get started?"

"Hold on. I'm in the middle of something."

While she finishes up whatever she's doing, I skim through the outline. "This doesn't look too bad. Basically, he wants us to—"

"Shh. I'm busy."

"Sorry," I say.

One minute passes, followed by two more. Finally, Jess turns off her phone and slips it in her backpack. She opens her lunch box and takes out a plastic spoon and a nonfat strawberry yogurt. As she's mixing in the mushy fruit chunks, she says rudely, "Are you going to tell me what we're doing?"

"To conclude our AP European History course, you will create a project that incorporates in-depth research on one of the topics we've covered this year," I read out loud. *"The final product will emphasize your topic's influence on Europe in present times. It will be of digital format and shared through a ten-minute video presentation. You will have in-class time until the exam date, which is when your project is due. Good luck!"*

Jess rolls her eyes. "Fun. What are the choices?"

I hand her the sheet, where roughly twenty events are listed below the synopsis in chronological order. "We should do one of the World Wars," I suggest. "It'll be easy since there are so many resour—"

"We're doing the Cold War," she interrupts. "My brother was in AP Euro three years ago, and that was his topic. He can help us."

"So . . . we're going to cheat?"

"Of course not. My brother is an idiot, so obviously we'll do better than him, but I've seen his Works Cited page, and there are a lot of good sources on there. We can use those for our research."

"Okay . . ."

"We'll probably have to do some artsy shit for the video." She takes a small bite of her yogurt, then pushes it to the side. "My father has a projector in his office, so if we make a Power-

Point, we can flash the slides behind us while we're filming. And—are you writing this down?"

I open my notebook to a blank page and begin scribbling down her suggestions.

"We should also create a diagram or something like that," she continues, "to show how the war progressed over time."

"That's a good idea."

"Well, duh. You need to think of one now—I've already come up with three."

"Uh . . ." As I'm racking my brain, the bell rings. "I'll have it by tomorrow. Do you want—"

"Tif, wait up!"

Jess snatches her backpack and hurries after her friend, knocking my pencil off the desk as she passes me. With a sigh, I pick it up and place it in my three-ring pencil pouch. That's when I realize that Jess forgot her notebook.

As much as I'm tempted to chuck it in the trash, I instead wedge it between my binder and my homework folder, so I can return it to her tomorrow. Then I carelessly push in my chair and leave the room, more than ready to go home. I'm walking through the A-Wing when my phone buzzes.

Mom: at guidance. see you soon!

"Dammit," I mumble. I'd been so preoccupied with my schoolwork, I completely forgot that my Planning and Placement Team meeting was scheduled for sixth period.

I turn around, nearly colliding with a boy in a Messi jersey, and reluctantly head to Guidance. In the conference room, Mom, Miss Dixon, Mrs. Perkenson, and Ms. Killion, the Pupil Services Coordinator, are seated around a rectangular table. I sit next to Mom, slouching in the mesh chair.

She nudges me. "Posture, Grace."

"Don't boss me around," I grouch.

Ms. Killion clears her throat. Once she has our attention, she opens a black briefcase and places her computer on the table. "We are here today for a PPT meeting for Grace Edwards to review her progress with her Individualized Education Plan and set goals for the upcoming school year."

"I want to keep my half-day schedule," I say.

"We'll get there, Grace," Ms. Killion assures me. "First, we need to evaluate how you're doing academically. Mrs. Perkenson, you have her grades, yes?"

Mrs. Perkenson nods. She's also brought her computer and is logging onto PowerSchool. I can tell by the reflection of the screen in the large window behind her. "Grace is doing well this quarter. She has a ninety-four in my class, an eighty-nine in chemistry, an eighty-three in math . . ."

As she's talking, I steal periodic glances at the clock above the door. The steady *tick-tock, tick-tock* seems to grow louder with every passing minute, whereas my teacher's voice merely becomes more grating. I know I have to be here because of my IEP, yet at the same time, I don't understand the point. My grades are progressively improving, my health, for the first time in months, is stable, and my goals are simple: earn my diploma and get the hell out of here.

"And how is she behaviorally?"

Mrs. Perkenson flashes me a kind smile. "Wonderful. She's a pleasure to have in class."

It takes every ounce of strength I have to hold my tongue. When I thought this morning couldn't get any more frustrating, it just did.

19

I'm beginning to dread family dinners again. From the stiff conversations to Mom commenting on my portions—either with praise or disapproval—to Jamie's relentless sulking, they have become my least favorite part of the day. Even school is more tolerable in comparison.

Tonight is no exception. After I've finished my slightly undercooked pasta and salad, I excuse myself and head to my room to start researching the Cold War. I briefly flip through Jess' notebook to see if she has any quality notes (I was in the hospital when Mr. Duffy taught the unit and had to rely solely on my textbook) but most of the pages are blank. Those that aren't are either illegible or irrelevant. Several have lists of numbers scribbled in no particular order: ninety, thirty-five, one-hundred-ten, so on and so forth.

Seeing them, I feel melancholic. After all, I used to make lists like that too. I would religiously record my caloric intake after every meal or snack: a skimpy bowl of cereal, an undressed salad, a handful of grapes, a sip of Vitamin Water. I still have those lists; they're stashed in my drawers or scribbled in the pretty pastel journals on my bookshelf. I haven't touched them in months, but then, I haven't gotten rid of them either.

With a sigh, I close Jess' notebook and turn on my computer. Jamie, who had borrowed it for a school assignment this afternoon, must have forgotten to shut it down, since the power button is still blinking.

"Eleven percent," I mumble under my breath. "Thanks a lot."

I plug my computer into its charger and open Chrome to see if Mr. Lipschitz has replied to the email I sent him about a question in our review packet. But when I type "g" into the search bar for "Gmail," it autocompletes to "gay test."

"What the hell?" Peering curiously at the screen, I pull up my history.

The Gay Test
How Gay Are You?
How to know if you're gay
Openly gay celebrities
Cristiano Ronaldo abs
Hot male models abs

A knock on my door makes me jump. I hastily drag the cursor to the top of the screen and click out of Chrome. "Come in!"

"Hey." Jamie stands in front of me wearing a white t-shirt and purple pajama pants. He flashes me a toothy grin. "I just want to say goodnight."

"You're going to sleep? At eight o'clock?"

"No, but I'm gonna get in bed and watch Netflix on my

phone. Sara said *Black Mirror* is really good, so I think I'll check it out."

"Spooky. Don't give yourself nightmares."

Jamie rolls his eyes. "Yes, Mom. Oh, can I use your computer again tomorrow? I have a stupid essay that's due on Thursday."

"Uh . . . yeah. That's fine."

"Thanks. 'Night, Grace."

"Goodnight, Jamie."

I wait until he's gone, closing my door behind him, to reopen Chrome. Mr. Lipschitz has yet to respond to my email—not that I'm surprised—so I move on to history without bothering to take another stab at the confusing equations. I spend the next twenty minutes watching YouTube videos on the Cold War, then ten more downloading a Red Hot Chili Peppers' song that popped up in my *Recommended*. With the music playing through my earbuds, I continue my research.

Around eight thirty, as my mind is beginning to drift from my schoolwork, a Gmail notification appears on the bottom right corner of my screen. *Email from Hubert Lipschitz*, it says. I bookmark the Wikipedia article I'm reading and open a new tab. "gay test" shows up in my search bar again, and I sigh. I know I should talk to Jamie about this, but I'm worried that I won't know what to say or, worse, I'll say the wrong thing, and he'll get upset.

But I don't have to make up my mind tonight. So, I snap a picture of my search history, clear my browsing data from the last twenty-four hours, and shut down my computer. It isn't until my screen is black that I realize I forgot all about Mr. Lipschitz's email.

"Did you get the invite to Matt's party?"

In response to Lou's question, I nod. "Yeah. Are you going?"

"I might. I heard his uncle's house is totally sick. Heather says the guy has an indoor swimming pool *and* a jacuzzi." She takes a gulp of her lemonade, then places the sky-blue *Stay Woke* mug on her nightstand. "How 'bout you?"

"Nah. I know I'll just get overwhelmed and will want to leave halfway through. Not to mention that everyone will be drunk."

"So?"

"So . . . I don't drink."

"Have a Coke then."

"I don't like soda."

Lou rolls her eyes. "Okay, fine. Be boring and stay home. I'll see if Cassie wants to come."

Now is my chance. "Um, Lou? Can I ask you something?" When she nods her head, prompting me to proceed, I hesitantly say, "This might sound weird, but when did you know you liked girls?"

Lou considers this. "Sixth grade. You remember Louise Moreau?"

"She was that French girl, right?"

"Yeah. I remember thinking that she was really hot, and whenever she'd talk to me, I'd get all flustered, like there were butterflies in my stomach. That's when I started to wonder if I was—no, wonder isn't the right word. That's when I knew."

"Did you ever go online and look up stuff?"

"You mean like porn?"

"No, like quizzes and articles. Stuff like that."

"Not really. I might have taken a quiz once, but that's about it. Why do you ask?"

"I think Jamie is gay," I explain. "He was using my computer the other day, and when I checked my history, there were these articles and gay quizzes and Cristiano Ronaldo pictures."

To my surprise, Lou begins to laugh. "Seriously? You're just figuring that out?"

"What do you mean?"

"It's so obvious that he's gay. I mean, he paints his nails and is into fashion and—"

"Stop stereotyping my brother," I interrupt. "Lots of guys like fashion."

"Grace . . ." Lou sighs. "Okay, say you're right, and he's just curious. Have you asked him?"

I shake my head. "Do you think I should?"

"Definitely. Knowing that he has someone to talk to, someone who cares, will make everything a lot easier. Coming out is scary and confusing and—and lonely. At least it was for me."

"You could have talked to me, Lou."

"I guess I was worried that you wouldn't understand or it would make things awkward between us. You were my best friend, and I didn't want to lose you."

"I'm not going anywhere," I assure her. "You don't have to worry."

"Thanks," she responds with a shy smile. "I really think you should talk to Jamie. He looks up to you. It would mean a lot to him."

"All right," I agree. "I'll do it."

Lou clamps her hand on my shoulder. "You're a good sister —even if you can be a little dense sometimes."

"Shut up!"

"You really didn't know?"

"I suppose part of me did," I admit, "but I never saw him as a label. He was just . . . Jamie. My kind, funny, fashionista brother."

"I wish more people thought that way," she says.

"Like your mom?"

Lou retracts her hand and stares at the floor. When she speaks again, her voice is softer; sadder. "I never told you this, but when we were younger, I was so jealous of your mom. I know you think she's a total pain, and obviously there's that thing with your dad, but at the same time, she's super supportive of you. But my mom? My mom will go out of her way to remind me of how much of a disappointment I am to her. Do you know the first thing she said when I told her about Cassie?"

I shake my head. "What's that?"

"That I was confused, and that all I needed to do was pray more, and God would cure me."

Her words make me sick to my stomach. "And your dad? What did he say?"

"Nothing. He never says anything. Ma runs her mouth, telling me I'm sick, I'm going to hell—and that's not even the worst of it—and he sits there like a fucking mute. It's pathetic."

"Lame dads suck," I gripe, thinking about my own emotionally unavailable father.

"At least we don't talk about it anymore," she says. "They're not gonna change their minds. I gave up on that years ago."

"What about Cassie? Are you talking to her again?"

Lou's smile returns. "I am. She's a lot more open with me now. She doesn't jump down my throat when I ask her how she is at least."

I chuckle. "Well, I'm happy for you."

"And how are things with Isaac? Do you think you'll find your Happily Ever After?"

"We'll see. We're meeting up in the Center tomorrow, so I'm sure we'll talk then."

"What do you think will happen?"

"I'm not sure. If there's one thing I know though, it's that I'm going to do what's right for me. It's time I started taking control of my life."

"That's my girl!" Lou raises her lemonade, and I reciprocate with my lime seltzer. "To Grace!" she exclaims.

I'm laughing as I clink my glass cup against her mug. "I don't want to jinx anything, but for some reason, I have a feeling that things are going to be okay. Is that crazy?"

"It's not crazy," Lou assures me. "It's hopeful. And everybody needs a little hope in their life, don't you think?" She takes another swig of her drink and peers at me with her dark eyes, waiting for my response.

"You know what?" I say. "I think I do."

MY HEART IS RACING AS I ASCEND THE STAIRCASE TO THE theater. The discolored concrete is slick from the raindrops that have been steadily falling from the grey sky for the past hour. At the top, I see Isaac; he's casually leaning against the brick wall where we shared our first kiss with his hands in the pockets of his skinny jeans. Whereas I'm wearing a raincoat, his button-down shirt does little to protect him from the messy weather.

A part of me wants to turn around; another wants to get this over with. Before I can commit to either, he looks up. It strikes me then how handsome he is: his pale skin is like satin, and his clear blue eyes sparkle in the dim lighting. He's still too thin, but he's packed on a considerable amount of muscle since I met him six months ago. I suppose those protein shakes he was always drinking at CADE had worked their magic after all.

"Hey," I say.

"Hey."

I stand next to him and direct my gaze to the marque overlooking the theater. Six movie titles, ranging from an animated fairytale to a trashy R-rated romcom that has received an abundance of hate from critics, are listed in no particular order.

"I heard *Empty* is supposed to be good," I say.

"I dunno. Evan saw it and said it was overrated."

"Oh. Never mind then."

"Do you want to go inside?" he asks.

I glance into the lobby, where a crowd of moviegoers are standing around; some in line to buy tickets, others impatiently waiting for their theater to clear out. "I'd rather stay here if that's okay."

"It's fine."

Isaac smooths down his damp hair with his hand, while I stare at my shoes, both of us waiting for the other person to say something. Anything.

"I'm sorry," we blurt out at the same time.

"You first," I say.

"I, um . . ." Isaac clears his throat. "I'm sorry if I made you uncomfortable. It wasn't right for me to pressure you, but I did, and I feel like shit about it." He tilts his head towards me. "Your turn now."

"I'm sorry for holding a grudge. And for ignoring your texts. And for deleting you on Snapchat. That wasn't mature." I take a deep breath. "Isaac, what you did was wrong, and I'm still not sure how I feel about the whole situation, but you should know that I'm not angry or upset. I just need time, that's all."

Isaac's blonde brows furrow. "What are you saying?"

"You see, I have a problem of putting other people's needs before mine. I've been like that for my entire life. But for once, I want to put myself first. I want to understand what it is that *I* need to feel okay."

"Are you breaking up with me?" he asks quietly.

I stare into his eyes, and to my surprise, they aren't filled with resentment, but compassion and understanding. "I think so."

Time stands still for several seconds. Finally, Isaac steps towards me and cups my chin in his hands. Pressing my back against the wall, he plants a kiss on my lips as raindrops stream down his face. Our kiss lasts for about ten seconds, and when we pull apart, I'm smiling despite the tears in my eyes. He touches his thumb to my lower lip, then wraps his arms around me.

"You'll be okay," he whispers in my ear.

I hold onto him a little tighter, embracing the familiar scents of his Axe body spray and cherry Chapstick for one last time. "So will you."

20

1 0. *Factor the expression:* $25y^2-9$

   a. $(5y-3)^2$

b. $(25y+1)(y-9)$

c. $(5y+3)^2$

d. $(5y+3)(5y-3)$

I stare down at the problem, desperately racking my brain for the formula Mr. Lipschitz taught us when he introduced factoring in April. But no matter how hard I try to remember, I keep drawing blanks. With a sigh, I hesitantly circle *c.* $(5y+3)^2$ and move on to the next question:

   11. *Solve the equation for x:* $log2(8x-x2)=4$

a. $x=-8$

b. $x=0$

c. $x=4$

d. $x=8$

Another sigh escapes my lips. "Hey, Mom?"

Mom looks up from the counter, where she's dicing vegetables for an orzo salad. "Yes?"

"How much algebra do you actually use in your adult life? Because if you ask me, it seems so impractical."

"Studying isn't going well?"

"I didn't say that. I just don't understand what the point of it is. Like, when am I ever going to have to know logarithmics? Seriously?"

Mom laughs. "I don't know. You might never. But classes like algebra that seem like a waste of time are scientifically proven to teach you valuable life skills."

"Like what?"

"Patience, problem-solving, time management, teamwork—your favorite."

"Yeah, right."

"I know it's hard—trust me, I've been there—but it's not for nothing. Plus, once you pass your final, you can put it all behind you."

"*If* I pass my final."

"Quit doubting yourself," she scolds. "Why don't you put away your review packet so we can have lunch?"

I eagerly reach for my homework folder. "Gladly."

"You can study more afterwards," she continues.

"And, you ruined it."

"You're so close, Grace. What kind of mother would I be if I let you slack off now?" She waits for me to respond, and when I don't, she changes the subject. "Can you set the table? I'll cut some cantaloupe."

"Okay." I place two mats, two napkins, two forks, and the

salt and pepper shakers on the table, then pour myself a glass of water while she heats up her second cup of coffee.

When she's finished slicing the melon, she places the bowl between the shakers and hands me the orzo salad. "Where are our plates?"

"I forgot."

"It's okay. You sit—I'll get them."

Once she's retrieved our plates, she takes a seat across from me and serves herself two heaping spoonfuls of salad. She watches as I attempt to replicate her hearty portion, biting her lip to refrain from interjecting. When I put back an olive, however, she clears her throat.

"Grace . . ."

"I don't like pimientos," I say. "You know that."

"Fair enough. I'll use kalamata next time." She stabs a mozzarella pearl with her fork and pops it in her mouth. "So, how are your other finals going?"

"Fine."

"What are you doing for Euro?"

I roll my eyes. "This girl and I are doing a project on the Cold War. We've been working on it in school, but I might have to go over to her house next week so we can use her dad's projector."

"That doesn't sound too bad."

"The bad part is that Mr. Duffy paired me with Jess. She's, like, the most stuck-up person I've ever met."

"You're going to have to work with a lot of people like Jess in your life," Mom begins to say, but I interrupt her.

"I know, I know. Teamwork."

Before she can respond, her phone buzzes. She flips it over

and glances at the number. "I have to take this. It's your brother's school."

"All right."

Mom holds the phone to her ear. "This is Kira." She pauses. "Okay." Another pause, this one longer than the first. "Oh, really?" In a matter of seconds, her entire demeanor shifts from curious to distressed. "Yes, I'm leaving right now. Thank you, Jeannette." She ends the call and drags her fingers through her hair. "Damn him!"

"What's going on?" I ask.

"Jamie is in the office," she responds flatly. "Apparently a student reported him using the girls' bathroom."

"Holy crap."

"Uh-huh." She sighs. "He has two weeks left of school. You think he could stay out of trouble for that long, you know?"

"Mom, there's something I need—"

"I have to go," Mom interrupts. She quickly scans my plate. "Good, you're almost done. Finish up, and then I'll head over."

I scarf down my last forkful of orzo salad. "When will you be back?"

"Not sure. Hopefully, this won't take too long."

Grabbing her keys off the counter, she stuffs her phone in the pocket of her khakis and hurries outside. Through the window, I watch her get in the car and whip out of the driveway, narrowly avoiding colliding with our recycle bin.

I place my plate in the sink, heft my ten-pound bookbag upstairs, and disappear into my room. There, I sit at my desk and take out my algebra review packet to have another go at it. Forty minutes and fifteen mind-boggling equations later, I hear the door open and Mom's authoritative voice say, "Jamie, it's not appropriate. You know that."

"I don't like the boys' bathroom," Jamie insists. "It's dirty, and—and it smells like marijuana. The girls' room isn't like that."

I hold my breath, wondering if Mom suspects that he's bull-shitting her. Even in middle school, I lost count of the number of times I caught a girl getting high in the bathroom.

"Jamie, where are you going?"

Her question is met by the sound of Jamie storming upstairs. Then the slam of his door. Then . . . nothing. I close my packet and place it next to my computer. He doesn't respond the first time I knock, so I try again.

"What?" Jamie's tone softens when he sees that it's me, not Mom. "Sorry. I thought—"

"It's fine. Sit with me?"

"Okay."

Jamie and I recline onto his lavender comforter. He clutches his hands to his chest, his white knuckles a stark contrast against his maroon t-shirt.

"What's going on?" I ask.

Jamie refuses to look me in the eyes. "I don't want to talk about it."

"I don't want to talk about stuff either, but I know if I keep it inside me, it'll only make things worse," I say. "I'm here for you, okay? I want to help."

With his gaze still trained on the floor, he sighs. "I—I don't know. It's all so . . . confusing."

I hear Lou's words in my head: *Talk to him. He looks up to you. It would mean a lot to him.*

"Jamie, um, remember when you used my computer the other day?"

"Yeah?"

"I, um . . ." I hesitate. "I saw my history. I know what you were looking at."

"Oh," he whispers. "Grace, I didn't—"

"It's no big deal if you're gay," I interrupt. "You don't have to be embarrassed. I mean, it's the twenty-first century. Things are changing."

"I'm not gay, Grace."

"You're not? But—"

"I thought I might be, but after taking those tests and reading those articles, I don't think I am."

"Then why are you confused?"

"I guess because I feel fake, like I'm trying to be someone I'm not. I look in the mirror, and I see these things about me, about my body, that I just don't like." Another shaky sigh escapes his lips. "I don't feel like a boy, but I don't feel like a girl either. It's like I'm stuck in between, if that makes sense."

I take a moment to process what he's said. "There's this kid in my English class—Remi, that's their name. They identify as gender neutral, meaning they also don't feel like a boy or a girl. They use different pronouns, and some days, they wear dresses or skirts, and other days, they wear guy's jeans and flannel shirts."

"They?"

"Yeah. A lot of gender-neutral people use the pronouns they/them. Remi's super chill about it; like this one time, we were working on a project together, and I referred to them as 'she,' and they politely corrected me. I know it's grammatically incorrect, but once you get the hang of it, it's not that hard to understand."

"Does she—sorry, *they*—ever get picked on?"

"Sometimes, yes, but the important thing is that Remi is true to themselves." When he doesn't respond, I say, "I'm not telling you that you should identify as gender neutral, but if you do, that's perfectly fine. It doesn't make you less of a person, and anyone who tries to tell you otherwise is an asshole."

"And Mom?"

"Mom's not mad at you—I promise."

"How do you know?"

"She told me. She's just worried. She wants you to be okay."

"Oh."

"And you will," I continue. "I know it might not seem like it now, but you're going to be okay."

"Like you are?"

I can't tell if he's being sarcastic or genuine, so I say, "I'm getting there. Do you want to know how?"

He nods.

I adjust my position on his bed so we're facing each other and reach for his hands. His turquoise nail polish is chipped, but his cuticles are in much better condition than they were when we visited Manhattan. "We're going to play a game. It's called *Jamie and Grace: Minute by Minute*. Basically, the only thing we have to think about is the next minute—that's it."

"Did you just come up with this?" he asks.

I shake my head. "Lou taught me how to play when I was in a very dark place. Now whenever I get stressed out about the future, I remember the game, and it makes everything seem a lot more manageable."

"And you think it could help me too?"

"One-hundred-percent," I respond firmly. "So, are you in?"

Jamie finally raises his head. His eyes, once so sad and scared, now twinkle with small flickers of hope. He smiles. "All right. I'm in."

"Did you get the link I sent you?"

"To your brother's video?"

Jess nods. "Did you get it?"

"I did."

"And? What'd you think?"

"It was, uh . . ." I hesitate, contemplating how honest I should be with her. "It sucked."

"Yeah, well, my brother's a moron. He had some good facts though—he aced that part of the rubric."

"You said we weren't going to copy him."

"We aren't. We're going to use what worked and change everything that didn't. I began making a PowerPoint in English. I'll share it with you."

"Okay. Is there anything I can do?"

"Start working on the diagram. You can draft it on Docs and copy it onto a Tri-Board later. Do you have those at home?"

"I don't think so."

"Then I'll ask my dad for one." She tries to turn on her computer, but the screen remains blank. "What the fuck?" she mutters, pressing the keys in frustration. "Dammit, I must have forgotten to charge this thing. It's such a piece of shit."

"You can use mine," I offer. "I'll draft on my phone."

"Cool." She snatches my computer off my desk without thanking me—not that I would expect any shred of decency from her. "What's your password?"

"Illmatic02. Capital I."

Jess shoots me a deprecating look. "That's a stupid password."

I don't respond. I know that nothing I say will help her understand how exceptionally rude and obnoxious she is.

"Something is wrong with your Wi-Fi," she asserts. "Oh, never mind. It was on Airplane Mode. Have you started the diagram?"

"Not yet."

"Well, get to it." She closes my computer and stands on her high heeled sandals, teetering ever-so-slightly. "Otherwise you'll have to do it over the weekend."

"Are you going somewhere?" I ask.

"I need to use the bathroom."

She pushes in her chair and walks out of the room, while I open Google Docs to begin drafting the diagram. I paraphrase the information I'd gathered from my research and play around with the formatting to create a theme that's relevant to the time period. I'm adding the final touches to my outline by the time Jess returns nearly ten minutes later.

When I show her what I've created, she nods in approval. "I'll bring the board on Monday. If we have time, we can go to the library and print out pictures."

"Did you share the slides with me?"

"Shit, I forgot. I'll do it this weekend. I already shut down your computer."

"All right."

With one minute until the bell rings, Jess begins to pack up her belongings. "Tif?" she calls to her friend, who's doodling in a cat-patterned notebook at the table to our left. "Do you need a ride to the party?"

Tiffany closes her notebook, inadvertently reminding me that I still haven't returned Jess', and shakes her head. "Tommy is driving me. We're going a little later, like around nine."

"Okay. I just thought I'd ask."

"I heard that Matt's older brother invited his friends," Tiffany says. "They're the ones bringing the beer."

"Thank God!" Jess exhales deeply. "I so need this after this fucking exhausting week."

Tiffany laughs. "Literally same."

As they're talking, I glance at Jess. She isn't lying about being exhausted; I can tell by the bags under her wide blue eyes and the dullness in her voice. She's certainly not the only one— lately it seems like all my classmates are checked-out, myself included.

Two more weeks, I remind myself. *Just two more weeks, and then I'm free.*

After the strenuous year I've had, surviving two weeks should be a breeze.

21

On Saturday morning, despite planning to stay in bed for as long as possible, I wake up bright and early at seven thirty. I try to fall back asleep, but after several unsuccessful minutes, I surrender. I toss aside my covers, throw on blue sweat shorts and a white *California Republic* t-shirt, and head downstairs. I hear Mom showering in the basement, so I plop down on the couch in the TV room and turn on Netflix. I'm a third of the way through a *How to Get Away with Murder* episode when she enters the room.

"You're up early," she remarks.

"I know. I kept having these dreams where I was in the hospital again." I shudder. "Oh well. I have a ton of studying to do, so it's probably a good thing that I'm up."

"I can't believe your finals are in two weeks. This year is flying by."

"Less than two weeks," I correct. "English is a week from Wednesday, but I'm not too worried about that one."

"Why is that?"

"It's an easy class. You heard Mrs. P. at my PPT; my grade is great, and I'm a pleasure."

"If she only knew," Mom jokes. "Do you want to have breakfast now or after your show?"

"Now. I'll finish it later."

"Okay. Are you in the mood for eggs?"

"Eggs are fine. Did you get more soy bacon?"

"Yes, but it's a different brand. I hope that's all right."

"It's fine."

I turn off the television and join her in the kitchen, where she's heating up a pan on the stove. Two eggs are on the counter, as well as four slices of the new bacon. Unlike our usual brand, which is crispy, light-red, and rectangular, this maroon-colored meat alternative is much smoother and is shaped like its Canadian counterpart.

I'm suddenly reminded of a story Dad told me about the time that he and a couple of his college friends visited Vancouver over spring break. On morning, they went to a diner, and Dylan, Dad's dimwitted roommate, ordered Canadian bacon, to which the waiter replied, "We're in Canada! It's just 'bacon!'"

Dad and I laughed and laughed about the story until our stomachs hurt. In retrospect, the story itself wasn't the funny part; it was how he told it. Dad could make anything, no matter how boring or insignificant, seem interesting. If he hadn't gone into medicine, he said, he would have been a professional storyteller.

"Hey, Mom?" I ask.

Mom cracks an egg on the side of the pan and discards the shell in the compost. "Yes?"

"When did you stop eating meat?"

"My second year of college."

"When you met Dad?"

"No, it was a couple months before that. I got sick from an undercooked burger, and afterwards, I just didn't see the point. It wasn't like I craved meat. I never ate that much to begin with."

"Not even when you were younger?"

She shakes her head. "My mom was very busy, so she'd usually make pasta or something easy like that. Whenever she did buy meat, she didn't know how to cook it properly. She'd use too little seasoning or the wrong pan—one time, she forgot to take a steak out of the oven. The whole house smelled like fire for weeks!"

"And your father?" I ask.

"My father worked late at Bellucci's, so he ate there."

"Bellucci's?"

"An Italian restaurant. It went out of business the year I left home. Spatula?"

I find the spatula in the utensils drawer and hand it to her so she can flip the eggs. "How come I've never met your parents?"

"You have met them. When you were two, they visited your father and me in California. They wanted to see you."

I recall discovering a photo a few years ago on Mom's computer when I was compiling pictures for a customized birthday calendar. It was captured on Ventura Beach, and in it, an older woman was cradling me in her arms while an older man stood next to her. At the time, I had no idea who they were. Now, however, it's all starting to make sense.

"And that was it?" I ask. "That was the only time?"

She nods. "I thought maybe we'd reconnect when we came to the East Coast, but then I found out that they'd moved to Florida. They hadn't even bothered to tell me."

"Why though? What happened to make you hate each other so much?"

"We don't hate each other. We just don't get along. Sometimes that happens in a family." She changes the subject before I can respond. "How do the eggs look? Are they cooked enough?"

I peer into the pan. "Uh-huh. Where's the bacon?"

"Damn, I forgot to cook it with the eggs. If you're eager to eat, we can microwave it. It'll only take a minute."

"It's a good thing you can't undercook soy, huh?" I say.

Mom smiles. "Thank God for that."

I SPEND THE REST OF THE DAY ALTERNATING BETWEEN studying for my finals and watching television. I go on a one-mile walk after lunch as well. By nine o'clock, I'm exhausted, so I bookmark my page in *The Handmaid's Tale* and head to the bathroom to brush my teeth. When I return to my room, two missed calls from Lou light up the lockscreen of my phone. I immediately call her back.

"Hello? Grace?"

I hear laughter in the background; she must be at Matt's party. "Hey. What's up?"

"I, um, I need to crash at your place," she slurs.

"For God's sake, Lou. Are you drunk?"

"No. I only had, uh . . ." She giggles. "Shit, I can't remember. But—but you can't tell because Ma thinks I'm studying with you."

"She what? You could have given me a heads up."

"Didn't I?"

"No!"

"Huh. I thought I did."

"Forget it. You can crash here."

"Girl, you are my saving grace." She bursts out laughing. "Get it? It's funny, 'cause your name is Grace."

"Yeah, I got it. Look, is there someone who can give you a ride?"

"I can dr—drive."

"No, Lou, don't drive. I'll come get you . . . somehow." I sigh. "Just stay where you are, okay?"

"Okie-doke."

I end the call with another sigh. Slipping my phone in the pocket of my shorts, I return to the kitchen, where Mom is cleaning the kitchen counter. Her hair is piled in a messy bun, and her ruby nail polish has started to chip. Even her outfit—a grey sweatshirt and loose-fitting jeans—alludes to her fatigue.

Nevertheless, I ask, "Mom?"

She turns around. "Yes, hon?"

"I, um . . ." I take a deep breath. "I need your help."

MATT'S UNCLE'S MANSION REMARKABLY SATISFIES THE countless rumors I've heard about it. Three stories tall with a massive lawn, an outdoor swimming pool, and a four-car garage, the entire estate is at least triple, maybe even quadruple, the size of mine. Inside, I hear Nelly's *Hot in Herre*, while out on the lawn, teens with red Solo cups talk in small groups or dance to the music. Tommy Kershaw has scaled the six-foot stone wall encircling the property and is pounding his chest like Tarzan.

"Arrived," Siri's robotic voice announces.

Mom stops her car between two life-sized lion sculptures and turns off her phone. "This brings back memories," she says. "When I was your age, one of my girlfriends invited me to a party like this. It got so out of hand that her neighbor called the police. I had to hide under the porch for two hours so I wouldn't get caught. I didn't even have my shoes with me—how crazy is that?"

I'm about to ask where her shoes were when my phone buzzes. "That's Lou. She says she's on her way."

"How bad is she?"

"I'm not sure. She was slurring a lot over the phone, but mostly she's afraid that her mom will find out. Mrs. Jackson would murder Lou if she knew about this."

Mom doesn't respond.

"You won't tell, right?"

"I—"

Before she can finish, Lou raps on my window. Mom unlocks the door for her, and she steps—stumbles—in, whacking her purse against my knee in the process. I feel her phone collide with my patella and wince. Although I've managed without my brace for months, my knee still isn't entirely healed.

"H—hi, Ms. Sinclair," Lou slurs. In a loud whisper, she asks, "You came with your mom? Are you crazy?"

"You know I don't have my license," I respond. "How else was I supposed to get you?"

Mom, who's observing our exchange in the rearview mirror, clears her throat. "Grace, can you help Lou with her seatbelt?"

"Sure." I reach across my friend to buckle her in, wrinkling my nose at the repulsive smells of alcohol and vomit on her fuchsia minidress. "We're good."

Lou is strangely quiet as we drive home. I keep my distance from her, worried that she'll throw up, but she holds it in until she gets out of the car. That's when she hurls in our neighbor's newly planted rose bush.

"Grace, go find her something to wear," Mom says. She wraps her arm around Lou and guides her into the house. "I think I have some old shirts in my closet."

Leaving Lou in Mom's care, I dash upstairs. Jamie is standing in his doorway, his expression conveying both confusion and concern. Behind him, I notice Kevin sitting on his bed. Eight cards are fanned out in his hand, while the rest are strewn across the crumpled sheets.

"What's going on?"

"Lou's having a rough night."

He follows me into Mom's room. "Is she okay?"

"She'll be fine," I say. "She just needs to cool off."

In Mom's closet, I find an oversized Guns 'N Roses t-shirt and plaid pajama shorts. I tuck them under my arm and hurry back downstairs. Mom has moved Lou to the bathroom and is patting her face with a damp towel as she sits on the closed toilet seat. Her minidress and sheer tights are in a clump on the floor.

"Here are the clothes."

"Thanks. Lou, honey, put these on. I'll set up an air mattress in Grace's room."

"Okay," Lou whispers.

"Do you need help?" I ask Lou once Mom is gone.

"I—I think I can do it." She tries to stand up, only to collapse back onto the toilet seconds later. "Fuck!"

"It's all right. I don't mind."

As I'm pulling the shirt over her head, Lou clears her throat. "Thank you—for everything. You didn't have to."

"Yes, I did," I say. "Consider it payback for all the times you've helped me."

Lou smiles shyly. "I'll do that."

"But, um, can I ask you something?"

She nods, prompting me to proceed.

"I know you've had beer before, but I've never seen you like this. Why is this time different?"

"I got in another fight with Ma," she admits. "I said something that was really shitty, and then I got in my car and drove to the party. I guess I was still upset about it, and that's why I drank so much."

"What did you say?"

"I said . . ." Lou closes her eyes. When she reopens them, a tear slips down her mascara-stained cheek. "I said I wished she'd hurry up and die."

"Oh."

"I know; I'm a horrible person."

"You're not a horrible person."

"Yes, I am," she tearfully insists.

"We all say things we shouldn't," I respond. "I've lost count of how many times I told Mom I hated her and that I wished she wasn't my mother. I said those things, and I can't take them back —no matter how shitty I feel. So, I had to move on. There's no point in beating yourself up about the past. What's done is done."

Lou, who has been attentively nodding along, suddenly lurches forward and throws up all over my shirt. More tears pool in her eyes as she wipes vomit off her mouth. "I'm so sorry."

I breathe through my mouth to avoid catching a whiff of the rancid stench. As I'm patting her back, I'm reminded of something that she told me not too long ago: payback surely is a bitch.

———————

I wake up at nine forty-five to Lou's noisy snoring. She's passed out on an air mattress on my floor with her face buried in a pillow. I get out of bed and carefully step over her so I don't disturb her—not that the odds of that are likely. After the chaos of last night, I wouldn't be surprised if she slept all day.

Downstairs, Mom is reading the newspaper at the kitchen table. She glances up when she hears me walk into the room. "Good morning."

"Morning," I echo. "Did you eat yet?"

She nods. "Can I fix you anything?"

"No, I'll have cereal." I grab a box of Special K Red Berries, shake some into a bowl, and add milk, accidently sloshing several drops onto the counter. "Dammit."

"How's Lou?" Mom asks as I retrieve a paper towel from the roll from under the sink.

"Not sure. She's still asleep."

"Well, if she's not up by noon, I'll wake her. She'll need to let her mom know how long she's planning to stay here. I can't imagine she'll want to go home hungover."

"Will you tell?"

Mom hesitates. "I know I should but . . ."

"But what?"

"But I've been in her shoes. I know how hard it is to feel like you're a disappointment to your parents. Everyone makes mistakes, but if there's one thing I know about the Jacksons, it's that they won't get over this—at least not for a while. That's not fair to Lou."

"Thank you," I say. "You have no idea how much that means to me."

"That said, if this happens again, I'll have no choice but to tell them."

"I understand. I'll keep an eye on her—I promise."

Mom smiles. "You're a good friend, you know that?"

"I try," I say. "The thing is, I don't know where I'd be without her. I was in a bad place when we moved here, Mom. I was upset about what happened with Dad, and I was nervous about going to a school where I didn't know anyone. I thought I wasn't going to make friends, but then I met Lou. We were so different—we still are—but at the same time, I could be myself around her; like, I could say almost anything to her and not worry that she'd hold it against me. I'd never felt that with another person before."

"When I was in the hospital, and she wouldn't answer my calls, I was terrified it was over; that I'd messed up things irreversibly. That week was one of the longest and hardest weeks of my life. For the first time since the move, I was alone, and the worst part was, it was all my fault."

Mom is quiet for a couple seconds. "You were never alone," she says finally. "You had me."

"I know. I'm sorry I didn't realize it then."

"You had me too!" Jamie calls from the TV room.

"Christ, Jamie!" I exclaim. "How long have you been in there?"

Jamie walks into the kitchen with an empty plate in his hands. Miscellaneous seeds—remnants of an everything bagel—are scattered across the white ceramic. "Like fifteen minutes. I was texting Sara."

"Sara?" Mom asks, but both Jamie and I ignore her.

"Then I guess you heard everything, huh?"

Jamie nods. "I'm glad you're in a better place. You know, when you weren't home, I felt alone too."

"And now?"

Jamie glances towards Mom, then back at me. "It's different now. And when I do feel alone, I know what to do."

I wrap my arm around his shoulders, feeling the soft fabric of his pink sleeping shirt rub against my skin. "What's that?"

He grins. "I play the game."

22

"It's after ten, and you're still in bed? You can't be *that* hungover anymore."

On the other end of the phone, Lou laughs. "Says the girl who's never had a drink in her life."

"Well, while you were sleeping, I had a quiz *and* a reading check."

"How did that go?"

"Eighty-five." I leave Guidance, holding the door for a girl in a Chuckles' cheerleader uniform, and walk through the Music Wing. Inside the band room, the Freshmen Band is playing an offbeat tune that vaguely resembles *Seven Nation Army*. "I'd say that's pretty good—considering I didn't have time to read all the chapters."

"Why? Because of me?"

"Something like that, yeah."

Lou laughs again. "Bitch."

"Are you coming tomorrow?" I ask.

"I don't know. Maybe on Wednesday. I should really get hungover more often. Ma can't bother me if she thinks I'm sick."

"Are you going to talk to her about . . . you know?"

"Grace, you gotta be more specific."

"Your fight. That thing you said."

"We'll see. For now, I'm just gonna rest. I was in the middle of an episode of *Elite* when you called."

"Then I'll let you get back to it. See ya."

"Later."

Shaking my head in amusement, I pocket my phone and continue to the library. Like the Music Wing, the central hallway is quiet, as it typically is between periods. The library, on the other hand, is a different story. Despite the *No Talking* and *This is a Quiet Zone* signs plastered across the grey walls, the spacious area is buzzing with chatter. Mr. Chadwick sits at the front desk with a defeated look in his coffee-colored eyes.

"Hi, Mr. C.," I say, punching my six-digit ID into the check-in computer.

"Hi, Grace. Sorry about the noise."

"It's okay. I brought my earbuds."

Once the computer has processed my ID, I navigate to the back of the library, where there are fewer students. I sit at a circular table across from a girl whose nose is buried in a book, insert my buds, and drown out the sounds of talking and laughter with my favorite alternative songs until the period is over.

When I walk into history, the first thing I notice is Mr. Duffy's hair—or lack thereof. Gone are his gelled black curls; now, his head is as smooth and shiny as a polished bowling ball.

Lou will love to hear about this, I think.

I take a seat at my desk and watch my classmates saunter in; some in groups, others alone. To my surprise, Tiffany is one of the loners. Her appearance as well—disheveled hair, baggy clothing, smudged makeup—is a stark contrast to how put-together she usually is.

When the bell rings, Mr. Duffy stands at the Smartboard, impatiently waiting for the talking to cease. "All right, get with your partner," he instructs once the room is quiet. "You only have seven more days to finish your projects, so I'd better see you staying on task."

In front of me, Tiffany's face is flat against her desk. "Hey, Tiffany?"

"Yeah?"

"Where's Jess?"

Without looking up, she shrugs. "Don't know."

"Thanks for nothing," I mumble sarcastically. I walk to the front of the room, where Mr. Duffy has returned to his desk to grade essays. I watch as he draws a large D above a student's name with a red pen. "Mr. Duffy?"

"Yes, Grace?"

"Do you know where Jess is?"

"I'm not sure. I believe attendance marked her absent."

"Well, can I have a pass to the library? We were going to print pictures for our project."

He jots the date and time onto a green slip of paper, scribbles his messy signature at the bottom, and hands it to me. "Be back by the end of class, all right?"

I nod. "I will."

While he continues grading essays, I grab my bookbag and head to the library. I spend the rest of the period in the computer lab printing out pictures of the Cold War: two grue-some battle shots, two landmarks, three political leaders, and one satirical cartoon. After I've compiled eight, I take a photo and Facebook message Jess.

Grace: Here's what I found. Let me know what you think.

I hang out in the lab for a few more minutes, waiting for her to respond, and when she doesn't, I slip the pictures in my homework folder and return to class. Everyone is standing at the door, all packed up to leave.

"It's eleven forty-five, Mr. Duffy," Julian says. "Can we go?"

"Yeah, the bells are slow today," Heather pipes in.

Mr. Duffy runs his hand over his head, momentarily forget-ting that his hair is gone. This elicits snickers from several kids. "All right. I'll see you tomorrow."

As I'm following my classmates out the door, my phone vibrates with a text from Mom.

Mom: got hung up at work. be there soon.

Grace: ok.

I wait for the message to send before repocketing my phone and continuing to the front office. I'm passing through the A-Wing when I notice Bianca talking to a girl in front of a gender-neutral bathroom. She's also wearing her cheerleading uniform under a pink zip-up hoodie. Figuring Mom will be at least another five minutes, I approach her.

"Bianca?"

"I'll catch you later," Bianca tells the girl. Turning to me, she says, "Hey. What's up?"

"Do you know where Jess is? We were supposed to work on our history final, but she wasn't in class, and she's not responding to my texts."

Bianca bites her lip. "Um . . . I'm not supposed to talk about it. Sorry."

"Please, Bianca," I beg. "I'm kind of relying on her. If I get below a seventy-two on this project, I'll have to retake the class over the summer, so if you could just tell me where she is—"

Bianca sighs. She grabs my hand and pulls me into the bathroom, locking the door behind her. "You can't tell anyone, okay?"

"I won't. I swear."

Bianca stares into my eyes for a couple uncomfortable seconds. "I'm trusting you on this," she says finally. "You'd better not screw me over."

"You have my word," I reiterate.

"You know that party at Matt's?"

"Yeah. What about it?"

"Jess has been under a lot of stress lately. She had too much to drink, and then she got in her car to drive home. I offered to take her since I'd only had one beer, but she said she was fine; that I shouldn't worry." Bianca shakes her head. "I wish I'd stopped her. I don't know why I didn't."

"Did she . . ."

With her gaze trained on her white sneakers, Bianca nods. "She was half a mile from her house when she swerved off the road and hit a tree. She's been in the hospital ever since."

"Oh my god. Is she okay?"

"I'm not sure. I'm not allowed to visit her. Her parents haven't told the school or Matt's family or anyone, I don't think. I'm not supposed to know either, but her brother filled me in. I called him when I couldn't get a hold of Jess."

"How bad was it?"

"I'm not sure of that either. I mean, she's in the hospital, so I assume . . ." Bianca takes a deep breath, then shakily exhales. "Fuck me. If I hadn't been so stupid . . ."

I tentatively place my hand on her shoulder. "It's not your fault, B. You know that, right?"

Bianca is about to respond when the bell rings. "I have to get to calc. I'll see you around."

She pulls her hood over her black hair and disappears into the hallway. Once she's gone, I open Instagram and click on Jess' profile. I hadn't paid attention to her post from the party— or anyone's for that matter—as I was too preoccupied with helping Lou. Looking at it now, however, at how happy she seemed with her arm slung around Tiffany's shoulders and a broad grin on her gaunt face, I feel a trace of sympathy for the same girl who five minutes ago, I could care less about.

Even though I've never been in a car accident, I know how sad and scary hospitals are. I wish there was something that I could do, but since I'm not sure what, I simply like her post, leave the bathroom, and head outside to wait for Mom.

A few minutes later, she pulls up next to me. Her window is partially rolled down, and her eyes are hidden behind a pair of oversized sunglasses. "How was school?" she asks when I join her in the car.

Ignoring her question, I lean across the console and awkwardly wrap my arms around her. Our embrace lasts for several seconds, and when we pull apart, Mom is smiling.

"What was that?"

"Something I should have done a long time ago," I say. "Can we go home?"

Mom glances behind us at the only other vehicle in the lane:

a white van with *CT Landscaping LLC* written on the side. Two buff men are hauling a ladder out of the back. "Do you want me to show you how?"

"To drive?" When she nods, I say, "I'm not really in the mood, but if it's not too late, you can sign me up for that class over the summer."

"All right," she agrees. "I'll call AAA after lunch."

As she navigates out of the parking lot, rambling on about her busy morning, a beam of sunlight travels across my arms. I glance at my fair skin, and I'm surprised to discover how faint my scars are. For the first time since I began hurting myself, I have to squint to see them.

One month ago, Isaac told me that he couldn't understand why someone would purposely harm themselves. What he didn't realize was that mental illness, as a whole, is confusing to anyone who hasn't experienced it firsthand. Take anorexia for example. The concept of deliberately depriving yourself of food, the building block of our survival, seems irrational, illogical, and, as I've heard time and time again, crazy.

But anorexia is much more than an unhealthy obsession with losing weight, just like self-harm is more than a cry for attention. Before I was sick, I, too, believed those misconceptions. Now that the tables have turned, I'm no longer that naïve girl. I used to wish that this was a nightmare, and that I'd wake up one morning having never been afflicted with mental illness. But I'm not so sure I do anymore.

Isaac also told me that I'm stronger because of what I went through. Kevin said the same thing about his sister. And although I still have my doubts, I'm starting to realize that perhaps they were right all along.

"I hardboiled eggs yesterday." Mom's voice snaps me back to reality. "I know egg salad is one of your challenge foods, so if you're up for it, I could make some for lun—hey, are you okay?"

When I look away from my scars, she's watching me skeptically. "I'm good, Mom. You don't have to worry."

"Worry? Me?" She laughs. "So, what do you think about the egg salad?"

In the past, the chances of me willingly trying any food outside of my comfort zone were next to nothing. But now, I merely shrug. "All right. Egg salad it is."

———

"To want?"

"Easy. *Querer*."

"To accept?"

"*Aceptar*."

"To worry?"

"Wait, I know this one. It's, uh . . . *preocupar*, right?"

Mom looks up from my Spanish review sheet and nods. "You've been studying."

"Why do you sound surprised?" I ask.

"I'm not. I'm proud of you—that's all. A few months ago, I wasn't sure you'd get through this school year, and now you're going to pass with flying colors."

"That's pushing it," I joke. While my grades have certainly improved, as far as I'm concerned, I can still perform much better. "I know what you mean though. I used to think I wouldn't make it either."

Mom smiles sadly. "I can only imagine how hard that must have been."

"I'm just glad it's behind me. And in a couple days, this stupid final will be too. I hope it's as easy as English was."

"Well, you've always done well in English. Speaking of which, how do you feel about taking a writing course this summer? Our community college is offering a program for high school seniors in August. It could be fun."

"But I'm not that good at writing. I always make stupid grammar errors."

"*Grammatical* errors," she corrects.

"See! That's exactly what I mean."

"At least think about it. The deadline isn't for another few weeks."

"Okay," I agree. "No guarantees though."

"Of course not." Mom glances at her watch. "I should get going. We can review the rest of the words later. There are only . . ." she does a quick count, "twelve left."

"Where are you going?"

"I'm picking up Jamie from school. Believe it or not, he agreed to go to the barbershop—under one condition."

"What's that?"

"We get our nails done afterwards."

I laugh. "Why am I not surprised?"

"Do you want to come with us?"

"Thanks, but I'll pass. What time will you be home?"

"Around four. Are you okay having snack on your own?"

After a brief hesitation, I nod. "I am."

She kisses my cheek. "Text me if you need anything. I love you."

"Love you too," I call as she walks out the door.

Once she's gone, I put away my Spanish sheet and move on to a seven-page chemistry packet. I'm skimming through my bulleted notes on atomic structure when my phone lights up with a text from an unrecognizable number. The sender writes: *hey. whats up?*

Two seconds later, an ellipsis appears under the message. I stare at my phone, curiously waiting for another text, and when it comes, my heart skips a beat: *this is Liam btw.*

I'm contemplating whether or not I should reply when the doorbell rings. Figuring Mom forget her keys, I roll my eyes and open the door to let her in. But to my surprise, it's not Mom standing on the porch; it's Lou. She's dressed in a floral romper and mismatched Birkenstocks—one black and one coral.

"What are you doing here?" I ask.

"I was listening to the news while I drove to the Center. They were talking about—well, you'll see."

Leaving my phone on the table, I follow her into the TV room. There, she flips on the television and scrolls to our local news station. "Lou, I don't under—"

"A student from Chuck L. Everett High School was involved in an automobile accident on Saturday night," a reporter wearing a violet dress informs us. "The seventeen-year-old female was driving home when she swerved off the road into a tree."

"Holy shit," Lou says. "Who do you think it is?"

I remember my conversation with Bianca. "No idea."

"The student is currently in the hospital," the reporter continues. "At this time, her condition is unknown."

Lou's eyes are glued to the television. "That could have

been me," she whispers. "If you hadn't come get me, I'd . . ." A tear trickles down her cheek.

I also feel myself well up at the thought of Lou's motionless body slumped behind the wheel of her car. "But it's not," I remind her. "I swear, Lou; I would never let anything like that happen to you. Friends protect each other."

"I didn't protect you when you weren't eating," she says. "I knew something was wrong, but I didn't do shit about it. And look at what happened to you."

"That wasn't your fault. I was sick, and I wouldn't let anyone in—not you, not my mom, not even the doctors. I was afraid of what would happen if you found out that I was . . ."

"Hurting yourself?"

I nod. "So I pushed you away. I pushed everyone away. That's on me. But I've decided I'm going to start trusting again. Nobody knows what's going to happen. I mean, look at the news." I gesture to the television, where another reporter—a tall man in a navy suit—is introducing a story of a bomb threat at a middle school in Massachusetts. "The world could end tomorrow, and all this fear and hatred would be for nothing. I used to be so afraid. I would pretend to be someone I wasn't because I didn't want to be judged."

"I remember," Lou says.

"That's my point. Now, on the other hand, maybe I'll get hurt or people will take advantage of me, but at least," I reach for her hand and hold on tightly, "I'll be okay."

If you or anyone you know is suffering from mental illness, please call 1-800-950-6264 or visit nami.org for more information.

ACKNOWLEDGMENTS

I learned many valuable lessons throughout the process of writing and publishing *Changing Ways*. I learned how to be patient and flexible, two previous weaknesses of mine. I learned how to accept imperfection. I learned that I'm more capable than I give myself credit for. But the most important lesson I took away was the significance of teamwork. *Changing Ways* wouldn't be the same had I not had support from so many incredible people, and neither would *Breaking Free*. So, I want to thank everyone who helped make my dream come true.

Thank you to my two mothers, Mom and Mama, for supporting me not only with my writing but with my recovery as well. I honestly don't know where I'd be today without you. You held me when I was weak, fought for me when I'd lost hope, and listened to me vent about my problems—even if you didn't always understand them. Your wisdom and insight have shaped *Breaking Free* into a comprehensive story that encapsulates the journey our family has been on for the past six years.

Thank you to my incredible team of editors. Thank you to Karin Stahl, author of the haunting memoir *The Option*, Bailey Francis, Jennifer Bassett, and Kari Karp, teen room librarians at Lucy Robbins Welles Library and Noah Webster Library, and Judy Goldfarb, a close family friend and former teacher, for dedicating your time and attention to *Breaking Free*. Your meticulous edits and thoughtful suggestions greatly enhanced my novel, and your kindness and generosity reminded me why working together is so important. A special thanks to Liza Kurchavykh, a sophomore at Farmington High School, for strengthening my writing with your sophisticated teen perspective. I enjoyed collaborating with you, and I'm excited to see where your passion for literature takes you.

Thank you to Kate Conway, author of the best-selling *Undertow* series, for offering to design and format *Breaking Free*. I'm in awe of your talent and grateful for all that you have done to help me navigate the complicated publishing world. I attribute a great deal of my success as a new author to you.

Thank you to my treatment team for guiding me through the ups and downs of recovery. From nerve-wracking book events to surviving my last year of high school to now preparing for college, you have been with me every step of the way, and I know that you will continue to support me as I embark on this next chapter of my life.

Finally, this wouldn't be complete without thanking my cat Chibi. Even on tough days, I know I can rely on you to make me feel okay. I love you, Little Bear.

ABOUT THE AUTHOR

Julia Tannenbaum published her debut novel *Changing Ways* when she was only eighteen years old. She has since been featured in newspapers and magazines, interviewed on television and radio stations, and actively works with mental health organizations to spread awareness and eliminate stigma. She is open about her personal journey to overcome mental illness and often incorporates elements of her real life into her fictional writing. Tannenbaum currently lives in West Hartford, Connecticut with her family and four cats .

Website: wackywriter.com
Instagram: julia.tannenbaum
Twitter: julia_tann

Made in the
USA
Middletown, DE